SPY STORY
was originally published in the U.S.A.
by Harcourt Brace Jovanovich, Inc.

SPY STORY

by LEN DEIGHTON

PUBLISHED BY POCKET BOOKS NEW YORK

SPY STORY

Harcourt Brace edition published 1974

POCKET BOOK edition published July, 1975

Ł

This POCKET BOOK edition includes every word contained
in the original, higher-priced edition. It is printed from
brand-new plates made from completely reset, clear, easy-to-
read type. POCKET BOOK editions are published by POCKET
BOOKS, a division of Simon & Schuster, Inc., 630 Fifth
Avenue, New York, N.Y. 10020. Trademarks registered
in the United States and other countries.

Standard Book Number: 671-80058-2.
Library of Congress Catalog Card Number: 74-3124.
This POCKET BOOK edition is published by arrangement
with Harcourt Brace Jovanovich, Inc. Copyright, ©, 1974,
by Len Deighton. All rights reserved. This book, or portions
thereof, may not be reproduced by any means without permission of the original publisher: Harcourt Brace Jovanovich, Inc., 757 Third Avenue, New York, N.Y. 10017.

Printed in the U.S.A.

Acknowledgments

The author would like to acknowledge the help and assistance of Major Berchtold, U.S. Army (retired), and the staff of the Institute of War Studies, London, and in particular the permission given for the inclusion of extracts and quotations from the Institute's previously unpublished confidential reports and private papers. All such extracts are subject to full copyright protection provided by the Berne Convention and the Copyright Act of 1956. No part of these extracts may be reproduced, stored in a retrieval system or stored in any form or by any means, either electronic, electrical, chemical, mechanical, optical, photocopying, recording or otherwise without the prior permission of the copyright owners.

11383

But war's a game, which, were their subjects wise,
Kings would not play at.

William Cowper, 1731–1800

SPY STORY

Chapter 1

As each bound ends, units cease to be operative until commencement of next bound.

RULES. ALL GAMES. STUDIES CENTRE. LONDON

Forty-three days without a night: six pale-blue fluorescent weeks without a sniff of air, sky, or a view of the stars. I drank in a cautious half-lungful of salty mist and smelled the iodine and seaborne putrefaction that seaside landladies call ozone.

H.M.S. *Viking*, a deep water anchorage in western Scotland, is no place to celebrate a return to the real world. The uninhabited islands, a mile or more out in the Sound, were almost swallowed by sea mist. Overhead, dark clouds raced across the water to dash themselves upon the sharp granite peaks of Great Hamish. Then, in threads, they tumbled down the hillside, trailing through the stones and walls that had once been a Highland croft.

There were four submarines alongside the one from which I emerged. Out at the anchorage were more of them. The lash of the westerly wind made them huddle close to the mother ships and their crooning generators. The yellow deck lights were visible through the grey mist, and so were the flocks of gulls that screamed and wheeled and shrieked as they fell upon the kitchen garbage.

The wind brought gusts of rain, whipping up crested waves that awoke the subs. Underfoot I felt the great black hull strain against its moorings. The brow tilted. Stepping from the edge of each horizontal fin to the next was easier if I didn't look down.

Now the next hull groaned, as the same wave sucked and gurgled at its bow. The forecast had been reasonably right for once: overcast, low cloud, drizzle and wind westering. The rain scratched at the slop-coloured sea and crept into my sleeves, boots and collar. My rubber shoe slipped but I recovered my balance. I shook the water off my face and cursed pointlessly.

"Steady on," said Ferdy Foxwell behind me, but I cursed again and built his name into one of the inversions.

"At least the navy is on time," said Ferdy. There was an orange-coloured Ford on the jetty. The door opened and a slim man got out. He was wearing a Burberry and a tweed hat but I knew he'd be the British naval officer from the police office. He bent his head against the rain. The armed U.S.N. sentry at the end of the gangway poked his head out of his shelter to check the pass. I recognized the officer as Frazer, a lieutenant. He made his way along the slippery walk towards us, stepping across the gaps with commendable agility.

"Let me take that." He extended a hand, and then smiled in embarrassment as he noticed that the shiny metal case was padlocked to a shoulder-chain under my coat.

"Help Mr Foxwell," I said. "He never fastens his."

"Neither would you if you had any sense," puffed

Foxwell. The man squeezed past me and I had a chance to look down at the oily scum, and smell the diesel, and decide that Ferdy Foxwell was right. When I reached the brow—the horizontal fin—of the next submarine I rested the box and looked back. The young officer was bowed under the weight of Ferdy's case, and Ferdy was stretching his arms to balance his two hundred pounds of compact flab, teetering along the gangway like a circus elephant balancing on a tub. Six weeks was a long time to spend in a metal tube, no matter about sun lamps and cycling gear. I picked up the case loaded with spools and tape recordings, and remembered how I sprinted across these brows on the outward journey.

A red Pontiac station wagon came along the jetty, slowed at the torpedo store and rolled carefully over the double ramps. It continued along the front until turning off at the paint shop. It disappeared down between the long lines of huts. The curved huts were shiny in the rain. Now there was no human movement, and the buildings looked as old as the black granite hills that shone rain-wet above them.

"Are you all right?" Frazer asked.

I shouldered the wet case as I started down the companionway to the jetty. The hatch in the sentry hut slid open an inch or two. I could hear the radio inside playing Bach. "O.K., buddy," said the sailor. He slammed the hatch shut as a gust of wind hammered the hut with rain.

There was a panel van behind the Ford. A bad-tempered Admiralty policeman grumbled that we were two hours late and about how the Americans couldn't make tea. He scowled as he signed for the cases and locked them in the safe in the van. Ferdy shot him in the back of the head with a nicotine-stained finger. Frazer saw the gesture and permitted himself a thin smile.

"Perhaps a tot?" said Frazer.

"I wish I had your job," said Ferdy Foxwell.

Frazer nodded. I suppose we all said that to him.

There was the clang of a steel door. I looked at the nuclear submarine that had taken us to the Arctic and back. We civilians were always permitted to leave first. Now there was a deck party assembling forward of the conning tower, or what I'd learned to call a sail. They faced several more hours of work before the sub's second crew arrived and took her to sea again.

"Where is everyone?"

"Asleep, I shouldn't wonder," said Frazer.

"Asleep?"

"A Russian sub came down through the North Channel and into the Irish Sea on Wednesday morning . . . big panic—hunter killers, sonar buoys, County Class destroyers, you name it. Yards of teleprinter. Seventy-two hours of red alert. We were only stood-down last night. You missed the pantomime."

"They were frightened it was going to put guns ashore in Ulster?" Ferdy asked.

"Who knows what?" said Frazer. "There were two Russian intelligence trawlers and a destroyer off Malin Head, too. You can see they'd be worried."

"So?"

"We stopped Class A Radio traffic for five and a half hours."

"And the sub?"

"They tracked it out past Wexford yesterday after-

noon. Looks like they were just taking our pulse."
He smiled as he unlocked the door of his car. It was
well cared for, and all dressed up in black vinyl,
Lamborghini-style rear-window slats, and even a
spoiler.

"They're tricky bastards!" said Ferdy resignedly. He
blew on his hands to warm them. "Who said something about splicing that damned mainbrace?"

Frazer got into the driver's seat and twisted round
to unlock the rear doors. "It might have been me,"
he said.

I reached under my oilskin coat and found a dry
handkerchief to polish the rain off my spectacles. Frazer
started the car.

Ferdy Foxwell said, "Never mind the dollars and
the cinnamon toast and grain-fed steaks . . . six weeks
without a drink: it's positively unnatural."

Frazer said, "Not all the skippers are as bad as
Fireball."

Ferdy Foxwell settled back into the rear seat of the
car. He was a huge man, well over six feet tall and
broad enough to carry it. He was in his early fifties but
still had enough brown wavy hair to visit a smart
barber once a month. But his hair was no more an
advert for the barber than were his rumpled suits for
his Savile Row tailor, or his curious inability to spell
for the famous public school to which he'd also sent
his two sons. "A drink," said Ferdy. He smiled. His
crooked, gapped teeth needed only gold wire to complete the image of a mischievous child.

The Admiralty van containing our tapes went at the
regulation fifteen miles an hour. We followed at the
same pace, all the way to the exit. It was a double

compound, with a large check-point at each gate, and
the wire twenty feet tall. Newcomers were always told
that H.M.S. *Viking* had been a prison camp during
the war but they were wrong, it had been an experi-
mental torpedo testing unit. But it would have done,
it would have done.

The dog handlers were drinking hot coffee in the
guard tower and the dogs were howling like were-
wolves. The sentry waved us through. We turned on to
the coast road and went down past the housing, the
Officers Club and cinema. The streets were empty but
the coffee-shop car park was full. The lights of the
housing were lost in a flurry of sea mist that rolled in
upon us. The Admiralty van continued along the
coast road to the airport. We took the high road, climbing steeply up the narrow road that leads to the moors
and the pass over the Hamish.

Defoliated by Iron Age farmers, the land is now
good for nothing but a few black-faced sheep. This
ancient tilted ~dge of Scotland has only a scattering
of poor soil upon the hard granite that does not weather.
I felt the wheels hesitate on an ice patch, and ahead
of us the higher ground was grey with last week's
snow. Only the red grouse can survive outdoors on
this sort of moorland, sheltering under the heather and
feeding upon its shoots, moving gently all the time so
that the snow does not bury them.

From here the valley formed an enormous stadium,
roofed by the hurrying black clouds. Halfway up its
steep far side there was a huddle of grey stone cottages
smudged with smoke from open fires. One of them was
a cramped little pub.

"We'll stop for a drink at The Bonnet?"

"You'll not get me past it," I said.

"My God, it's cold," said Ferdy, and rubbed the condensation from the window to see how far it was to the pub.

"There's the one I'm going to get next year," said Frazer. A large light-blue BMW was on the road behind us. It had a lefthand drive. "Second-hand," Frazer added apologetically. "It shouldn't cost me more than a new one of these. My next door neighbour has one. Says he'll never buy another English car."

Cars, politics or climate, for a Scotsman they were English if bad, British if good. Perhaps he sensed my thoughts. He smiled. "It's the electrics," he said.

I could hear it now, just a faint burr of the Highlands. It would make sense for the navy to use a local man for this kind of job. Strangers could still find a barrier of silence once the cities were left behind.

Frazer took the hairpin bends with exaggerated care. On one of the turns he stopped, and reversed, to pull tight enough to avoid the snow-banked ditch. But the blue BMW stuck with us, following patiently. Following more patiently than was natural for a man who drives such a car.

Frazer glanced in his mirror again. "I think we should," he said, voicing our unspoken thoughts, and Ferdy wrote down the registration number in his crocodile-covered note pad. It was a Düsseldorf registration, and even while Ferdy was writing it, the BMW gave a toot and started to overtake.

Whatever was the extent of his intention, he'd chosen his moment well. The BMW squeezed past us in a spray of powdery snow from the drift on our left, and Frazer's nervous reaction was to swerve away from the flash of light blue and the hard stare of the bearded man in the passenger seat.

The road was downhill and the ice was still hard and shiny up here on the top of the Hamish. Frazer fought the wheel as we swung round—as slowly as a boat at anchor—and slid almost broadside down the narrow mountain road.

We gathered speed. Frazer pumped the brake pedal, trying vainly to snatch at the road. I could see only the sheer drop, down where a clump of firs was waiting to catch us a thousand feet below.

"Bastards, bastards," mumbled Frazer. Ferdy, flung off-balance, grabbed at the seat back, the roof and the sun visor, so as not to grab at Frazer and kill us all.

There was a thump as the rear wheel struck some stones at the road edge, and the tyres for a moment gripped enough to make the differential whine. Frazer was into bottom gear by now, and at the next patch of stones the car whimpered and ceded to his brake pedal enough for him to narrow the angle at which we were sliding. The road was more steeply downhill and the low gear had not slowed us enough to take the steep bend ahead. Frazer hit the horn in two loud blasts before we hit the banked snow that had collected around the edge of the hairpin, like piped icing round a birthday cake. We stopped with a bang of hollow steel, and the car rocked on its suspension.

"My God," said Ferdy. For a moment we sat still. Praying, sighing or swearing according to inclination.

"I hope you're not going to do that every time someone tries to overtake," I said.

"Just foreign registrations," said Frazer.

Frazer started the engine again. Gently he let in the

clutch and the car waddled out of the drift. He took the middle of the road, and at no more than twenty-five miles an hour we went all the way down to the bridge and up the next climb all the way to The Bonnet.

He pulled into the yard there. There was a crunch of gravel and a soft splintering of ice. The BMW was already parked but none of us remarked upon the way its driver had nearly killed us.

"I'm not sure I'd enjoy it," said Frazer, talking of the voyage but studying our faces as if to see the effect the near-accident had had on us. "I'm a destroyer man myself . . . like to keep my head above water."

I would have described Frazer as an office-boy, but if he wanted to play Long John Silver it was all right by me.

"Peace time," pronounced Ferdy, "a submarine trip north is no different to trailing Russians round the Med in an intelligence trawler."

"In winter the Med's a damned site rougher," I said.

"You're right," said Ferdy. "As sick as a dog, I was, and I could see that Russian cruiser as steady as a rock all the time."

"Your second trip, wasn't it?" asked Frazer.

"That's right."

"Well, you chaps never do more than one a year. It's over and done with, eh?"

"Are you buying?" Ferdy Foxwell asked him.

"Then it'll be small ones," said Frazer. The wind bit into us as we stepped from the car but there was a fine view. The hills at the other end of the valley obscured the anchorage, but to each side of the summit I could see the Sound and the mist-shrouded islands that continued all the way to the grey Atlantic breakers. The wind sang in the car aerial and tugged at the chimney smoke. We were high enough to be entangled in the fast moving underside of the storm clouds. Ferdy coughed as the cold wet air entered his lungs.

"All that air-conditioned living," said Frazer. "You'd better take your briefcase—security and all that, you know."

"It's only dirty underwear," said Ferdy. He coughed again. Frazer went around the car testing each door-lock and the boot too. For a moment he looked down at his hand to see if it shook. It did, and he pushed it into the pocket of his trench-coat.

I walked across to the BMW and looked inside it. There was a short oilskin coat, a battered rucksack and a stout walking-stick: a walker's equipment.

It was a tiny cottage. One bar; a front parlour except for the warped little counter and flap scorched by cigarettes and whittled with the doodles of shepherds' knives. On the whitewashed walls there was a rusty Highlander's dirk, an engraving of a ship in full sail, a brightly shone ship's bell and a piece of German submarine surrendered in May 1945. The landlord was a shaggy-haired giant, complete with kilt and beer-stained shirt.

There were two customers already drinking, but they had taken the bench near the window so we could stand around the open peat fire and slap our hands together and make self-congratulatory noises about its warmth.

The beer was good: dark and not too sweet, and not crystal clear like the swill that the brewers extol on TV. The Bonnet's had flavour, like a slice of wheat loaf. Frazer knew the landlord well but, with the formality that Highland men demand, he called him Mr MacGregor. "We'll have another fall of snow before the day's through, Mr MacGregor."

"Is it south you're heading, Mr Frazer?"

"Aye."

"The high road is awful bad already. The oil delivery could not get through that way: he made the journey by the road along the Firth. It never freezes there. It's a wicked long journey for the boy." He prodded the peat fire with a poker and encouraged the smoke to turn to flame.

"You are busy?" asked Frazer.

"Travellers. People walk, even in winter. I don't understand it." He made no attempt to lower his voice. He nodded impassively at the two customers by the window. They were looking at large-scale walker's maps, measuring distances with a tiny wheeled instrument that they rolled along the footpaths.

"Travellers, walkers and spies," said Frazer. The wind banged on the tiny window panes.

"Ahh, spies," said the landlord. He came as near as I'd ever seen him to laughing: the two men in the window seat looked like some inept casting director's idea of Russian spies. They had black overcoats and dark tweed hats. Both wore coloured silk scarves knotted at their throats and one man had a closely trimmed grizzled beard.

"We'll have the other half, Landlord," said Ferdy.

With infinite care the landlord drew three more pints of his special. In the silence I heard one of the other men say, "In our own good time." His voice was soft but his accent had the hard spiky consonants of the English Midlands. In the context of our remarks the sentence hung in the air like the peaty smoke from the fireplace. What in their own good time, I wondered.

"Well, what's been happening out here in the real world?" said Ferdy.

"Nothing much," said Frazer. "Looks like the German reunification talks are going ahead, the papers are full of it. Another car workers' strike. The Arabs put a bomb in the Tokyo Stock Exchange but it was defused, and Aeroflot has started running its own jumbos into New York."

"We get all the big news," said Ferdy. "And American hometown stuff. I could tell you more about the climate, local politics and football scores of the American heartland than any other Englishman you could find. Do you know that a woman in Portland, Maine, has given birth to sextuplets?"

It had begun to snow. Frazer looked at his watch. "We mustn't miss the plane," he said.

"There's time for one from this man's stone bottle," said Ferdy.

"The stone bottle?" said MacGregor.

"Come along, you hairy bastard," said Ferdy. "You know what I'm talking about."

MacGregor's face was unchanging. It would have been easy to believe him deeply offended, but Ferdy knew him better than that. Without taking his eyes from Ferdy, MacGregor took a packet of Rothmans from his pocket. He lit one and tossed the packet on to the counter.

MacGregor went into his back parlour and reappeared with a jar from which he poured a generous measure. "You've a good palate—for a Sassenach."

"No one would want the factory stuff after this,

Mac," said Ferdy. MacGregor and Frazer exchanged glances.

"Aye, I get my hands on a little of the real thing now and again."

"Come along, MacGregor," said Ferdy. "You're among friends. You think we haven't smelled the barley and the peat fire?"

MacGregor gave a ghost of a smile but would admit to nothing. Ferdy took his malt whisky and tasted it with care and concentration.

"The same?" asked MacGregor.

"It's improved," said Ferdy.

Frazer came away from the fireplace and took his seat at the counter. MacGregor moved the malt whisky towards him. "It will help you endure the cruel blows of the west wind," he said.

So he must have rationalized many such drinks up here on the bare slopes of the Grampians' very end. A desolate place: in summer the heather grew bright with flowers, and so tall that a hill walker needed a long blade to clear a lane through it. I turned an inch or two. The strangers in the corner no longer spoke together. Their faces were turned to watch the snow falling but I had a feeling that they were watching us.

MacGregor took three more thimble-sized glasses, and, with more care than was necessary, filled each to the brim. While we watched him I saw Frazer reach out for the packet of cigarettes that the landlord had left on the counter. He helped himself. There was an intimacy to such a liberty.

"Can I buy a bottle?" asked Ferdy.

"You can not," said MacGregor.

I sipped it. It was a soft smoky flavour of the sort that one smelled as much as tasted.

Frazer poured his whisky into the beer and drank it down. "You damned heathen," said the landlord. "And I'm giving you the twelve-year-old malt too."

"It all ends up in the same place, Mr MacGregor."

"You damned barbarian," he growled, relishing the r's rasp. "You've ruined my ale and my whisky too."

I realized it was a joke between them, one that they had shared before. I knew that Lieutenant Frazer was from R.N. security. I wondered if the landlord was a part of it too. It would be a fine place from which to keep an eye on strangers who came to look at the atomic submarines at the anchorage.

And then I was sure that this was so, for Frazer picked up the packet of cigarettes from which he'd been helping himself. The change of ownership had been a gradual one but I was sure that something more than cigarettes was changing hands.

Chapter 2

In games where the random chance programme is not used, and in the event of two opposing units, of exactly equal strength and identical qualities, occupying same hex (or unit of space), the first unit to occupy the space will predominate.

RULES. "TACWARGAME." STUDIES CENTRE. LONDON

The London flight was delayed.

Ferdy bought a newspaper and I read the departures board four times. Then we drifted through that perfumed limbo of stale air that is ruled by yawning girls with Cartier watches, and naval officers with plastic briefcases. We tried to recognize melodies amongst the rhythms that are specially designed to be without melody, and we tried to recognize words among the announcements, until finally the miracle of heavier-than-air flight was once again mastered.

As we climbed into the grey cotton wool, we had this big brother voice saying he was our captain and on account of how late we were there was no catering aboard but we could buy cigarette lighters with the name of the airline on them, and if we looked down to our left side we could have seen Birmingham, if it hadn't been covered in cloud.

It was early evening by the time I got to London. The sky looked bruised and the cloud no higher than the high-rise offices where all the lights burned. The drivers were ill-tempered and the rain unceasing.

We arrived at the Studies in Hampstead just as the day staff were due to leave. The tapes had come on a military flight and were waiting for me. There is a security seal when tapes are due, so we unloaded to the disapproving stares of the clock-watchers in the Evaluation Block. It was tempting to use the overnight facilities at the Centre: the bathwater always ran and the kitchen could always find a hot meal, but Marjorie was waiting. I signed out directly.

I should have had more sense than to expect my car to sit in the open through six weeks of London winter and be ready to start when I needed it. It groaned miserably as it heaved at the thick cold oil and coughed at the puny spark. I pummelled the starter until the air was choked with fumes, and then counted to one hundred in an attempt to keep my hands off her long enough to dry the points. At the third bout she fired. I hit the pedal and there was a staccato of backfire and judder of one-sided torque from the oldest plugs. Finally they too joined the song and I nudged her slowly out into the evening traffic of Frognal.

If the traffic had been moving faster I would probably have reached home without difficulty, but the sort of jams you get on a wet winter's evening in London gives the *coup de grâce* to old bangers like mine. I was just a block away from my old place in Earl's Court when she died. I opened her up and tried to decide where to put the Band-aid, but all I saw were raindrops sizzling on the hot block. Soon the raindrops no longer sizzled and I became aware of the passing traffic. Big expensive all-weather tyres were filling my shoes with dirty water. I got back into the car and stared at an old packet of cigarettes, but I'd given them up for six weeks and this time I was determined to make it stick. I buttoned up and walked down the street as far as the phone box. Someone had cut the hand-piece off and taken it home. Not one empty cab had passed in half an hour. I tried to decide between walking the rest of the way home and lying down in the middle of the road. It was then that I remembered that I still had the door-key of the old flat.

The Studies Centre was turning my lease over the following month. Possibly the phone was still connected. It was two minutes' walk.

I rang the doorbell. There was no answer. I gave it an extra couple of minutes, remembering how often I'd failed to hear it from the kitchen at the back. Then I used the old key and let myself in. The lights still worked. I'd always liked number eighteen. In some ways it's more to my taste than the oil-fired slab of speculator's bad taste that I'd exchanged it for, but I'm not the sort of fellow who gives aesthetics precedence over wall-to-wall synthetic wool and Georgian-style double-glazing.

The flat wasn't the way I'd left it. I mean, the floor wasn't covered with *Private Eye* and *Rolling Stone,* with strategically placed carrier bags brimming with garbage. It was exactly the way it was when the lady next door came in to clean it three times a week. The furniture wasn't bad, not bad for a furnished place, I mean. I sat down in the best armchair and used the phone. It worked. I dialled the number of the local mini-cab company and was put up for auction. "Anyone do a Gloucester Road to Fulham?" Then, "Will anyone do a Gloucester Road to Fullham with twenty-five pence on the clock?" Finally some knight of the road deigned to do a Gloucester Road to Fulham with seventy-five pence on the clock if I'd wait half an hour. I knew that meant forty-five minutes. I said yes and wondered if I'd still be a non-smoker had I slipped that pack into my overcoat.

If I hadn't been so tired I would have noticed what was funny about the place the moment I walked in. But I was tired. I could hardly keep my eyes open. I'd been sitting in the armchair for five minutes or more when I noticed the photo. At first there was nothing strange about it, except how I came to leave it behind. It was only when I got my mind functioning that I realized that it wasn't my photo. The frame was the same as the one I'd bought in Selfridges Christmas Sale in 1967. Inside was almost the same photo: me in tweed jacket, machine washable at number five trousers, cor-blimey hat and two-tone shoes, one of them resting on the chromium of an Alfa Spider convertible. But it wasn't me. Everything else was the same—right down to the number plates—but the man was older than me and heavier. Mind you, I had to peer closely. We both had no moustache, no beard, no sideboards and an out-of-focus face, but it wasn't me, I swear it.

I didn't get alarmed about it. You know how crazy things can sound, and then along comes a logical, rational explanation—usually supplied by a woman very close to you. So I didn't suddenly panic, I just started to turn the whole place over systematically. And then I could scream and panic in my own good, leisurely, non-neurotic way.

What was this bastard doing with all the same clothes that I had? Different sizes and some slight changes, but I'm telling you my entire wardrobe. And a photo of Mr Nothing and Mason: the creepy kid who does the weather print-outs for the war-games. Now I was alarmed. It was the same with everything in the flat. My neck-ties. My chinaware. My bottled Guinness. My Leak hi-fi, and my Mozart piano concertos played by my Ingrid Haebler. And by his bed—covered with the same dark green Witney that I have on my bed—in a silver frame: my Mum and Dad. My Mum and Dad in the garden. The photo I took on their thirty-fifth wedding anniversary.

I sat myself down on my sofa and gave myself a talking-to. Look, I said to myself, you know what this is, it's one of those complicated jokes that rich people play on each other in TV plays for which writers can think of no ending. But I haven't got any friends rich and stupid enough to want to print me in duplicate just to puzzle me. I mean, I puzzle pretty easily, I don't need this kind of hoop-la.

I went into the bedroom and opened the wardrobe to go through the clothes again. I told myself that these were not my clothes, for I couldn't be positive they were. I mean, I don't have the sort of clothes that I can be quite sure that no one else has, but the combination of Brooks Brothers, Marks and Sparks and Turnbull and Asser can't be in everyone's wardrobe. Especially when they are five years out of fashion.

But had I not been rummaging through the wardrobe I would never have noticed the tie rack had been moved. And so I wouldn't have seen the crude carpentry done to the inside, or the piece that had been inserted to make a new wooden panel in the back of it.

I rapped it. It was hollow. The thin plywood panel slid easily to one side. Behind it there was a door.

The door was stiff, but by pushing the rackful of clothes aside I put a little extra pressure on it. After the first couple of inches it moved easily. I stepped through the wardrobe into a dark room. Alice through the looking-glass. I sniffed. The air smelled clean with a faint odour of disinfectant. I struck a match. It was a box room. By the light of the match I found the light switch. The room had been furnished as a small office: a desk, easy chair, typewriter and polished lino. The walls were newly painted white. Upon them there was a coloured illustration of Von Guericke's air thermoscope given as a calendar by a manufacturer of surgical instruments in Munich, a cheap mirror, and a blank day-by-day chart, stuck to the wall with surgical tape. In the drawers of the desk there was a ream of blank white paper, a packet of paper clips, and two white nylon jackets packed in transparent laundry packets.

The door from the office also opened easily. By now I was well into the next apartment. Adjoining the hall there was a large room—corresponding to my sitting-room—lit by half a dozen overhead lights fitted behind frosted glass. The windows were fitted with light-tight wooden screens, like those used for photographic dark rooms. This room was also painted white. It was spotlessly clean, walls, floor and ceiling, shining and dustless. There was a new stainless-steel sink in one corner. In the centre of the room there was a table fitted with a crisply laundered cotton cover. Over it there was a transparent plastic one. The sort from which it's easy to wipe spilled blood. It was a curious table, with many levers to elevate, tilt and adjust it. Rather like one of the simpler types of operating table. The large apparatus alongside it was beyond any medical guess I could make. Pipes, dials and straps, it was an expensive device. Although I could not recognize it, I knew that I'd seen such a device before, but I could not dredge it up from the sludge of my memory.

To this room there was also a door. Very gently, I tried the handle, but it was locked. As I stood, bent forward at the door, I heard a voice. By leaning closer I could hear what was being said. ". . . and then the next week you'll do the middle shift, and so on. They don't seem to know when it will start."

The reply—a woman's voice—was almost inaudible. Then the man close to me said, "Certainly, if the senior staff prefer one shift we can change the rota and make it permanent."

Again there was the murmur of the woman's voice, and the sound of running water, splashing as if someone was washing his hands.

The man said, "How right you are; like the bloody secret service if you ask me. Was my grandmother born in the United Kingdom. Bloody sauce! I put 'yes' to everything."

When I switched off the light the conversation suddenly stopped. I waited in the darkness, not moving. The light from the tiny office was still on. If this door was opened they would be certain to see me. There was the sound of a towel machine and then of a match striking. Then the conversation continued, but more distantly. I tiptoed across the room very very slowly.

I closed the second door and looked at the alterations to the wardrobe while retreating through it. This false door behind the wardrobe puzzled me even more than the curious little operating theatre. If a man was to construct a secret chamber with all the complications of securing the lease to his next door apartment, if he secretly removed large sections of brickwork, if he constructed a sliding door and fitted it into the back of a built-in wardrobe, would such a man not go all the way, and make it extremely difficult to detect? This doorway was something that even the rawest recruit to the Customs service would find in a perfunctory look round. It made no sense.

The phone rang. I picked it up. "Your cab is outside now, sir."

There are not many taxi services that say "sir" nowadays. That should have aroused my suspicions, but I was tired.

I went downstairs. On the first-floor landing outside the caretaker's flat there were two men.

"Pardon me, sir," said one of the men. I thought at first they were waiting for the caretaker, but as I tried to pass one of them stood in the way. The other spoke again. "There have been a lot of break-ins here lately, sir."

"So?"

"We're from the security company who look after this block." It was the taller of the two men who'd spoken. He was wearing a short suede overcoat with a sheepskin lining. The sort of coat a man needed if he spent a lot of time in doorways. "Are you a tenant here, sir?" he said.

"Yes," I said.

The taller man buttoned the collar of his coat. It seemed like an excuse to keep his hands near my throat. "Would you mind producing some identification, sir?"

I counted ten, but before I was past five the shorter of the men had pressed the caretaker's buzzer. "What is it now?"

"This one of your tenants?" said the tall man.

"I'm from number eighteen," I prompted.

"Never seen him before," said the man.

"You're not the caretaker," I said. "Charlie Short is the caretaker."

"Charlie Short used to come over here now and again to give me a break for a couple of hours. . . ."

"Don't give me that," I said. "Charlie is the caretaker. I've never seen you before."

"A bloody con man," said the man from the caretaker's flat.

"I've lived here for five years," I protested.

"Get on," said the man. "Never seen him before." He smiled as if amused at my gall. "The gentleman in number eighteen has lived here for five years but he's much older than this bloke—bigger, taller—this one would pass for him in a crowd, but not in this light."

"I don't know what you're up to . . ." I said. "I can prove . . ." Unreasonably my anger centred on the man who said he was the caretaker. One of the security men took my arm. "Now then, sir, we don't want any rough stuff, do we?"

"I'm going back to *War and Peace*," said the man. He closed the door forcefully enough to discourage further interruption.

"I never had that Albert figured for a reader," said the taller man.

"On the telly, he means," said the other one. "So—" he turned to me, "you'd better come and identify yourself properly."

"That's not the caretaker," I said.

"I'm afraid you're wrong, sir."

"I'm not wrong."

"It won't take more than ten minutes, sir."

I walked down the flight of stairs that led to the street. Outside there was my taxi. Screw them all. I opened the cab door and had one foot on the ledge when I saw the third man. He was sitting well back in the far corner of the rear seat. I froze. "Do get in, sir," he said. It should have been a mini-cab, this was a taxi. I didn't like it at all.

One of my hands was in my pocket. I stood upright and pointed a finger through my coat. "Come out," I said with a suitable hint of menace. "Come out *very* slowly." He didn't move.

"Don't be silly, sir. We know you are not armed."

I extended my free hand and flipped the fingers up to beckon him. The seated man sighed, "There are three of us, sir. Either we all get in as we are, or we all get in bruised, but either way we all get in."

I glanced to one side. There was another man standing beside the doorway. The driver hadn't moved.

"We won't delay you long, sir," said the seated man.

I got into the cab. "What is this?" I asked.

"You know that flat is no longer yours, sir." He shook his head. The driver checked that the door was closed and drove off with us, along Cromwell Road. The man said, "Whatever made you trespass there, at this time of night? It's brought all three of us out of a bridge game." The taller man was sitting on the jump seat. He unbuttoned his sheepskin coat.

"That really reassures me," I told them. "Cops playing poker might frame you. Cops playing pontoon might beat you to death. But who could get worried about cops who play bridge?"

"You should know better," said the tall man mildly. "You know security has tightened since last year."

"You people talk to me like we are all related. I've never seen you before. You don't work with me. Who the hell are you, dial-a-cop?"

"You can't be that naïve, sir."

"You mean the phone has always been tapped?"

"Monitored."

"Every call?"

"That's an empty flat, sir."

"You mean—'Anyone do a Gloucester Road to Fulham with fifty pence on the clock' was your people?"

"Barry was so near to winning the rubber," said the second man.

"I just went in to use the phone."

"And I believe you," said the cop.

The cab stopped. It was dark. We had driven across Hammersmith Bridge and were in some godforsaken hole in Barnes. On the left there was a large piece of open common, and the wind howled through the trees and buffeted the cab so that it rocked gently. There was very little traffic, but in the distance lights, and sometimes a double-decker bus, moved through the trees. I guessed that that might be Upper Richmond Road.

"What are we waiting for?"

"We won't delay you long, sir. Cigarette?"

"No, thanks," I said.

A black Ford Executive came past, drew in and parked ahead of us. Two men got out and walked back. The man with the sheep-skin coat wound down the window. A man from the other car put a flashlight beam on my face. "Yes, that's him."

"Is that you, Mason?"

"Yes, sir." Mason was the one who did the weather print-outs and got himself photographed with strangers wearing my clothes.

"Are you in on this, then?" I said.

"In on what?" said Mason.

"Don't bullshit me, you little creep," I said.

"Yes, that's him," said Mason. He switched off the light.

"Well, we knew it was," said the first cop.

"Oh sure," I said. "Or else I would have got you with only twenty-five pence on the clock." How could I have been so stupid. On that phone if you dialled TIM you'd hear the tick of the Chief Commissioner's watch.

"We'd better get you home," said the cop. "And thank you, Mr Mason."

Mason let the driver open the door of the Executive for him as if to the manner born. That little bastard would wind up running the Centre, that much was clear.

They took me all the way home. "Next time," said the cop, "get car-pool transport. You're entitled to it after a trip, you know that."

"You couldn't get one of your people to collect my Mini Clubman—between games of bridge, I mean."

"I'll report it stolen. The local bobbies will pick it up."

"I bet sometimes you wish you weren't so honest," I said.

"Goodnight, sir." It was still pouring with rain. I got out of the cab. They'd left me on the wrong side of the street. U-turns were forbidden.

Chapter 3

All time is game time . . .

RULES. ALL GAMES. STUDIES CENTRE. LONDON

I let myself into the flat as quietly as possible. Marjorie turned up the heating whenever I was away, and now the stale air, heavy with fresh paint and unseasoned timber smells, hit me like a secondhand hangover. It would be a long time before I'd get used to living here.

"Is that you, darling?"

"Yes, love." I prodded at the pile of mail, pushing the unsealed buff envelopes aside until there remained only a postcard from a ski resort, *Cross and Cockade* magazine and a secondhand book about the Battle of Moscow. On the silver-plated toast rack—a place kept for urgent messages—there was a torn piece of hospital notepaper with "Please go to Colonel Schlegel's home on Sunday. He'll meet the ten o'clock train" written on it in Marjorie's neat handwriting. I'd have gone Monday except that Sunday was underlined three times, in the red pencil she used for diagrams.

"Darling!"

"I'm coming." I went into the sitting-room. When I was away she seldom went in there: a quick bout with the frying pan and a briefcase full of post-graduate

28

medical studies on the bedside table were her routine. But now she'd got it all tidied and ready for my return: matches near the ashtray and slippers by the fireplace. There was even a big bunch of mixed flowers, arranged with fern and placed in a jug amid her copies of *House and Garden* on the side table.

"I missed you, Marj."

"Hello, sailor."

We embraced. The lingering smell of bacon I'd encountered in the hall was now a taste on her lips. She ran a hand through my hair to ruffle it. "It won't come loose," I said. "They knit them into the scalp."

"Silly."

"Sorry I'm late."

She turned her head and smiled shyly. She was like a little girl: her large green eyes and small white face, lost somewhere under that dishevelled black hair.

"I made a stew but it's a bit dried up."

"I'm not hungry."

"You haven't noticed the flowers."

"Are you working in the mortuary again?"

"Bastard," she said, but she kissed me softly.

In the corner, the box was keeping up its bombardment of superficial hysteria: British Equity outwits fat German extras shouting *Schweinhund*.

"The flowers were from my mother. To wish me many happy returns."

"You're not rerunning that twenty-ninth birthday again this year?"

She hit me in the ribs with the side of the hand and drew enough anatomy to make it hurt.

"Take it easy," I gasped. "I'm only joking."

"Well, you save your lousy jokes for the boys on the submarine."

But she put her arms round me and grabbed me tight. And she kissed me and stroked my face, trying to read her fortune in my eyes.

I kissed her again. It was more like the real thing this time.

"I was beginning to wonder," she said, but the words were lost in my mouth.

There was a pot of coffee clipped into an electric contraption that kept it warm for hours. I poured some into Marjorie's cup and sipped it. It tasted like iron filings with a dash of quinine. I pulled a face.

"I'll make more."

"No." I grabbed her arm. She made me neurotic with all this tender loving care. "Sit down, for God's sake sit down." I reached over and took a piece of the chocolate bar she'd been eating. "I don't want anything to eat or drink."

The heroes on the box got the keys to a secret new aeroplane from this piggy-eyed Gestapo man, and this fat short-sighted sentry kept stamping and giving the Heil Hitler salute. The two English cats Heil Hitlered back, but they exchanged knowing smiles as they got in the plane.

"I don't know why I'm watching it," said Marjorie.

"Seeing these films makes you wonder why we took six years to win that damned war," I said.

"Take off your overcoat."

"I'm O.K."

"Have you been drinking, darling?" She smiled. She'd never seen me drunk but she was always suspecting I might be.

"No."

"You're shivering."

I wanted to tell her about the flat and the photographs of the man who wasn't me, but I knew she'd be sceptical. She was a doctor: they're all like that. "Did the car give you trouble?" she asked finally. She wanted only to be quite certain I wasn't going to confess to another woman.

"The plugs. Same as last time."

"Perhaps you should get the new one now, instead of waiting."

"Sure. And a sixty-foot ocean racer. Did you see Jack while I was away?"

"He took me to lunch."

"Good old Jack."

"At the Savoy Grill."

I nodded. Her estranged husband was a fashionable young pediatrician. The Savoy Grill was his works canteen. "Did you talk about the divorce?"

"I told him I wanted no money."

"That pleased him, I'll bet."

"Jack's not like that."

"What *is* he like, Marjorie?"

She didn't answer. We'd got as close as this to fighting about him before, but she was sensible enough to recognize male insecurity for what it was. She leaned forward and kissed my cheek. "You're tired," she said.

"I missed you, Marj."

"Did you really, darling?"

I nodded. On the table alongside her there was a pile of books: *Pregnancy and Anaemia, Puerperal Anaemia,* Bennett, *Achresthic Anaemia,* Wilkinson, *A Clinical Study,* by Schmidt and *History of a Case of Anaemia,* by Combe. Tucked under the books there was a bundle of loose-leaf pages, crammed with Marjorie's tiny writing. I broke the chocolate bar lying next to the books and put a piece of it into Marjorie's mouth.

"The Los Angeles people came back to me. Now there's a car and a house and a sabbatical fifth year."

"I wasn't . . ."

"Now don't be tempted into lying. I know how your mind works."

"I'm pretty tired, Marj."

"Well, we'll have to talk about things some time." It was the doctor speaking.

"Yes."

"Lunch Thursday?"

"Great," I said.

"Sounds like it."

"Sensational, wonderful, I can't wait."

"Sometimes I wonder how we got this far."

I didn't answer. I wondered too. She wanted me to admit that I couldn't live without her. And I had the nasty feeling that as soon as I did that, she'd up and leave me. So we continued as we were: in love but determined not to admit it. Or worse: declaring our love in such a way that the other could not be sure.

"Strangers on a train," said Marjorie.

"What?"

"We are—strangers on a train."

I pulled a face, as if I didn't understand what she was getting at. She pushed her hair back but it fell forward again. She pulled a clip from it and fastened it. It was a nervous movement, designed more to occupy her than to change her hair.

"I'm sorry, love," I leaned forward and kissed her gently. "I'm really sorry. We'll talk about it."

"On Thursday . . ." she smiled, knowing that I'd promise anything to avoid the sort of discussion that she had in mind. "Your coat is wet. You'd better hang it up, it will wrinkle and need cleaning."

"Now, if you like. We'll talk now, if that's what you want."

She shook her head. "We're on our way to different destinations. That's what I mean. When you get to where you're going, you'll get out. I know you. I know you too well."

"It's you who gets offers . . . fantastic salaries from Los Angeles research institutes, reads up anaemia, and sends polite refusals that ensure an even better offer eventually comes."

"I know," she admitted, and kissed me in a distant and preoccupied way. "But I love you, darling. I mean really . . ." She gave an attractive little laugh. "You make me feel someone. The way you just take it for granted that I *could* go to America and do that damned job . . ." She shrugged. "Sometimes I wish you weren't so damned encouraging. I wish you were bossy, even. There are times when I wish you'd insist I stayed at home and did the washing-up."

Well, you can't make women happy, that's a kind of fundamental law of the universe. You try and make them happy and they'll never forgive you for revealing to them that they can't be.

"So do the washing-up," I said. I put my arm round her. The wool dress was thin. I could feel that her skin was hot beneath it. Perhaps she was running a fever, or perhaps it was passion. Or perhaps I was

just the icy cold bastard that she so often accused me
of being.

"Are you sure you wouldn't like a bacon sandwich?"

I shook my head. "Marjorie," I said, "do you remember the caretaker at number eighteen?" I walked
across to the TV and switched it off.

"No. Should I?"

"Be serious for a moment . . . Charlie the caretaker.
Charlie Short . . . moustache, cockney accent—always
making jokes about the landlords."

"No."

"Think for a moment."

"No need to shout."

"Can't you remember the dinner party . . . he climbed
in the window to let you in when you'd lost your key?"

"That must have been one of your other girls," said
Marjorie archly.

I smiled but said nothing.

"You don't look very well," said Marjorie. "Did
anything happen on the trip?"

"No."

"I worry about you. You look pretty done in."

"Is that a professional opinion, Doctor?"

She screwed her face up, like a little girl playing
doctors and nurses. "Yes, it is, honestly, darling."

"The diagnosis?"

"Well it's not anaemia." She laughed. She was very
beautiful. Even more beautiful when she laughed.

"And what do you usually prescribe for men in my
condition. Doc?"

"Bed," she said. "Definitely bed." She laughed and
undid my tie.

"You're shaking." She said it with some alarm. I was

shaking. The trip, the journey home, the weather, that damned number eighteen where I was now in mass production, had all got to me suddenly, but how do you explain that? I mean, how do you explain it to a doctor?

Chapter 4

The senior officer in Control Suite at commencement of game is CONTROL. Change of CONTROL must be communicated to Red Suite and Blue Suite (and any additional commanders), in advance and in writing. CONTROL's ruling is final.

RULES. "TACWARGAME." STUDIES CENTRE. LONDON

You might think you know your boss, but you don't. Not unless you've seen him at home on Sunday.

There are only three trains to Little Omber on Sunday. The one I caught was almost empty except for a couple of Saturday-night revellers, three couples taking babies to show Mums, two priests going to the seminary and half a dozen soldiers connecting with the express.

Little Omber is only thirty-five miles from central London but it is remote, and rural in a general way: frozen fish fingers, and picture-window housing-estates for the young executive.

I waited at the deserted railway station. I hardly knew Charles Schlegel the third, Colonel U.S. Marine Corps Air Wing (retired), so I was expecting anything from a psychedelic Mini to a chauffeured Rover. He'd taken over the Studies Centre only ten days before I'd gone off on my last sea trip, and our acquaintance had been limited to a Charles Atlas handshake and a blurred glimpse of a pin-striped Savile Row three piece, and a Royal Aero Club tie. But that didn't mean that he hadn't already scared the shit out of half the staff, from the switchboard matron to the night door-keeper. There was a rumour that he'd been put in to find an excuse for closing the Centre down, in support of which he was authoritatively quoted as saying we were "an antediluvian charity, providing retired limey admirals with a chance to win on the War Games Table the battles they'd screwed up in real life."

We all resented that remark because it was gratuitous, discourteous and a reflection on all of us. And we wondered how he'd found out.

Bright red export model XKE—well, why didn't I guess. He came out of it like an Olympics hurdler and grasped my hand firmly and held my elbow, too, so that I couldn't shake myself free. "It must have got in early," he said resentfully. He consulted a large multifaced wristwatch of the sort that can time high-speed races under water. He was wearing charcoal trousers, hand-made brogues, a bright-red woollen shirt that exactly matched his car, and a shiny green flying jacket, with lots of Mickey Mouse on sleeves and chest.

"I screwed up your Sunday," he said. I nodded. He was short and thickset, with that puffed-chest stance that small athletes have. The red shirt, and the way he cocked his head to one side, made him look like a gigantic and predatory robin redbreast. He strutted around the car and opened the door for me, smiling as he did so. He wasn't about to apologize.

"Come on up to the house for a sandwich."

"I have to get back," I argued without conviction.

"Just a sandwich."

"Yes, sir."

He let in the clutch, and heel-and-toed like a rally driver. He gave the car the same sort of attention that I suppose he'd given his F-4 or his B-52 or his desk, or whatever it was he flew before they unleashed him onto us. "I'm glad it was you," he said. "You know why I say that?"

"Man management?"

He gave me a little you'll-find-out-buddy smile.

"I'm glad it was you," he explained slowly and patiently, "because I haven't had a chance of a pow-wow with you or Foxwell, on account of the mission."

I nodded. I liked the glad-it-was-you stuff. You'd have thought the message said anyone who'd like a free train ride to Little Omber this Sunday could go.

"Goddamned imbecile," he muttered as he overtook a Sunday driver tooling down the white line, chatting with his kids in the back seat.

Close to Schlegel, I could see that the sun-lamp tan was there to disguise the complicated surgery he'd had on his jaw. What from a distance might look like the legacy of acne was a pattern of tiny scars that gave one side of his face the permanent hint of a scowl. Sometimes his face puckered enough to bare his teeth in a curious lopsided humourless smile. He did one now. "I can imagine," he said. "Yank trouble-shooter, hundred missions in Nam. They probably are saying I'm a hatchet man." He paused. "Are they saying that?"

"I've heard it whispered."

"What else?"

"They are saying that you are taking the staff aside one by one and giving them a working over." They

weren't saying that—as far as I knew—but I wanted
to get his reaction.

"Like this?"

"Let's wait and see."

"Huh." He did that crooked smile again. He slowed
to go through the village. This was really home-counties
stuff: six shops and five of them selling real estate. It
was the kind of authentic English village that only Germans, Americans and real-estate men can afford. At the
far end of the village there were four locals in their
Sunday clothes. They turned to watch us pass. Schlegel
gave them a stiff-armed salutation like the ones in that
old English war film. They nodded and smiled. He
turned off the road at a plastic sign that said "Golden
Acre Cottage. Schlegel" in ye olde English lettering.
He gunned the motor up the steep track and fired
gravel and soft earth from the deep-tread tyres.

"Nice place," I said, but Schlegel seemed to read
my thoughts. He said, "When they cut my orders they
said I must be within easy access of NATO/A.S.W.
down the road at Longford Magna. Your government
won't let us Yanks buy a place to live—by law, by
law! And half the country is owned by the same
English lord who's got his finger in my eye." He
slammed on the brakes and we slid to a halt inches
short of his front door. "A goddamn lord!"

"You haven't started Chas off about the landlord, I
hope," said a woman from the doorway.

"This is my bride, Helen. There are two daughters
and a son around the house someplace."

He'd parked outside a large thatched cottage, with
black cruck-frame timbers and freshly whitened plaster.
Placed on the front lawn there was a very old single-

furrow plough and over the front door there was a
farming implement that I didn't recognize. The daughters arrived before I was even half out of the car.
Slim, fresh-faced, clad in jeans and brightly coloured
lambswool sweaters, it was difficult to tell wife from
teenage daughters.

"What a wonderful thatching job," I said.

"Plastic," said Schlegel. "Real thatch harbours ver-
min. Plastic is cleaner, quicker and longer lasting."

Mrs Schlegel said, "Gee Chas, you should have told
me. I was only doing B.L.T.s for lunch."

"B.L.T.s, Helen! You want to send him into a state
of shock? These Brits strike into roast beef with all the
trimmings for Sunday lunch."

"A bacon, lettuce and tomato sandwich will be fine,
Mrs Schlegel."

"Helen, call me Helen. I sure hope Chas hasn't been
too rude about our English landlord."

The Southern United States—its climate and terrain
so suitable for training infantry and aviators—has
played a part in moulding the character of American
military men. And it is there that so disproportionately
many of them met their wives. But Mrs Schlegel was
no Southern belle. She was a New Englander, with all
the crisp assurance of that canny breed.

"He'd have to be a lot ruder before he could hope
to offend me . . . er . . . Helen." The sitting-room had
a big log fire perfuming the centrally heated air.

"A drink?"

"Anything."

"Chuck made a jug of Bloody Marys before going to
meet you." She was no longer young, but you could
have prised that snub nose and freckled face out of a

Coke commercial. The teenager's grin, the torn jeans and relaxed hands-in-pocket stance made me happy to be there.

"That sounds just right," I said.

"You Englishmen . . . that cute accent. That really gets to me. Do you know that?" she asked her husband.

"We'll go into the den, Helen. He's brought me some junk from the office."

"Take the drinks with you," said Mrs Schlegel. She poured them from a huge frosted glass jug. I sipped at mine and coughed.

"Chas likes them strong," said Mrs Schlegel. At that moment a small child came through the sitting-room. He wore a Che Guevara sweatshirt, and, with arms outstretched, dumped small clods of garden earth upon the carpet while emitting a steady high-pitched scream.

"Chuckie!" said Mrs Schlegel mildly. She turned to me. "I suppose here in Britain any mother would beat the daylights out of a child for doing that."

"No, I believe there are a still a few who don't," I told her. We could hear the scream continue out into the garden and around the back of the house.

"We'll be up in the den," said Schlegel. He'd downed half of his drink and now he poured himself more and added some to my glass too. I followed him through the room. There were black timber beams across the ceiling, each one decorated with horse brasses and bridle fittings. I hit my head on the lowest one.

We went up a narrow wooden staircase that creaked at each step. Off the passage at the top of it there was a small box room with a "Do not disturb" label from the Istanbul Hilton. He pushed the door open with his elbow. The screaming child came nearer. Once inside Schlegel bolted the door.

He sat down heavily, and sighed. He had a rubbery face, well suited to his habit of pummelling it with his hands, pushing at his cheeks, bending his nose and then baring his teeth, as if to be sure that all the muscles were in working order. "I hate lords," he said. He fixed me with an unwinking stare.

"Don't look at me," I said.

"Aw, I don't mean that," he said. "Hell, no one would take you for a lord."

"Oh well," I said, trying to sound indifferent.

From Schlegel's den there was a view of the surrounding country. A clump of poplar trees was bare, except for bunches of mistletoe, and the birds that rested there before coming down to join in the feast of holly berries. The gate to the next field was open, and the cart tracks shone with ice all the way round the side of the hill over which the steeple of Little Omber church could be seen. Its bell began striking twelve. Schlegel looked at his watch. "Now that damned village clock is fast too," he said.

I smiled. That was the essence of Schlegel, as I was to find out.

"Bring good stuff this time?"

"I'll let you know when we see the analysis."

"Can't you tell when you're out there monitoring it?"

"One trip last year they found the Russians working a new Northern Fleet frequency. The monitor leader got permission to change the cruise route to get cross-bearings. They brought in forty-three fixed-position Russian radio stations. There was talk of some kind of citation."

"And . . . ?" said Schlegel.

"Buoys. Meteorological stations, some of them unmanned."

"But it wasn't you."

"I've always been on the cautious side."

"It's not a word you'd want on your fitness report in the Marine Corps."

"But I'm not in the Marine Corps," I said.

"And neither am I any longer—is that what you were about to say?"

"I wasn't going to say anything, Colonel."

"Drink up. If your new stuff is anything like the analysis I've been reading, I want to War Game the results and submit them for next summer's NATO exercises."

"It's been suggested before."

"It's a hardy annual, I know that. But I think I might do it."

If he was expecting a round of applause he was disappointed.

He said, "You'll see some dough pumped into the Centre if they agree to that one."

"Well, that's just fine for the controller of finance."

"And for the Studies Director, you mean?"

"If we ever use the stuff we're picking up on these trips as a basis for NATO fleet exercises, you'll see the Russians really light up and say tilt."

"How?" He bit into a cigar and offered them. I shook my head.

"How? For starters the C.-in-C. will recognize the NATO movements as their alert scheme, and he'll guess that these sub trips must be collecting! He'll hammer

the First Deputy who will get the War Soviet into a
froth . . . bad news, Colonel."

"You mean this is all something we should be at
pains to avoid."

"Then you are reading me correctly," I said. "They'll
know for certain that we have subs on the ocean floor
outside Archangel, they'll surmise about the Amderma
and Dikson patrols. And then maybe they'll guess what
we are doing in the River Ob. Bad news, Colonel."

"Listen, sweetheart, you think they don't already
know?" He lit the cigar. "You think those babies aren't
sitting on Norfolk, Virginia, taping our signals traffic
from under our water?"

"Colonel, I think they *are* sitting outside Norfolk.
For all I know they are up the Thames as far as Strat-
ford, and sending liberty crews ashore to see Ann
Hathaway's cottage. But so far, both sides have kept
stumm about these operations. You base NATO exercises on a real Russian Fleet alert, and Russian Northern Fleet are going to get roasted. And the price they'll
have to pay for returning life to normal will be nailing
one of our pig-boats."

"And you like it cosy?"

"We're getting the material, Colonel. We don't have
to rub their noses in it."

"No point in getting into a hassle about something
like this, son. The decision will be made far above this
level of command."

"I suppose so."

"You think I've come into the Centre to build an
empire? . . ." He waved a hand. "Oh, sure. Don't deny
it, I can read you like a book. That's what riles Foxwell too. But you couldn't be more wrong. This wasn't

an assignment I wanted, feller." The athletic Marine Colonel sagged enough to show me the tired old puppeteer who was working the strings and the smiles. "But now I'm here I'm going to hack it, and you'd just better believe."

"Well, at least we both hate lords."

He leaned forward and slapped my arm. "There you go, kid!" He smiled. It was the hard, strained sort of grimace that a man might assume when squinting into the glare of an icy landscape. Liking him might prove difficult, but at least he was no charmer.

He swivelled in his chair and clattered the ice cubes in the jug, using a plastic swizzle stick with a bunny design on the end. "How did you get into the Studies, anyway?" he asked me, while giving all his attention to pouring drinks.

"I knew Foxwell," I said. "I saw him in a pub at a time when I was looking for a job."

"Now straighten up, son," said Schlegel. "No one looks for a job any more. You were taking a year off to do a thesis and considering a lot of rather good offers."

"Those offers would have to have been damn near the bread line to make Studies Centre the best of them."

"But you've got your Master's and all those other qualifications: math and economics; potent mixture!"

"Not potent enough at the time."

"But Foxwell fixed it?"

"He knows a lot of people."

"That's what I hear." He gave me another fixed stare. Foxwell and Schlegel! That was going to be an inevitable clash of wills. No prizes for who was going to buckle at the knees. And what with all this lord-hating stuff . . . Ferdy wasn't a lord, but he'd no doubt do for Schlegel's all-time hate parade until a real lord came by in a golden coach. "And Ferdy fixed it?"

"He told Planning that I'd had enough computer experience to keep my hand from getting jammed in the input. And then he told me enough to make it sound good."

"A regular Mr Fixit." There was no admiration in his voice.

"I've earned my keep," I said.

"I didn't mean that," said Schlegel. He gave me the big Grade A—approved by the Department of Health —smile. It wasn't reassuring.

From the next room there came the shouts of children above the noise of the TV. There was a patter of tiny feet as someone screamed through the house, slammed the kitchen door twice and then started throwing the dustbin lids at the compost heap. Schlegel rubbed his face. "When you and Ferdy do those historical studies, who operates the computer?"

"We don't have the historical studies out on the War Table, with a dozen plotters, and talk-on, and all the visual display units lit up."

"No?"

"A lot of it is simple sums that we can do more quickly on the machine than by hand."

"You use the computer as an adding machine?"

"No, that's overstating it. I write a low-level symbolic programme carefully. Then we run it with variations of date, and analyse the output in Ferdy's office. There's not much computer time."

"You write the programme?"

I nodded, and sank some of my drink.

Schlegel said, "How many people in the Studies Group can write a programme and all the rest?"

"By all the rest, you mean, get what you want out of storage into the arithmetic, process it and bring it out of the output?"

"That's what I mean."

"Not many. The policy has always been . . ."

"Oh, I know what the policy has been, and my being here is the result of it." He stood up. "Would it surprise you to hear that I can't work the damn thing?"

"It would surprise me to hear that you can. Directors are not usually chosen because they can work the computer."

"That's what I mean. O.K., well I need anyone who knows what goes on in the Group and who can operate the hardware. What would you say if I asked you to be a P.A. for me?"

"Less work, more money?"

"Don't give me that stuff. Not when you go in to do Ferdy's historical stuff for free nearly every Saturday. More money maybe, but not much."

Mrs Schlegel tapped on the door and was admitted. She'd changed into a shirt-waist dress and English shoes and a necklace. Her dark hair was tied back in a tail. Schlegel gave a soft low whistle. "Now there's a tribute, feller. And don't bet a million dollars that my daughters are not also in skirts and fancy clothes."

"They are," said Helen Schlegel. She smiled. She was carrying a tray loaded with bacon, lettuce and tomato toasted sandwiches, and coffee in a large silver vacuum jug. "I'm sorry it's only sandwiches," she said again.

"Don't believe her," said Schlegel. "Without you here

we would have got only peanut butter and stale crackers."

"Chas!" She turned to me. "Those have a lot of English mustard. Chas likes them like that."

I nodded. It came as no surprise.

"He's going to be my new P.A.," said Schlegel.

"He must be out of his mind," said Mrs Schlegel. "Cream?"

"There's a lot more money in it," I said hurriedly. "Yes, please. Yes, two sugars."

"I'd want the keys to the mint," said Mrs Schlegel.

"And she thinks I've got them," explained Schlegel. He bit into a sandwich. "Hey, that's good, Helen. Is this bacon from the guy in the village?"

"I'm too embarrassed to go there any more." She left. It was clearly not a subject she wanted to pursue.

"He needed telling," said Schlegel. He turned to me. "Yes, clear up what you are doing in the Blue Suite Staff Room . . ." He picked a piece of bacon out of his teeth and threw it into an ashtray. "I'll bet she did get it from that bastard in the village," he said. "And meanwhile we'll put a coat of paint on that office where the tapes used to be stored. Choose some furniture. Your secretary can stay where she is for the time being. O.K.?"

"O.K."

"This history stuff with Foxwell, you say it's low-level symbolic. So why do we use autocode for our day to day stuff?"

I got the idea. My job as Schlegel's assistant was to prime him for explosions in all departments. I said, "It makes much more work when we programme the machine language for the historical studies but it keeps the machine time down. It saves a lot of money that way."

"Great."

"Also with the historical stuff we nearly always run the same battle with varying data to see what might have happened if . . . you know the kind of thing,"

"But tell me."

"The Battle of Britain that we're doing now . . . First we run the whole battle through—Reavley Rules . . ."

"What's that?"

"Ground scale determines the time between moves. No extension of move time. We played it through three times using the historical data of the battle. We usually do repeats to see if the outcome of a battle was more or less inevitable or whether it was due to some combination of accidents, or freak weather, or whatever."

"What kind of changed facts did you programme into the battle?" said Schlegel.

"So far we've only done fuel loads. During the battle the Germans had long-range drop tanks for the single-seat fighters, but didn't use them. Once you programme double fuel loads for the fighters, there are many permutations for the bombing attacks. We can vary the route to come in over the North Sea. We can double the range, bringing more cities under attack and so thinning the defences. We can keep to the routes and attacks actually used, but extend fighter escort time over the target by nearly an hour. When you have that many variations to run, it's worth bringing it right the way down, because machine time can be reduced to a quarter of autocode time."

"But if you were running it only once?"

"We seldom do that. Once or twice we've played

out a battle like a chess game but Ferdy always wins. So I've lost enthusiasm."

"Sure," said Schlegel, and nodded in affirmation of my good sense.

There was a silence in the house, and the countryside was still. The clouds had rolled back to reveal a large patch of clear blue sky. Sunlight showed up the dust of winter on the austere metal desk at which Schlegel sat. On the wall behind it there was a collection of framed photographs and documents recording Schlegel's service career. Here was a cocky crew-cut trainee in a Stearman biplane on some sunny American airfield in World War Two; a smiling fighter pilot with two swastikas newly painted alongside the cockpit; a captain hosed-down after some final tropical-island mission; and a hollow-cheeked survivor being assisted out of a helicopter. There were half a dozen group photos, too: Marine flyers with Schlegel moving ever closer to the centre chair.

While I was looking at his photos there was the distant roar of a formation of F-4s. We saw them as dots upon the blue sky as they headed north.

Schlegel guessed that they were going to the bombing range near King's Lynn. "They'll turn north-west," he said, and no sooner had he spoken the words than the formation changed direction. I turned back to the sandwiches rather than encourage him. "Told you," he said.

"Ferdy didn't want to give anyone the excuse to say that the machine time was costing too much."

"So I hear, but this historical stuff . . . is it worth *any* machine time?"

I didn't react to the provocation. A man doesn't give up his spare time working at something he believes not worth continuing. I said, "You're the boss, that's what you'll have to decide."

"I'm going to find out what it's costing. We can't go on eating our heads off at the public trough."

"Strategic Studies is a trust, Colonel Schlegel. Under its terms, historical studies were a part of its purpose. We don't have to show a profit at the end of the year."

He pinched his nose as a pilot might to relieve sinus pressure. "Have another sandwich, kid. And then I'll run you down to the station for the two twenty-seven."

"Foxwell is a historian, Colonel, he's given quite a few years to this historical research. If it was cancelled now it would have a bad effect on the whole Studies Group."

"In your opinion?"

"In my opinion."

"Well, I'll bear that in mind when I see what it's costing. Now how about that sandwich."

"No mayonnaise this time," I said.

Schlegel got up and turned his back on me as he stared out of the window after the fading echoes of the Phantoms. "I'd better level with you, son," he said over his shoulder. "Your screening's not through, but I can block in the plan. The trustees have relinquished control of the Studies Centre, although they will still be on the masthead of the Studies Centre journal and mentioned in the annual accounts. From now on, control is through me from the same naval warfare committee that runs the U.S.N. TACWAR Analysis, your British Navy's Undersea Warfare Staff School and NATO Group-North at Hamburg."

"I see."

"Oh, you'll be able to carry on with the historical

games, if that's what you want, but gone are the days of the horse and buggy—and you'd better be sure Foxwell knows it."

"I'm sure it will become evident, Colonel."

"You're damn right it will," said Schlegel. He consulted his watch. "Maybe we'd better get your coat—remember that damn station is running fast."

Chapter 5

No game decisions or plays are valid or binding except those made in writing during game time.

RULES. "TACWARGAME." STUDIES CENTRE. LONDON

Ferdy Foxwell had this solid fuel stove in his office. He was some kind of fire freak, because he'd bribed five successive porters to bring him coal from next door without a chit. I thought the porters changed over just to make him go through the bribe business all over again, but Ferdy said that was just my nasty mind.

Anyway, he had this stove and I liked to go into his office in the winter time because I was a fire freak, too, in a small way of business.

When I entered I found Ferdy reading *Red Star,* the Soviet Defence Review, designed by Smersh to kill by boredom.

"There are one hundred and twenty military academies in Russia," said Ferdy. "And that's not counting technical staff colleges." He turned the page and folded it into a small wad again, turning it in his hands as he read down the column. He looked up as he got to the end. "Is Schlegel Irish?"

"That's it," I said. "One of the Boston O'Schlegels."

"I thought he must be," Ferdy said.

"That last programme failed, Ferdy. They'd set the bloody label twice. When one of the boys corrected it, it read-in but then stopped. The intermediate print-out is on its way."

"Ummm."

"Someone will have to stay tonight."

"What for?"

"If we don't finish today, we won't have machine time again until Thursday. Unless you know some way of fiddling the computer charges."

Our programmes were written in FORTRAN (Formula Translation Language) and fed into the computer on tape together with a "processor tape" that translates it into instructions of a sort the machine can comply with. By means of the FORTRAN, certain common errors (like the double printed label that was Ferdy's fault) were programmed to respond on the print-out. On this tear-off sheet the machine had written: "I'm only a bloody machine but I know how to print a label once only."

I thought Ferdy would laugh, and I pushed the sheet across the desk to him, half expecting that he would pin it up on his board. He looked at the machine's message, screwed it into a ball and tossed it in the direction of his waste-basket.

"Bomber bloody Schlegel will have to hear about it, I suppose."

"He looks at the sheets every day."

"Only because you take them up to him."

I shrugged. Ferdy had no need to do these pro-grammes personally, but since he'd done this one it was his error and a stupid one. There was no way to hide it from Schlegel.

There was no real need for a clash to come between

Ferdy and the boss, yet it seemed to have an inevitability that they had both recognized already. Foxwell regarded my job as Schlegel's personal assistant as blacklegging; Schlegel was convinced that I spent half my working hours covering up for the incompetence of my cronies.

Ferdy dropped the wadded journal into his out-tray and sighed. He'd not been reading it, he'd been waiting for me to come back from the computer. He got to his feet with a lot of creaking and groaning. "Fancy a drink?"

"At the Lighthouse?"

"Wherever you like."

Ferdy was usually more imperious in his invitations. I interpreted it as a plea. I said, "As long as I'm not too late home."

It was a cold evening. The Lighthouse was crowded: regulars mostly, some medical students and a Welsh Rugby club that had been infiltrated by hard-drinking Australians. "I knew he'd turn out a bastard," said Ferdy, pulling a cashmere scarf tight around his throat. The drinks came and he pushed a pound across the counter. "Have one with us, Landlord."

"Thank you, Mr Foxwell, a small bitter," said the barman. Characteristically, Ferdy chose a sheltered piece of bar counter under one of the huge sherry casks that formed one wall.

"You're the only one who can run the Russian desk, Ferdy," I told him. "Why don't you talk to Schlegel tomorrow? Tell him that if he doesn't give you the two girls and your programmer back you'll do something drastic."

"Drastic?" said Ferdy. "You mean the old karate chop: Zap! Pow! Wallop!"

"Well he couldn't get anyone else for weeks, Ferdy. And they couldn't leave the desk unmanned, could they? Hell, you don't need the money anyway. I don't know why you've stuck it as long as this."

"Zap, pow, wallop, Schlegel," said Ferdy experimentally. "No, I don't think that's my style."

"More my style, you mean?"

"I didn't say that, old chap."

Ferdy twisted up his face and gave an impression of Schlegel. "And cut out this zap, pow, wallop crap, Foxwell. You show me a good loser and I'll show you a loser." He let a trace of Schlegel's suppressed Southern drawl creep in at the end. I dreaded to think what Ferdy did to imitate me when I wasn't around.

I said, "You should get some of your titled relatives down to your place one weekend . . ."

"And invite Schlegel and his 'bride.' You know I had considered even that . . ."

"Big heads think the same."

"But it's a bit feeble, isn't it?"

"You know your relatives better than I do."

"Yes, well, not even my bloody titled relatives deserve a weekend of Schlegel. Drink up, old lad, he's bringing some more."

Ferdy had ordered more drinks by raising an eyebrow at a garrulous barman that he treated like an old family retainer. I paid for them, and Ferdy laid into his brandy and soda as though he didn't want to risk it being knocked over. "What's the difference," he said, after draining it. "It's obvious the bloody Yanks are going to close us."

"You're wrong there," I told him.

"Time will tell," he said portentously.

"No need to wait. I can tell you that they are pumping a couple of million into the Studies Group over the next six months. We're going to have five hours a day computer time, including Saturdays and Sundays."

"You can't be serious."

But Ferdy knew that I was in a position to tell him. "Scenarios," I said. Instead of the studies, we were going to do projections forward: strategic guesses on what might happen in the future.

Ferdy is only a few inches taller than me but he is able to make me feel like a dwarf when he leans forward to murmer in my earhole. "We'd need all the American data—the real hard stuff," he said.

"I think we're going to get it, Ferdy."

"That's pretty high-powered. Scenarios would be top level security. Joint Chiefs level! I mean we'd be running alive with Gestapo! . . . plastic credit cards with our photos, and Schlegel looking at our bank balances."

"Don't quote me, but . . ." I shrugged.

Ferdy tucked into his brandy and soda. "O.K.," Ferdy muttered, "industrial action it is then."

As if on cue Schlegel came into the saloon bar. I saw him look round for us. Systematically he checked everyone along the counter and then came through into the public bar. "I'm glad I found you," he said. He smiled to indicate that he'd overlook the fact that it was still office hours.

"Brandy and soda for me," said Ferdy. "And this is a Barley Wine."

"O.K.," said Schlegel; he waved his hand to indicate

that he'd understood. "Can you do the Red Admiral tomorrow for some visiting firemen from CINCLANT?"

"Zap, pow, wallop," said Ferdy.

"How's that again?" said Schlegel cupping his ear.

"Bit short notice," said Ferdy. He shuffled his feet and bit his lip as if trying to work out the difficulties involved, although we all knew that he'd have to do it if Schlegel asked.

"So was Pearl Harbor," said Schlegel. "All I'm asking for is a simple A.S.W. run-through, to show these idiots how we work."

"Anti-Submarine Warfare run-through," said Ferdy patiently, as though encountering the expression for the very first time. It was easy to understand why Schlegel got angry.

"Anti-Submarine Warfare run-through," said Schlegel, without concealing the self-restraint. He spoke as if to a small child. "With you acting as the C.-in-C. of the Russian Northern Fleet and these NATO people running the Blue Suite to fight you."

"Which game?"

"The North Cape Tactical Game, but if it escalates we'll let it go."

"Very well," said Ferdy, after stretching his silence to breaking point.

"Great!" said Schlegel, with enough enthusiasm to make some of the Welsh Rugby club stop singing.

He looked at the two of us and gave a big smile. "There'll be Admiral Cassidy and Admiral Findlater: top brass from CINCLANT. Well, I've got a lot to do before they arrive." He looked around the pub as if to check on our associates. "Don't be late in the morning."

Ferdy watched him all the way to the door. "Well

at least we know how to get rid of the bastard," said Ferdy. "Ask him to buy a round of drinks."

"Give it a rest, Ferdy."

"Oh, don't think I don't know what's going on. You come out and buy me a drink and soften me up for him."

"O.K., Ferdy," I said. "You have it your way." Just for a minute I was about to blow my top, the way I would have done in the old days. But I had to admit, I was Schlegel's assistant, and it could have looked like that. I said, "Just four beats to the bar, Ferdy. Remember?"

"Sorry," said Ferdy, "but it's been a bloody awful week."

"Why?" I asked.

"I'm sure they are watching the house again."

"Who?"

"Our burglary last May; could be the same people."

"Oh, burglars."

"Oh yes, I know you all think I go on about it."

"No, Ferdy."

"You wait until you've been burgled. It's not so damned funny."

"I never said it was."

"Last night there was a taxi outside the house. Driver just sat there—nearly three hours."

"A taxi?"

"Say it was waiting for a fare. Ask me if the meter was on—it was on. But that doesn't mean it wasn't a burglar. What's a cab doing out there in the mews at three o'clock in the morning?"

It was a good time to tell Ferdy about my visit to number eighteen. I'd have to tell someone sooner or later and so far I'd not even told Marjorie. It was then that I remembered that I'd not seen Mason—the one who'd identified me—in the office lately. "Do you remember that little creep named Mason? Did the weather print-outs. Had that tiny dog in his office some days, the one that crapped in the hall and that Italian Admiral trod in it."

"Mason, his name was."

"That's what I said: Mason."

"He's gone," said Ferdy. "Doubled his salary, they say. Got a job with some German computer company . . . Hamburg or somewhere . . . good riddance if you ask me."

"How long ago?"

"While we were on the trip. A month or so. You didn't lend him any money did you?"

"No."

"That's good, because I know he went off only giving personnel twenty-four hours notice. Personnel were furious about it."

"They would be," I said.

"He came to us from Customs and Excise," said Ferdy, as if that explained everything.

The best was was probably to mention the number eighteen business to Ferdy like this, over a drink. What was the alternative: suspect everyone—paranoia, madness, sudden death, and into the big King Lear scene.

"Ferdy," I said.

"Yes."

I looked at him for a full minute but didn't speak. Confiding is not one of my personality traits: it's being an only child, perhaps. That's Marjorie's theory, anyway. "Brandy and soda, wasn't it, Ferdy?"

"That's it, brandy and soda." He sighed. "You wouldn't want to come back while I look at that programme again?"

I nodded. I'd already told Marjorie that I'd have to stay. "It will be quicker if both of us do it."

*   *   *

When I finally left the Centre I didn't drive directly home. I went over to Earl's Court and cruised past my old flat. At the end of the road I parked and thought about it for a minute or two. For a moment I wished I had confided in Ferdy and perhaps brought him here with me. but it was too late now.

I walked back on the other side of the street. It was a fine night. Above the crooked rooftops there was a pattern of stars. The crisp polar air that had driven away the low clouds made the traffic noises, and my footsteps, abnormally loud. I trod warily, moving past each of the parked cars as if looking for my own. I need not have been so cautious. I saw them fifty yards ahead and long before they might have seen me. It was an orange Ford: black vinyl top, rear-window slats and that absurd spoiling device to stop the rear wheels lifting at speeds above Mach One. Frazer. There were undoubtedly others like it, but this was Frazer's car. The long whip aerial and finally the silhouetted triangle of the Admiralty permit on the windscreen confirmed it. It would be just like Frazer to want a mileage allowance instead of using a car from their pool.

There was a girl with him. They were smoking and talking. but they were situated perfectly to watch the entrance to number eighteen.

They say that on his deathbed, Voltaire, asked to renounce the devil, said, "This is no time to be making new enemies." That's how I felt about Frazer, and whoever and whatever was behind him. I turned the ignition key and thought about home.

I wanted the end of the live concert on Radio 3 but got the news on Radio 4. On Monday the car workers would strike for a thirty-five per cent wage increase, and a six-week paid holiday. The Russians had announced the six-man team that would go to Copenhagen for the German reunification talks. Two of the Russian team were women, including its leader, who was in the running for chairman of the whole circus. (A proposal energetically supported by Women's Liberation, who planned to march to Westminster on Sunday afternoon.) There'd been a fire in a Finsbury Park hairdresser's, and a stick-up in a pay-office in Epsom. The weather forecast was frost, overcast skies and rain following. And I'd missed the best part of the concert.

Chapter 6

There is no limit to the number of staff officers or advisers in either Suite, nor need the Red and Blue Suite staffs be of equal size.

RULES. 'TACWARGAME.' STUDIES CENTRE. LONDON

The Studies Centre—now STUCEN LONDON—is a particularly appalling example of Gothic revival, that in anywhere but Hampstead would have been too conspicuous to house secrets.

"Caledonia," for such was deeply incised on its portals, was built by a nineteenth-century ironmaster to celebrate the Royal Navy's decision to reinforce the wooden walls of England with ironclads.

It was a three-storey maroon and mustard monolith, with turrets, domes and slots for bowmen. The main staircase would not have cramped Busby Berkeley, and the marine life depicted in mosaics in the hall might well have made Disney feel quite proud.

The smell of cheap metal-polish and warm machine-oil penetrated even to Ferdy's stove-heated den, and the carbolic that they used to swab down the hall was probably what was killing the winter lettuce that I was trying to grow in the conservatory.

But it was probably the ballroom—with its glazed

dome roof—that attracted the men who chose Caledonia as the Studies Centre. Most of its panelling was intact. And, although it had suffered under a decade or two of military footwear, the inlaid sprung floor would still have supported a light fantastic or two. The minstrel's gallery had been extended and glass-faced to make a long Control Room—or "god box"—from which the Director and his staff could look down upon the War Table.

The Table took up most of the ballroom. It was well over seven yards wide and at least twelve yards long. In the bottom left-hand corner there was the tiny Jan Mayen Island. The North Pole was halfway up the left of the table, the right showed the ragged northern coast of the Soviet Union, from the Laptev Sea and the New Siberian Islands right the way down to Murmansk and a slice of Norway.

The whole Table could be folded away and replaced by other latitudes, but this was our bread and butter. Sections of the Table hinged to give access to plotters who couldn't reach far enough across Lapland to find the Barents Sea. But conveniently close to the bottom edge of the board there was the almost land-locked White Sea which sheltered Archangel, where Soviet Undersea Warfare Command had built a large underground control centre, and a powerful series of transmitters to control the Northern Fleet submarines.

Only a few hundred miles away was the Northern Fleet's HQ at Murmansk, and farther along the Kola Fjord was Poliarnyi. Ice free almost all the year round, from here came the Russian Navy's Tupolev 16s: the gigantic "Badgers," noses full of guidance radar, slung with intelligence pods and Kennel air-breathers under each wing, so bedecked with missiles and gear that they'd had to extend the runway by five hundred metres to get them into the air. These were the boys that came sniffing into Hamish Sound and down even to the Thames Estuary and out to the Atlantic: timing the defences, listening to the radio traffic and watching the shipping all the way to eastern Canada.

From here too came the big jet flying boats, crammed with homing torpedoes and nuclear depth charges, patrolling the Northern Sea Route in summer, and in winter the Arctic ice. And here were helicopters of all shapes and sizes, from two-seaters to sky cranes. All nice kids without a doubt, but don't think they were staging their all-weather patrols in case some Russian Chris-craft owner needed winching to safety.

"Are we all here?" Ferdy asked, and waited while the last two visitors caught up with us.

It wasn't Ferdy's job to show visiting teams round the Centre, but, now that I was Schlegel's P.A., it wasn't mine either. We compromised; I stayed close to the tour while Ferdy shepherded them through the building.

They'd seen the Blue Suite, where they would sit for a week fighting the battle of the Northern seas. It was a fine room on the first floor, with chubby angels entwined each side of the fireplace and a crystal chandelier. So far the chandelier had survived the drastic changes that had made the elegant library into an Operations Room of the sort that one might find on a Guided Missile Destroyer, only with more central floor space. Adjoining it, a box room had been converted to a Sonar Control Room that we used for special tactical games that were subordinated to the main action. Today the shutters were open and Blue Ops was lighted by daylight, but tomorrow the room would be dark except for the visual displays and the side-lit plastic sheets that depicted the action, bound by bound.

The library—as we still called it—had a door opening on to the upper gallery. Its fine carved mahogany balustrade provided a place from which one could see the brightly coloured mosaic paving of the entrance hall below. It was easy to imagine it crowded with men in frocked coats, talking about Dreadnoughts, and women in ostrich feathers and silk, whispering about Edward VII's love life.

The room adjoining the library, once a small bedroom, was now a conference room with closed-circuit television showing the most vital displays from Blue Ops. This was where the visitors would spend most of their time, watching the V.D.U.s and agonizing over whether to resort to nuclear depth charges or abandon their advanced submarines. On the same level there were bathrooms, bedrooms, a well-stocked bar and a sentry to make sure none of the visitors tried to see what was displayed downstairs on the big War Table. For only the ballroom Table showed the true state of affairs for both sides. Blue Suite, just like Red Suite in the basement, had only the results of reports and analysis. And that was another name for guesswork.

"For the big strategic game we often assume that the coast of northern Norway has already been occupied by the Soviet Union," said Ferdy. "If war came, that would be inevitable—and we believe it would be fast."

Once he'd put it even more bluntly than that to a group of senior officers form AFNORTH at Kolsaas. None of them, especially the Norwegians, had proved readily convertible to Ferdy's instant strategy.

But today there were no Norwegians. I looked at them, all lined up along the War Table. Behind the two V.I.P. American admirals and their aides, there was the usual rag-bag: cocky thirty-year-olds, earnest forty-year-olds, desperate fifty-year-olds, career officers who, in their ill-chosen civilian suits, looked more like insurance salesmen. There were seldom any surprises. An elderly, soft-spoken New Zealand Captain from the purchasing commission, a bald Dutch senior intelligence officer, two American submarine captains, fresh from a staff tour at CINCPAC, a civilian war-game specialist from SACLANT (Striking Fleet), some embassy free-loaders and a one-eyed German who'd already confided to us twice that he'd sunk over a hundred thousand tons of Allied shipping. "During the war, of course," he added, but we had only his word on that.

"There's a problem with all these games," warned one of the embassy attachés, a Canadian. "If you don't introduce the element of chance—dice or random machine—you get no idea of what happens in war. But introduce it, and you're into the gambling business."

I winked at Ferdy but he had to keep a straight face while this Canadian mastermind was looking at him. We'd often said that no matter how slow you take the briefing, one of these hoorays is going to ask that very question. You could put it on the big machine and trip it for a print-out.

"It is not a war-game in that sense," said Ferdy. He smoothed his rumpled hair. "You do better to regard it as a historical reconstruction."

"I don't dig you," said the Canadian.

"Some history might be instructive, other aspects of history less so. If you learn from experience here, then that of course is splendid, but it's dangerous to start off thinking of the process as a future event."

"Is that why your set-up is civilian operated?"

"Perhaps it is," said Ferdy. Nervously he picked up one of the plastic plot markers from that morning's test run-through. "Let's be clear. We don't control any Fleet elements from here and neither do we predict what they might do in any future action. Once we made a strenuous effort to stop the word 'game' being used about anything we do here—'studies' is the operative word—but it was no use, people like 'game' better."

"That's because your material is too out of date by the time it's ready for the Table?" said the Dutchman.

"The material used here is collected from intelligence ships and aircraft. We probably could radio it back and have fairly recent data on the Table, but unless we processed the game at the same speed as an actual battle there would be little or no advantage."

"I'll tell you something, Mr Foxwell," said the German Captain. "If, God forbid, we ever have to start retransmitting electronic intelligence from the Barents Sea . . ." he tapped the War Table, ". . . I'll give you a dozen five-figure groups before they trip the nuclear minefields and end your game for ever."

The New Zealand officer said, "And game-time is always much slower than normal?"

"Yes, for many reasons it has to be. Tomorrow, when you are in the Blue Suite trying to control this ocean full of ships, submarines and aircraft, worrying about supplies and air cover for your bases—when you're trying to judge which of the sighting reports are a

Soviet strike force, and which are liver spots, you'll wish you had double the bound time that you'll get."

"But you'll fight us single-handed?" said the German.

"No," said Ferdy, "I'll have the same size staff that you'll have."

I interrupted him. "Mr. Foxwell is being modest," I said. "Red Suite Command Staff is a coveted assignment for those of us who want to catch up on their light fiction."

"I've been the Red Admiral many times by now," said Ferdy. "I can remember so many of the computer responses for my logistics. I can keep the overall line-up in my mind's eye more easily than you'll be able to. And I know all the tactics you are likely to pull out of the hat. By the way, have you decided which of you will be with me on the winning side?"

"Me," said one of the American submarine Captains.

"The confidence you display, Mr Foxwell." The German smiled acidly. "Is that because the standard of visiting staff officers is so low, or are you so expert?" He licked his lips as if tasting the last drips of lemon juice.

"I'll tell you my secret," said Ferdy. "You're mostly experienced naval men with many years of sea duty. All sailors are romantics. You look at this table and you see frigates, cruisers and nuclear subs. You hear the breakers, smell the warm diesel and hear the voices of old friends. Committing those units—and the men inside them—to battle is a traumatic experience for you. You hesitate, you vacillate, you die."

"And you are not a naval man, Mr Foxwell?" the German asked.

"As far as I'm concerned," said Ferdy, "you're just

a bag of plastic markers." He picked up one of the plot markers that gave the strength, direction and identity of a naval force steaming past the Jan Mayen Island. Gently he tossed it into the air and caught it. Then he hurled it into the far corner of the room where it landed with a noise of breaking plastic.

The War Room was silent. The two Admirals continued to look at Ferdy with the same polite interest with which champions eye contenders at weigh-ins.

"Then we'll see you all tomorrow, gentlemen," said Ferdy. "And come out fighting."

Chapter 7

The success or failure of ALL games will be measured ONIY by the lessons learned through post-game analysis (POGANA). In this respect the object of each game is not victory.

"NOTES FOR WARGAMERS." STUDIES CENTRE.
LONDON

When there was a game in progress, the Studies Centre became a different sort of place. The mess served forty lunches and there wasn't even standing room in the upstairs bar. My new job as Schlegel's personal assistant meant that I spent a great deal of time in the Control Room looking down from the balcony to the War Table. Also I was one of the few people permitted to visit both Blue Suite and Red Suite while the game was in progress.

Ferdy and his five deputies were in Red Ops in the basement. His conference room adjoining it was seldom used unless a real crisis occurred. Ferdy liked to be in the darkened Ops Room watching the Visual Display Units and arguing with the plotters. Even then he got bored sometimes, and would invent complex disputes just so that Schlegel would send me down there to sort it out. Not that there was ever an outward sign of the pandemonium that was in the staff's minds. Even in Blue Suite on the first day they were cool calm and collected, reading data print-outs or asking for clarification from one of the Technical referees.

Like the opening moves in a chess game, the first few bounds were predictable. The knight's opening—and its offensive-defensive posture—was directly comparable with both sides putting their nuclear subs up close to the coastal cities of the enemy. For such a move inhibited attacks on them (for fear the submarine's atomic missiles would be triggered by depth charges and their cities destroyed). Pulling the bishops out through the gaps could be likened to the fighting for the northern coastline of Arctic Norway, for the Russian Navy needed ice-free ports to utilize its full surface fighting strength in the Atlantic.

The winter struggle for ports below the drift-ice limits was more a matter of luck than judgment. The invasion of Norway by Russian land forces was not designed by Red Suite. Ferdy had to read it off the big computer. Its progress depended upon strategic games played by NATO and the U.S.N. at other places and other times. A Russian air-supplied move through the long finger of Finland that pointed at Tromsö leaves the naval arm to pursue its own war. But an amphibious bid for the port of Narvik relegates the submarines to defensive roles and puts Red Suite into the intricate business of ice-breaking, Northern Route patrols, convoy escorts; and it means devoting all the air to defensive umbrellas.

Ferdy was lucky; the current strategic theory was that Sweden and Finland would resist an overland movement, and this centred the fighting too far east to drain Northern Fleet resources. Ferdy breathed a sigh of relief when he read the Land Forces report off the teleprinter.

He offered me one of his best cigars. I waved it away. "I'm trying to stop."

"Bad timing," said Ferdy. He carefully cut the Punch Suprema and offered one to the American submariner who was acting as his aide. "A stogie, kid?"

"No thanks, comrade."

Ferdy puffed gently as the cigar started to glow. "And I'll want air recce and the exact limit of the drift-ice."

"We've got that," said the submariner.

"We've got the seasonal average. I want it exactly." He scribbled a request for the air reconnaissance and a clerk typed it onto the teleprinter that was connected to Schlegel's Control Balcony.

"The forecast is two miles with a four thousand foot ceiling," said the weather clerk.

The clerk at the teleprinter waited for Control to reply before reading off the answer. "They are giving us two Be-10 Mallow flying boats, out of Murmansk."

Ferdy ran a red chinagraph pencil across the map, making a line to divide the White Sea from the Barents Sea at its narrowest place. The clerk at the teleprinter took the Be-10's punch card and asked the computer the arming details of the jet flying boats that Ferdy was going to use. They were equipped with rockets, homing torpedoes and depth charges. Ferdy nodded and passed the print-out to the submariner.

"Put them up earliest," said Ferdy. He turned to me. "Schlegel will bring that cloud down and write those flying boats off, you see."

"Don't be stupid, Ferdy. That weather comes off the computer, you know that."

Ferdy smiled grimly.

I'd continued to use the personal locker in the Red Ops, more because clearing it might have offended Ferdy than because it was very convenient to me. I went through into the narrow locker room and let the door bang closed behind me before switching on the lights.

There were eight lockers there, one for each of the Ops Room staff, and a couple of spares. Mine had a *Playboy* nude stuck on the door, a legacy from its previous owner. The erotic effect was not enhanced by the portrait of Beethoven that Ferdy had carefully matched and pasted over the head of it. Or by the football boots that some unknown collage artist had added a week later. By that time, there were not so many people who didn't know whose locker it was. So now that the corner of the door had been bent at right angles with a blunt instrument, and the contents ransacked, I was inclined to take it personally.

"My locker's been forced, Ferdy."

"I noticed that," said Ferdy.

"Thanks a lot," I said.

"Shouting won't help things," said Ferdy.

"How's about letting me in on what will help things," I said.

"Is anything missing?" the American boy asked.

"No," I said. "Not as far as I can see."

"Well, there you are," said Ferdy.

"I'll toddle," I said.

"You'll tell Schlegel I want weather?"

"I'll tell him," I said. "But he'll get it off the computer like I told you."

"You put some weather on the line," said Ferdy. "Or don't bother about dinner tonight."

"You don't get out of it as easy as that," I said. "See you at eight."

Ferdy nodded. "Now we're going to put some sonobuoys into the Kara, and we'll start a search with the Mallow flying boats. Take a good look at the weather reports and then place them."

The young American submariner had removed his uniform jacket and now he loosened his tie. He pushed the plastic markers that were the Russian flying boats along the line of the ice-limits. The ocean, which had always seemed so empty to him, was now a network of detection stations and seabed sonar. The flying boats were the most effective weapon of all, for they could land on the water and lower their detectors into it to get the anticline of the layered water. Then they could bring out their short-range Magnetic Anomaly Detectors to confirm that it was a big metal sub down there, and not just a whale or a patch of warm water.

"What about the ice-limits?" the boy asked.

"Forget it—bang your flying boats down wherever you want them to start the search."

"On the ice?"

"They've got wheels—either the ice is thick enough to take the weight of them or they'll float."

The boy turned to me. "Did the Russians ever do that?"

"No," I said. "But it would certainly change the tactical maps if it was possible."

"It'd shake up the electronics," said the boy. "It's

about forty tons of airplane—she'd be a thin scattering of rivets and radio tubes if you did that with her." He held the plastic marker in his hand, hovering above the deep water channel where the attacking U.S. submarines would probably turn to reach the Russian coastline.

"Place those damned markers," said Ferdy. "This is a war, not a safety week."

"Jesus," whispered the boy, and now he was out there in the freezing ocean with those two Mallows, laden with A.S.W. equipment, right over him. "There's just no place to hide if you do that."

* * *

It's a rare event that I'm home early enough to worry about the parking regulations. Marjorie was even earlier. She was already dressed up and ready to go to Ferdy's dinner party that evening. She was relaxed and beautiful and determined to mother me. She made a big pot of coffee and added a plate of Florentina sticky cakes to the tray placed within arm's reach of my favourite chair. She offered to put her car in the lockup so that there would be room for mine on the meter. And before she went to move both cars herself, she told me for the third time that my suit was laid out on the bed and there was a clean shirt in the top drawer. And she was beautiful, clever and she loved me.

The bell rang only two minutes after she'd gone downstairs. I chuckled in that patronizing way that men do when women forget keys, can't open a tin or stall in traffic. "Put your door keys on the same ring . . ." I said, but when the door was open far enough, I saw two men in black overcoats and one of them carried a burnished metal case that might have contained soap samples.

"No thanks," I said.

But the sort of sales course these two had graduated from had "no thanks" as the first lesson. They were heavyweights: with big hats that bent the tops of their ears over, and the sort of teeth that went up in value whenever paper money slipped. They lowered their shoulders. I had the door almost closed when four hundred pounds of animal protein split the facing board almost without pause and sent me pirouetting down the hall.

By the light coming through the hall window I could see them better. One—a swarthy man, with a neatly trimmed beard and pigskin gloves—I'd seen before. He had been in the passenger seat of the blue BMW that had tried to force us off the Great Hamish road.

It was this one that tried to bear hug me now, and put his face low enough for me to elbow. He avoided the full force of it only by twisting his head, while I put my foot on his instep with enough force to make him grunt. He reeled back into his friend but my victory was short-lived. All three of us knew that I'd stand little chance if they backed me into the larger space of the lounge. They paused before the head-down charge, then together they gave me the sort of treatment that had worked so well on the door panels. My feet left the ground and I went right over the back of the sofa. As I came in to land on the carpet, I took with me the coffee tray, cakes and a blizzard of flying chinaware.

I was still full length as the clean-shaven one came

wading through the debris. I was only just fast enough
to ensure that his big, black, well-polished military
boot, with its lace double knotted, nicked my ear, instead of carrying away the side of my head.

I rolled away from him, raising myself up on my
knees. I grabbed the edge of the rug and fell forward
again still holding it. With one foot still raised he was
in the perfect pose. He went over like a brick chimney.
There was a thud as his head hit the glass front of the
TV, and a blast of song as his sleeve went down the
controls. For a moment he didn't move at all. On the
screen there were singing glove puppets, brutally com-
pressed and repeated across the screen in horizontal
slices.

The bearded one gave me no time to admire my
handiwork. He came at me even before I was fully
upright. One hand was ready to chop and the other
was looking for a wristlock. But the judo man is off
balance at the time he makes his grab. I jabbed him
hard. It was enough to make him step back a pace and
yell, although it might not have been had I not been
holding the brass-plated fire-tongs that Marjorie's
mother had given us for Christmas.

But I hadn't crippled either of them. I'd just slowed
them a little. Worse, I'd come to the end of my surprises: they were wary. The fellow under the TV was
already back on his feet and he was staring at the
flickering strips of glove puppet as if fearing for his
vision.

Then he turned and they came at me from different
sides. "Now let's talk," I said. "I've heard about hard-
sell techniques, but this is ridiculous."

The bearded one smiled. He was dying to put his

world-famous right cross on me. I could tell that from the way he was drawing the diagrams of how he'd do it. I taunted him twice, and then came in early to make him throw it. I took it on the forearm and it hurt like hell but not as much as the right jab I hung on his jaw.

He slewed as he fell, revealing the bald patch on his head. For a moment I felt ashamed, and then I thought maybe Joe Louis and Henry Cooper had bald patches, too. And by that time the other one was slamming short body punches into my ribs and I was making noises like an old concertina that had been dropped on the floor.

I punched him off, but baldy came back and took my left wrist with enough enthusiasm to make my nose touch my knees. And suddenly the whole world was sliced into horizontal slices and singing like glove puppets, and I could hear this voice shouting, "What did I tell you in the car. What did I tell you in the car." It was a very angry voice.

It wasn't Marjorie. It was a broad-shouldered elderly Soviet security Colonel named Stok. He was waving a pistol and threatening to do terrible things to his friends in Russian.

"He attacked us," said the hairy one.

"Get to work," said Stok. The bearded man picked up the metal case and went with it into the next room. "And fast," said Stok. "Very, very fast."

"There will be trouble," I said.

"We thought you both got into the car," said Stok.

"You'd better get new glasses before you trip off World War Three."

"We hoped you would be out," said Stok. "It would have been simpler."

"It's not complicated this way," I said angrily. "You let your gorillas out of their cage. oil your gun, rough up the citizens, break the furniture often enough. and soon life will be as simple here as it is in the Soviet Union."

Through the door I could see the two men getting drills and a hammer from the metal case. "They'll find nothing here," I told Stok.

"There is a conspiracy," Stok said. "A Soviet official is threatened."

"Why not tell the police?"

"How can we be sure the police are not the ones arranging it?"

"In your country, you can't," I said.

Stok's mouth moved as if he was about to argue but he thought better of it. He decided to smile instead but it wasn't a heart-warming smile. He unbuttoned his overcoat to find a handkerchief to wipe his nose. His suit was a well-cut Western one. With it he wore a white shirt and silver tie. The nervous hands and piercing eyes completed the Godfather look. "Five minutes. and we will be gone," he said.

From the next room there was a quick exchange in Russian too fast for me to understand even vaguely. "The medical bag?" said Stok to me. "What are you doing with a medical bag?"

"Marjorie's," I said. "The girl; she's a doctor."

Stok told them to carry on the search. "If the girl proves not to be a doctor we might have to return."

"If the girl proves not to be a doctor I might be dead," I said.

"You are not hurt," said Stok. He walked close to

me and looked at the tiny mark left by the welt of the
boot. "It is nothing," he said.

"By your standards nothing more than a good evening."

Stok shrugged. "You are under surveillance," he
said. "I warn you."

"The more the merrier," I said. "Tap the phone too
if it will make you feel good."

"It's not a joke."

"Oh! It's not. Well, I'm glad you told me that, before I split my sides laughing."

From the next room I could hear Stok's two friends
tapping and hammering, in pursuit of secret compartments. One of them brought him the file in which I
keep a record of my expenses. Stok put away his pistol
and put on his reading-glasses in order to scrutinize the
sheets but I knew there was nothing there that would
compromise security. I laughed. Stok looked up and
smiled and put the file back on the table.

"There's nothing," I said. "You're wasting your
time."

"Probably," agreed Stok.

"Ready," called the voice from the next room.

"Wait a minute," I said as I realized what they were
going to do. "I can explain about that—this flat be-
longed to a bookie. There's nothing in there now. Nothing at all."

I pushed Stok aside to get to the next room. His two
friends had fixed our Birmingham carpet upon the wall.
It covered the wall safe upon which they had affixed
six small charges. They triggered them as I got to the
doorway. The carpet billowed into a great spinnaker

before I heard the muffled bang. There was a rush of hot cordite-smelling air that hammered me backwards.

"Empty," said the bearded one; already he was throwing his odds and ends back into the metal case.

Stok looked at me and blew his nose. The other two hurried out through the front door but Stok delayed a moment. He raised a hand as if he was about to offer an apology or an explanation. But words failed him; he let the hand drop to his side, turned, and hurried out after his friends.

There was the sound of a scuffle as Frazer met the Russians on the stairs. But Frazer was no more of a match for them than I had been, and he came through the door dabbing at his nose with a blood-spotted handkerchief. There was a Special Branch man with him: a new kid who insisted upon showing me his card before photographing the damage.

Well, it had to be to Russians, I thought. There was something inimitable in it. Just like the business of forcing us off the road and then waiting in The Bonnet to show us who they were. Just like the intelligence trawlers that followed NATO ships, and the big Soviet Fleets that harassed us at sea. It was all part of the demonstration of their resources and their knowledge, an attempt to bully opponents into ill-considered action.

It was typical too that the security Colonel had arrived separately, taking no chances of being in the same car with the house-breaking tools and explosives. And that half-hearted gesture of regret—tough bastards, and I didn't like it. I mean, you go for a dip in the municipal baths, and you don't expect to catch sight of a shark fin.

They had all gone by the time Marjorie returned. At

first she didn't look through the bedroom door, to where the previous tenant's safe had its door dangling and its lock shredded into wire wool. Or at paper wrappings from the explosive charges or the twists of wire and dry batteries. And she didn't see the thick layer of old plaster that covered the bed and my suit and her dressing table. Or the carpet with its circular burn in the middle.

She saw me picking up the fragments of the china tea service her mother had given her and Jack for their wedding anniversary.

"I told you about the old man with the twisted hip," said Marjorie.

"What!" I said.

"Doing exercises. You'll do the same. You see! You'll be in the Emergency Ward with him: you're too old for press-ups."

I tossed the pieces of china on to the tray with the broken teapot.

"Well, if it wasn't exercises," said Marjorie, "what's happened?"

"A Colonel from the Russian embassy, and an explosives man, and a driver with gold teeth and a beard. And then there was the Navy and Special Branch taking photos."

She stared at me trying to see if I was joking. "Doing what?" she asked guardedly. She sniffed the burnt air and looked around the room.

"With a cast like that," I said, "who needs a plot?"

Chapter 8

Line reject. *To miss a move. Wargamers must remember that fuel, fatigue and all logistic support will continue to be expended during such a move. Continuous instructions (air patrols etc.) will be continued and naval units will continue on course unless halted by separate and specific instruction. Therefore, think twice before rejecting.*

GLOSSARY. "NOTES FOR WARGAMERS." STUDIES CENTRE. LONDON

There's a large piece of plush Campden Hill landscape trapped on the wrong side of Holland Park Avenue. That's where the Foxwells live. Past the police station there's a street of crumbling Victorian villas that West Indian tenants have painted pistachio green, cherry red and raspberry pink. See it in daylight and it's a gargantuan banana split, with a side-order of dented cars.

On the corner there's a mews pub: topless dancers Friday, Irish riots Saturday, on Sunday morning, advertising men and a sports car club. Alongside the pub there is the mews. At the mews's far end a gate opens onto the entirely unexpected house and garden that Foxwells have owned for three generations.

It was hard to believe that this was central London. The trees were bare, and sapless roses hung their shrunken heads. A hundred yards up the drive there was a large house just visible in the winter gloom. In front of it, well clear of the London planes, the gardener was burning the last of the fallen leaves. He raked the fire with great apprehension, as a man might goad a small dragon. A billow of smoke emerged and fierce embers crackled and glowed red.

"Evening, sir."

"Evening, Tom. Will it rain?" I went round and opened the car door for Marjorie. She knew how to operate it for herself, but when she had her hair up she liked to be treated like an elderly invalid.

"There's snow up there," said Tom. "Make sure your anti-freeze is in."

"I forgot to drain it out last year," I said. Feeling neglected, Marjorie put her hands in her pockets and shivered.

"That's cruel," said Tom. "She'll rust."

Ferdy's house sits on two acres of prime London building land. It makes the apples he grows in the orchard an expensive delicacy, but Ferdy is like that.

There were cars already there: Ferdy's Renault, a Bentley and an amazing vintage job: bright yellow, perhaps too ostentatious for Al Capone but certainly big enough. I parked my Mini Clubman next to it.

I hesitated for a moment before ringing the bell. These intimate little dinner parties of the Foxwells were planned with the special sort of skill that his wife gave to everything she did. Committees devoted to musical charities, societies for new music and, according to Ferdy, a trust that restored old organs. But in spite of such gags, Ferdy gave some of his time and money to the same charities. I knew that dinner would be followed by a short recital by some young singer or musician. I knew too that the performance would be Mozart, Schubert, Beethoven or Bach, because Ferdy had vowed never again to have me at one of the evenings the Foxwells dedicated to twentieth-century music. It was a disbarment for which I was eternally thankful. I guessed that the other guests that I saw at these dinners had similarly disgraced themselves by contributing to the discord.

Ferdy and Teresa were in deadly earnest about these musical soirées: they'd put me under real pressure to get me into my second-hand dinner suit. It made me look like a band leader waiting for a return of the nineteen thirties, but twice I'd gone along wearing my dark grey suit, and Teresa had told a mutual friend that I was a man delivering something from Ferdy's office—and she'd felt obliged to ask me to stay—democracy in action. I mean, I like the Foxwells, but everyone has their funny little ways. Right?

I pressed the bell.

Marjorie liked the house. She had an idea that one day, when we grew up, we'd be living in plastic and hardboard scaled-down versions of it. She stroked the door. It was set into an elaborate sea-shell canopy. On each side of it there was a lighted coach lamp. The burning leaves scented the night air. The Notting Hill traffic was no more than a soft purr. I knew that Marjorie was storing this moment in her memories. I leaned close and kissed her. She clutched my arm.

The door opened. I saw Ferdy, and behind him his wife Teresa. Out spilled the tinkles of music, laughter, and ice-cubes colliding with Waterford glass. It had everything, that house: suits of armour, stags' heads and gloomy portraits. And servants with lowered eyes who remembered which guests had hats and umbrellas.

There is a particular type of tranquil beauty that belongs to the very very rich. Teresa Foxwell had grown-up children, was on the wrong side of forty and gathering speed, but she still had the same melancholy beauty that had kept her photo in the society columns since she was a deb. She wore a long yellow and orange dress of marbled satin. I heard Marjorie's sharp intake of breath. Teresa knew how to spend money, there was no doubt of that.

Ferdy took my coat and handed it to someone off-stage.

Teresa took Marjorie's arm and walked her off. She must have seen the storm warnings.

"I'm so glad you're here," said Ferdy.

"Yes . . ." I said. "Well . . . good."

"You left early and there was a bit of a scene right after." He turned to a servant who was standing motionless with a tray of champagne. "Put the tray on the hall stand," said Ferdy.

"A tray of champagne," I said. "Now that's what I call hospitality."

Ferdy picked up two glasses and pushed one upon me. "Schlegel was rude," said Ferdy. "Damned rude."

I took off my champagne. I could see I was going to need it. "What happened?" I said.

And out it came: all the anxieties and resentments that Ferdy had been storing for goodness knows how long hit me in one long gabble of plaintive bewilderment.

"He doesn't have to come over the speaker with it, does he?"

"No," I said. "But perhaps you'd better take it from the beginning."

"Schlegel came through on the yellow phone, as soon as I put those M.A.D.'s into the Kara. Did I mean the Barents, kid. No, Kara, I said. You know where the Kara is, Ferdy kid, he says. You know where the Kara is."

Ferdy sipped some of his champagne, smiled, and as he continued slipped into his devastating impression of Schlegel's accent. "And those Mallow flying boats—you're making crushed ice out there, sweetheart, that's all you're doing—check those ice-limits, baby, and take another look at the Kara. Will you do that for me?"

Again Ferdy sipped his drink, by which time I'd almost drained mine. Ferdy said, "I didn't reply. Schlegel came through on the loudspeaker, shouting, Are you reading me, Foxwell kid, because if you're giving me that old time limey high-hat treatment I'll move your tail out of that chair so fast your tootsies won't touch the ground, got me."

I said. "Schlegel was probably getting a bad time from those CINCLANT admirals."

Ferdy putting those huge flying boats down on the ice was probably what was really worrying Schlegel. If the big computer showed them as landing safely, a lot of the Arctic strategy would have to be rethought, but meanwhile, Ferdy might wipe the floor with Schlegel's two V.I.P.s.

"What would you have done?" asked Ferdy.

"Kicked him in the crutch, Ferdy."

"Zap! Pow! Wallop!" he said doubtfully. "Yes, look here, drink up." He took a glass of champagne off the hallstand and handed it to me.

"Good health, Ferdy."

"Cheers. No, the little swine was angry because we got a contact. And because he was being such a little bastard I put three atomic depth charges in a tripod off the coast of Novaya Zemlya. I wiped out two subs. Schlegel was so angry that he tore the print-out off the machine and stalked out of the Control Room without saying goodnight." Ferdy spilled some of his drink without noticing. I realized he was a bit drunk.

"What will happen now, Ferdy?"

"There you are. I'm dashed if I know. I'm expecting the little swine any minute." He leaned over to pat the dachshund. "Good Boudin! There's a good little chap." But the dog backed under the hallstand, baring its teeth, and Ferdy almost overbalanced.

"Here?"

"Well, what was I supposed to do—run after him and cancel the invitation?" He spilled some champagne on his hand and kissed away the dribbles from it.

"Stand by for flying glass."

"Little swine." He held the brimming glass at chest height and lowered his head to it. He was like a great untidy bear and had all the clumsy strength of that much maligned creature.

"What were Blue Suite doing; two subs close together like that?"

Ferdy gave a knowing smile. He wiped his mouth with a black silk handkerchief from his top pocket. "Schlegel buttering up the admirals. Telling them how to win the game."

"Do yourself a favour, Ferdy. What happened today was just Blue Suite at their most typically inept. It wasn't Schlegel. If he decides to cheat on you, he's not going to muff it like that."

"Machine failure, then?" said Ferdy. He allowed himself a grin.

"That's about it, Ferdy." I drank some more champagne. Machine failure was our way of describing any of the more stupid sort of human errors. Ferdy shrugged and raised a hand to usher me into the drawing-room. As I passed him he touched my arm to halt me. "I've lost that damned Northern Fleet battle order."

"So what? You can get another."

"I think Schlegel stole it. I know he came into Red Ops while I was at lunch."

"He gets his own copy. He's only to ask for a dozen if he wants more."

"I knew I shouldn't have mentioned it." He patted his hair, then he picked up his drink and swallowed the whole of it before putting the glass down.

"I don't get it." I said.

"Boudin, Boudin." He crouched down and called the dachshund but it still didn't come to him. "Don't you see that it's just a devious way of getting me kicked out?" His voice came from under the hall stand.

"By inventing some sort of security stunt?"

"Well, it would work, wouldn't it?" He spat out the words and I knew that he'd not completely eliminated me from the conspiracy. Perhaps telling me was only his way of complaining to Schlegel.

"Life's too short, Ferdy. Schlegel's a bastard, you know that. If he wanted to get rid of you he'd just have you in the office, and give it to you right between the eyes."

Ferdy took another glass of champagne and handed

it to me, taking my empty in exchange. He said, "I keep telling myself that."

The door bell sounded. Ferdy looked anxiously at the front door. "Kick him in the crutch, you say?"

"Mind he doesn't grab your ankle."

He smiled. "It's all right, I'll attend to the door," he called. He picked up his drink and finished it. "We're having drinks in the library. See yourself in, will you? I think you know everyone."

It was a curious evening and yet there is no easy way to convey the atmosphere that was generated. Anyone might have guessed that attention would be on Schlegel. Not because he was Ferdy Foxwell's boss—not everyone present knew that, so perfunctory were Ferdy's introductions—but rather owing to Schlegel's personality. It was not entirely Schlegel's profligate expenditure of energy. Nor was it his resonant voice, that made shouting unnecessary. It was an atmosphere of uncertainty that he generated, and seemed to relish. For instance, there was what Schlegel did to the wood carvings.

Schlegel walked around the library, peering close at the engravings and the furniture and the ornaments and the bookcase. When he got to the medieval wooden pilgrim that stood five feet tall in the corner, Schlegel rapped it with his knuckles. "Damn nice, that," he said in a voice that no one missed.

"Let me give you a drink," said Ferdy.

"Is it real?"

Ferdy gave Schlegel another drink.

Schlegel nodded his thanks and repeated his question. "Real, is it?" He rapped the priest on the arm as he'd so often rapped me, and then he cocked his head to listen. Maybe he'd been checking on whether I was real.

"I believe so," said Ferdy apologetically.

"Yeah? Well they sell plaster jobs in Florence . . . just like that, you'd never tell."

"Really?" said Ferdy. He flushed, as if it might be bad form to have a real one when these plaster ones were so praiseworthy.

"Fifty bucks apiece, and you'd never tell." Schlegel looked at the Foxwells.

Teresa giggled. "You're a terrible tease, Colonel Schlegel."

"So maybe they are a hundred bucks. But we saw a couple of dandy angels—ninety-eight dollars the pair —beauts, I tell you." He turned and started to examine the Chippendale long-case clock. And people began talking again, in that quiet way they do when waiting for something to happen.

Marjorie took my arm. Mrs Schlegel smiled at us. "Isn't this a wonderful house."

Marjorie said, "But I was hearing all about your beautiful thatched cottage."

"We love it," said Mrs Schlegel.

"By the way," I said, "that thatched roof is beautiful. And it's real, not plastic."

"I should think it is real." She laughed. "Chas did ninety-five per cent of that roof with his own bare hands; the local thatcher works in a factory all the week."

It was then that the butler came to tell Teresa that dinner could be served.

I heard Schlegel say, "But as they say in the Coke commercials, you can't beat the real thing, Mrs Foxwell." She laughed, and the servants folded back the doors of the dining-room and lit the candles.

Schlegel's midnight-blue dinner suit, with braid edge collar, showed his athletic build to advantage, and Mrs Foxwell wasn't the only woman to find him attractive. Marjorie sat next to him at dinner, and hung on his every word. I knew that from now on I'd get little sympathy for my Schlegel horror stories.

There were enough candles on the table to make the silver shine, the women beautiful, and provide light enough for Schlegel to separate pieces of truffle from the egg, and line them up on the edge of his plate like trophies.

There was still a full decanter of wine on the table when the ladies were banished. Each of the men filled his glass and moved along the table nearer to Ferdy. I knew them all. At least, I knew their names. There was Allenby, a young professor of modern history from Cambridge wearing a lacy evening shirt and a velvet tie. He had a pale skin and a perfect complexion, and preceded most of his earnest pronouncements with, "Of course, I don't believe in capitalism, as such."

"Communism is the opiate of the intellectuals," Mr Flynn had told us in the soft accent of County Cork. "Grown, processed and exported from the U.S.S.R."

The Flynns built harpsichords in a refurbished Shropshire rectory. And there was the taciturn Mr Dawlish, who eyed me with the steely predatory stare that I'd once known so well. He was a high-ranking civil servant who never finished his wine.

The elegant Dr Eichelberger had found literary fortune, if not fame, after writing a scientific paper called "The physics of water layering and temperature varia-

tions in northern latitudes." All his subsequent literary
output being printed, classified, and circulated to a
select few by the underwater weapons research department of the U.S. Navy.

Finally, there was the vociferous guest of honour:
Ben Toliver, Member of Parliament, businessman and
bon viveur.

His low voice, wavy hair, piercing blue eyes and
well-fitting girdle had earned Toliver a starring role in
British politics in the late 'fifties and early 'sixties. Like
so many ambitious British politicians, he used slogans
from John F. Kennedy as his passport to the twentieth
century, and expressed belief in both technology and
youth. Toliver had long ago discovered that a well-
timed banality plus a slow news day equals a morning
headline. Toliver was available for any programme from
from "Any Questions" to "Jazz at Bedtime," and if he
wasn't at home someone knew a number where you'd
find him and don't worry about the holding hair spray,
he had a can of it in his briefcase.

I suppose all those 'B.T. for P.M.' buttons have been
put into the attic along with those suits with Chinese
collars, and the hula-hoops. But I still hear people
talking about how this Peter Pan, who runs his father's
factory at such big profits while expressing loud con-
cern about the workers, might have made the greatest
P.M. since the young Mr Pitt. Personally, I'd sooner
dust off the hula-hoops.

"Full bodied for a Pauillac, and that's what deceived
me," said Toliver, swirling his wine and studying its
colour against the candle flame. He looked around in-
viting comment, but there was none.

"Space research, supersonic travel and computer development," said Professor Allenby, resuming the conversation that Toliver had interrupted. "Also grown and processed in the U.S.S.R."

"But not yet exported?" Flynn asked, as if not sure that he was right.

"Never mind all that crap," said Schlegel. "The simple fact is that it takes five per cent of us Americans to produce such big food surpluses that we sell grain to the Russians. And the Russians use twenty-five per cent of their population in food production and screw it up so bad they have to buy from the United States. So never mind all that crap about what's cultivated in Russia."

The young professor tweaked the ends of his bow tie, and said, "Do we really want to measure the quality of life in output per cent? Do we really want to . . ."

"Stick to the point, buddy," said Schlegel. "And pass that port."

"Well, Russians might want to measure it like that," said Flynn, "if all they had to eat was American grain."

"Look here," said Professor Allenby. "Russia has always been beset by these bad harvests. Marx designed his theories round the belief that Germany—not Russia —would be the first socialist land. A unified Germany would provide a chance to see Marxism given a real chance."

"We can't keep on giving it a chance," said Flynn, "it's failed in half the countries of the world now. And the West Zone will swallow the East Zone if they unify. I don't like the idea of it."

"East Zone," said Ferdy. "Doesn't that date you?"

"The D.D.R., they call it," said Toliver. "I was there with a trade delegation the summer before last. Working like little beavers, they are. They are the Japs of Europe, if you ask me, and equally treacherous."

"But would the socialists support a reunification, Mr Toliver?" said Flynn.

"I don't think so," said Toliver. "Simply because in the present climate of talks it looks like a sell-out. It's a deal between the Americans and the Russians, out of which will come a bigger stronger capitalist Germany —no thanks. Those West German buggers are trouble enough already."

"And what's in this deal for us Yanks?" Schlegel asked sarcastically.

Tolliver shrugged. "I wish I could answer that, but it won't be any comfort for us British, and that you can be sure of." He looked round the others and smiled.

Professor Allenby said, "The official text says federation, not reunification. In the context of history, Germany was born out of a miscellany of principalities gathered around the royal house of Brandenburg. This is nothing new for them. Reunification is a dynamic process of historical reality leading inevitably to Marxism."

"You sure use fifty-dollar words," said Schlegel, "but don't talk about historical reality to guys who carried a gun from the beaches to Berlin. Because you might get a swift kick in the principalities."

The professor was used to flamboyant hectoring. He smiled and continued calmly. "The common language of the two Germanys is not a lubricant but an irritant. Most of the East-West tensions are simply extended, amplified versions of purely parochial arguments. Reunification is inevitable—lie back and enjoy it."

"Never," said Flynn. "A reunited Germany that moved closer to the West would make the Russians very nervous. If Germany moved closer to the East they'd make *us* nervous. If, and this is more likely, Germany decided to play man in the middle, the worst days of the cold war could be remembered with nostalgia."

"The Russians have made up their minds," said Toliver. "The American's don't care. There's not much chance for anyone else. The mere fact that the Russians have agreed to talk in Copenhagen shows how keen they are."

"Why?" asked Flynn. "Why are they so keen?"

"Come along, George," Ferdy coaxed, and everyone turned to look at Dawlish.

"My goodness," said the elderly grey-haired man, who had so far said so little. "Old codgers like me are not privy to such secrets."

"But you were in Bonn last week and Warsaw the month before," said Ferdy. "What are they saying?"

"Being there and being told anything are two different matters," he said.

"A diplomatic offensive," said Toliver, availing himself of Dawlish's reluctance to explain. "A small group of Russian whizz-kids have pushed these proposals. If the unification goes through it will be such a triumph for that faction that they'll assume command of Russian foreign policy."

"Surely it should have been debated," said Ferdy.

"The Germans have debated it," said Eichelberger. "They want it. Is it right that foreigners should interfere?"

"You can't trust the Germans," said Toliver. "Let

them all get together and they'll be electing another Hitler, mark my words."

"We've got to trust someone," said Professor Allenby, without going further to remind Toliver that in the space of five minutes he'd condemned the Americans, the Russians, the Germans—East and West—and the Japanese. But the taunt was obvious to the men present, and there was a long silence during which Ferdy opened his boxes of cigars and passed them down the table with a maximum of displacement activity.

I resisted and passed them to Schlegel. He took one. He rolled it in his fingers and listened to its sound. Only when he had everyone's attention did he bite the end off it. He lit it with a match that he struck with one hand, using his thumbnail. He fixed me with his beady eyes. "Big snafu at the Table today, after you left. Did you hear?"

"Port for anyone who'd like some," said Ferdy nervously.

"My informant said jackpot," I replied.

"A host's prerogative," said Schlegel. He inhaled, nodded and blew a perfect smoke ring. "No time now to pull the back off and probe the balance spring."

Toliver waved away Schlegel's cigar smoke and with measured care sipped enough of the Pauillac to commit its flavour to memory. "I'm glad there are still some people who serve a Bordeaux with game," he said. He finished his wine, then took the port decanter and poured himself some. "What kind of a meal can I expect if I visit your Studies Centre? Does your influence obtain there, Foxwell?" He touched his wavy hair and moved it a fraction off his forehead.

"You needn't worry about the food," said Schlegel. "We don't run tours."

Toliver's knuckles whitened as he grasped the neck of the decanter. "I'm not exactly a *tourist,*" he said. "An official visit . . . on behalf of the House."

"No tourists, no journalists, no free-loaders," said Schlegel. "My new policy."

"Musn't bite the hand that feeds you," said Toliver. Dawlish watched the exchange. Gently he took the port decanter from Toliver's clenched hand, and passed it to Eichelberger.

"I'm not quite sure I understand your duties at the Studies Centre," said Dr Eichelberger to Ferdy. He took the decanter, poured himself some port and passed it.

"War Games," said Ferdy. He was relieved to deflect the collision course of Toliver and Schlegel. "I usually do the Russian Navy side of it."

"That's funny," said Toliver, "you don't look Russian." He looked round and then laughed heartily with every one of his perfect white teeth.

"But what does he *do?*" Eichelberger asked Schlegel.

"He introduces the element of human fallibility," said Schlegel.

"And very important, too," said Eichelberger, and nodded seriously.

"The nuclear submarine," said young Professor Allenby, "is the most perfect symbol of imperialistic aggression. It is designed solely for long-range use to distant countries and can only destroy the civilian populations of large cities."

He fixed me with his bright eyes. "I agree," I said,

"and the Russians have more of them than the American, British and French fleets combined."

"Nonsense," said the professor.

"A palpable hit," said Mr Flynn.

"What's more," said Schlegel, poking a finger at Allenby, "your goddamn red buddies are building at a rate of one a week, have been for years, and show no sign of slowing construction."

"My goodness," said Flynn, "the seas must be filled with the awful things."

"They are," said Schlegel.

"It's probably time we joined the ladies," said Ferdy, dreading an argument among his guests.

Dawlish stood up politely and so did I, but Schlegel and his new-found enemy, Professor Allenby, didn't give up so easily. "A typical example of propaganda from the rearmament lobby," said Allenby. "Isn't it obvious that the Russians need more submarines: their coastline is incredibly long and they need naval forces for their land-locked seas."

"Then what the hell are they doing all over the Med, the Atlantic, the Red Sea and the Indian Ocean?"

"Just showing the flag," said Allenby.

"Oh, pardon me," said Schlegel. "I thought only crypto-fascist reactionary imperialists did that."

"I don't know why you Yanks should be so frightened of the Russians," said Allenby. He smiled.

"You Brits should be a little more frightened of them, if you ask me," said Schlegel. "You depend upon imports just in order to eat. Hitler came in the war with twenty-seven long-range submarines. He sank enough of your merchant shipping to make it touch and go whether you could continue the war. Today, with a Royal Navy no longer visible to the naked eye, the Russian Navy has about four hundred subs, many of them nukes. Maybe they are just for showing the flag, Prof, but you want to start asking yourself where they are planning to run it up."

"I think we really should join the ladies," said Ferdy.

Coffee was served in the drawing-room. It was a fine room; tapestries, placed to absorb stray sounds, made its acoustics as good as any recital room. There were a dozen delicate gilt chairs placed equidistant upon the pale-green Afghan carpet. The Bechstein grand piano had been stripped of family photos and cut flowers, and placed under the huge painting of Ferdy's grandfather's favourite horse.

The pianist was a handsome youth with an evening shirt even frillier than those currently *de rigueur* at Oxford, and his tie was bright red and droopy. He found every note of one of the Beethoven Opus 10 Sonatas, and held many of them for exactly the right duration.

Coffee was kept hot in a large silver samovar— O.K., don't tell me, but it was Ferdy's samovar—and thimble-sized demi-tasses were positioned alongside it. Dawlish held his cigar in one hand and the coffee cup and saucer in the other. He nodded his thanks as I operated the coffee tap for him.

I held up the jug of hot milk and raised an eyebrow.

"Worcester," said Dawlish, "late eighteenth century, and damned nice too."

The old idiot knew that I was asking him if he wanted milk, but he was right. Holding a hundred pounds-worth of antiques in your hand to pour hot milk was part of the miracle of the Foxwells' lifestyle.

"Mozart next," said Dawlish. He was wearing an old-fashioned dinner suit with a high wing collar and a stiff-fronted shirt. It was difficult to know if it was an heirloom or whether he had them made like that.

"So I read on the programme," I said.

"That's my car outside, that Black Hawk Stutz."

"Come along, you chaps," called Toliver from behind us. "Move along there. Can't stand milk in coffee —ruins the whole flavour. You might just as well have instant if you're going to put that stuff in it."

"I know you're interested in motors," said Dawlish. On the far side of the room I heard the strident voice of the history professor proclaiming how much he liked cowboy films.

"He's going to play the Mozart A Major in a minute," said Dawlish.

"I know," I said, "and I quite like that."

"Well then . . ."

"It better have a heater."

"Our friend wants to look at the motor," he told Ferdy, who nodded silently and looked around to see if his wife Teresa was likely to see us abandon their protégé.

"He's had more practice with the Mozart," said Ferdy.

"It's a thirsty beast," said Dawlish. "Seven or eight miles to a gallon is good going."

"Where are you going?" said Marjorie.

"To see my motor," said Dawlish. "Overhead camshaft: eight cylinders. Do come, but put a coat on. They tell me it's beginning to snow."

"No, thank you," said Marjorie. "Don't be long."

"Sensible girl, that," said Dawlish. "You're a lucky man."

I wondered what climatic conditions he'd have invented had she accepted his invitation. "Yes, I am," I said.

*   *   *

Dawlish put on his spectacles and looked at the instruments. He said, "Black Hawk Stutz, nineteen twenty-eight." He started the engine and so got the primitive heater to work. "Straight eight: overhead camshaft. She'll go, I'll tell you that." He struggled to open the ash tray. Then he inhaled on his cigar so that his rubicund face loomed out of the darkness. He smiled. "Real hydraulic brakes—literally hydraulic, I mean. You fill them up with water."

"What's all this about?"

"A chat," he said. "Just a chat."

He turned in order to tighten the already firmly closed window. I smiled to myself, knowing that Dawlish always liked to have a sheet of glass between himself and even the remotest chance of a parabolic microphone. The moon came out to help him find the handle. By its light I saw a movement in a grey Austin 2200 parked under the lime trees. "Don't fret," said Dawlish, "a couple of my chaps." A finger of cloud held the moon aloft and then closed upon it like a conjurer's dirty glove upon a white billiards ball.

"What are they here for?" I asked. He didn't answer before switching on the car radio as another precaution against eavesdroppers. It was some inane request programme. There was a babble of names and addresses.

"Things have changed a lot since the old days, Pat." He smiled. "It is Pat, isn't it? Pat Armstrong, it's a good name. Did you ever consider Louis to go with it?"

"Very droll," I said.

"New name, new job, the past gone forever. You're happy and I'm glad it all went so well. You deserved that. You deserved more than that, in fact, it was the least we could have done." A fleck of snow hit the windscreen. It was big, and when the moonlight caught it it shone like a crystal. Dawlish put a finger out to touch the snowflake as if the glass was not there. "But you can't wipe the slate clean. You can't forget half your life. You can't erase it and pretend it never happened."

"No?" I said. "Well, I was doing all right until this evening."

I sniffed his cigar smoke enviously but I'd held out for about six weeks and I'd be damned if it was Dawlish who'd make me weaken my resolve. I said, "Was this all arranged? Us both being invited tonight?"

He didn't answer. Music began on the radio. We watched the snowflake as the heat from his fingertip melted it. It slid down the glass in a dribble of water. But already another snowflake had taken its place, and another, and another after that.

"And anyway there's Marjorie," I said.

"And what a beautiful girl she is. But good grief, I wouldn't think of asking you to get mixed up in the rough and tumble side of it."

"There was a time when you pretended that there was no rough and tumble side of it."

"A long time ago. Regrettably, the rough parts have

become much rougher since then." He didn't elaborate on the tumbles.

"It's not just that," I said. I paused. No point in hurting the old boy's feelings but already he had me on the defensive. "It's simply that I don't want to become part of a big organization again. Especially not a government department. I don't want to be just another pawn."

"Being a pawn," said Dawlish, "is just a state of mind."

He fumbled in his waistcoat pocket and produced a small multi-bladed device that I'd seen him use for everything from picking a despatch box lock to reaming his pipe. Now he used the pin of it to probe the vitals of his cigar. He puffed at it and nodded approval. He looked at the cigar as he began to talk. "I remember this boy—young man perhaps I should say—phoning me one night . . . This is a long time ago now . . . public call box . . . he said there'd been an accident. I asked if he wanted an ambulance, and he said it was worse than that . . ." Dawlish puffed at the cigar and then held it up for us both to admire the improvement he'd wrought. "Do you know what I told him?"

"Yes, I know what you told him."

"I told him to do nothing, stay where he was until a car came for him . . . He was whisked away . . . a holiday in the country, and the whole business never got into the papers, never went into the police files . . . never even went on record with us."

"That bastard was trying to kill me."

"It's the sort of thing the department can do." He gave the cigar a final adjustment and then admired it again, as proud as some old ferry-boat engineer putting an oily rag over an ancient turbine.

"And I admire the way you've done it all," said Dawlish. "Not a whisper anywhere. If I went back into that house and told Foxwell—one of your closest friends —to say nothing of your good lady, that you used to work in the department, they'd laugh at me."

I said nothing. It was typical of the sort of moronic compliment that they all exchanged at the Christmas party, just before that stage of inebriation when the cipher girls get chased round the locked filing cabinets.

"It's not a *cover*," I said. "Nothing to admire: I'm O.U.T."

"We'll need you for the Mason business, though," he said.

"You'll have to come and get me," I said. From the radio came the voice of Frank Sinatra, change partners and dance with me.

"Just an hour or so for the official inquiry. After all, it was you and Foxwell they were impersonating."

"While we were away?"

"Stupid, wasn't it? They should have chosen some-one more remote, one of the radio-room clerks, per-haps."

"But it nearly came off." I was fishing for informa-tion and he knew it.

"It did indeed. It seemed so genuine. Your old flat, your address in the phone book and one of them even looking a bit like you." He puffed smoke. "Ninety thousand pounds they would have collected. Well worth the money spent on those retouched photos. Beauti-fully done, those photos, eh?" He gave the cigar another adjustment and then held it up for us both to look at it.

"For what?"

"Oh not just the A.S.W. Task Force procedures. A whole lot of stuff—radio fuse diagrams, the latest SINS modifications, lab reports from Lockheed. A rag-bag of stuff. But no one would have paid that sort of money for it if they hadn't set up all the pantomime of it coming from you and Foxwell."

"Very flattering."

Dawlish shook his head. "There's a lot of dust still in the air. I was hoping to soft-soap your Colonel this evening but I judged it not opportune. He'll be angry, of course." He tapped the polished wooden dashboard. "They don't make them like that any more."

"Why should he be angry?"

"Why indeed, but that's how it always is, you know that. They never thank us for getting onto these things . . . slack security, the change of directors, your trip, the empty flat, no proper co-ordination: it's the old story."

"And?"

"There will probably be a trial, but their lawyers will do a deal if they have any sense. Don't want it all over the papers. Delicate situation at the moment."

"Schlegel asked me how I got the job at the Centre."

"What did you say?"

"I said I bumped into Ferdy in a pub . . ."

"Well, that's right, isn't it?"

"Can't you ever give a straight answer?" I said angrily. "Does Ferdy know—must I pry every last syllable . . . Schlegel is quite likely to bring it up again."

Dawlish waved away his cigar smoke. "Don't get so agitated. Why the devil should Foxwell know anything?" He smiled. "Foxwell: our man at the Studies Centre, you mean?" He laughed very softly.

"No, I didn't mean that exactly."

The front door of the house opened. In the rectangle of yellow light, Toliver swayed as he tied his scarf and buttoned his overcoat to the neck. I heard the voices of Toliver and Ferdy as the two men walked across to Toliver's shiny new two-door green Bentley. It was icy underfoot and Toliver grabbed Ferdy's arm to steady himself. In spite of the closed windows I heard Ferdy's "Goodnight. Goodnight. Goodnight."

Dawlish had made it sound ridiculous. Why would Dawlish have an agent in the Studies Centre when he could have the analysis delivered every month merely for the asking.

He said, "Another extraordinary thing, after all the procedures we've been through, we've gone right back to routing our phone connections through the local engineers into Federal exchange."

"Don't tell me, I don't want to hear about it," I said. I opened the catch of the car door. It made a loud click but he gave no sign of noticing it.

"Just in case you want to get in touch," he said.

Write in today for the Dawlish system: sent in a plain sealed envelope and it might change your life. But not for the better. I could see it all now. The Dawlish gambit—a piece sacrificed and then the real move. "Not a chance," I said. "Not. A. Chance."

And Dawlish heard that new tone in my voice. He frowned. On his face there was bewilderment, hurt feelings, disappointment and a sincere attempt to understand my point of view. "Forget it," I said. "Just forget it." You may never want to change partners again,

sang Sinatra, but he had an arranger and a big sob-
bing string section.

Dawlish knew then that I'd slipped the hook. "We'll
have lunch one day," he said. It was as near to ad-
mitting defeat as I'd ever seen him. At least, I thought
so at the time. For a moment I didn't move. Toliver's
car leaped forward, almost stalled and then swung
round, missing the next car by only inches. It revved
loudly as Toliver changed gear and then lumbered out
through the gate. After only a few moments the Austin
2200 followed it.

"Nothing's changed," I said, as I got out. Dawlish
continued smoking his cigar. I'd thought of all the
things I'd rather have said by the time I got to the
front door. It was ajar. From the end of the corridor
there was the music of the piano: not Mozart but Noel
Coward. It was Ferdy doing his fat-rich-boy-makes-
good act. "The Stately Homes of England . . ." sang
Ferdy gaily.

I helped myself to another cup of coffee: Dawlish
hadn't followed me. I was glad of that. I didn't believe
Dawlish's glib explanations specially designed so that
I had to drag the lies out of him. But the fact that
Dawlish was even interested made me nervous. First
Stok and now Dawlish . . .

"Shall I tell you something?" said Schlegel. He was
rocking on the two rear legs of the delicate gilt chair
and beating time to the music with his cigar. "This is
a whole new side of Foxwell. A whole new side of him."

I looked at Ferdy, who required all his concentration to play the piano and remember the words too.
He fitted in a hasty smile as he came to the end of the
line. Somewhere under that Savile Row evening suit

with the silk collar there was a history graduate, farm owner, man about town and skilled amateur strategist, who could talk for an hour about the difference between digital and analog computers. No wonder the suit didn't fit very well.

"To prove the upper classes always have the upper hand." He sang it with all the astringent bravura of the maestro, and Helen Schlegel called encore so enthusiastically that he did a repeat performance.

I went to sit next to Marjorie. She said, "He wasn't trying to sell you that hideous car, was he?"

"I've known him for ages. We were just chatting."

"Did that awful Toliver drive himself home?"

"I don't know where he was headed, but he was sitting behind the wheel when he left here."

"It would serve him right if he was caught. He's always half-cut."

"How do you know?"

"He's on the hospital board. He's constantly in and out of our place. He tries to recruit staff for his nursing home."

"He'd be a delight to work for."

"Good pay, they say."

"It would have to be."

As if by magic, when Ferdy's piano music stopped a servant came in with jugs of coffee and chocolate. It was a gracious way of telling your guests to go home. Schlegel was enthusiastic about Ferdy's piano playing. I formed the impression that Ferdy was going to spearhead Schlegel's attempt to squeeze more funds out of CINCLANT. I could imagine Ferdy being paraded through a schedule of Norfolk, Virginia, parties. With Schlegel announcing him like a fairground barker.

I said that to Marjorie on the way home but she would have none of it. "Give me the Schlegels every time," she said. "At present in my department there is a row going on about teaching payments—there's always a lot of teaching in the pathology departments— and the professor isn't speaking to the senior assistant and the staff have divided into two camps and no one will say honestly that it's all about money. They want to pretend they are arguing about the extension to the mortuary. Give me the Schlegels every time."

"Extension to the mortuary. It sounds like a title for a Hammer film. How can you *like* working in pathology?"

"Pat, I've told you a thousand times, I *hate* working there. But it's the only department I can get into which gives me a normal nine to five day. And you know how unbearable you are about my shift work."

"That Toliver!" I said. "Boy can he pack it away: second helpings of everything and always it's not quite salty enough, or not quite as good as he gets in the south of France."

"He looks ill," said Marjorie, overtaken by professionalism.

"He certainly does. I can understand him coming in the Path Lab. What I don't understand is how they let him out."

"Last week I heard him having a terrific row with my professor."

"My professor now, is it? I thought he was the one you called Jack the Ripper. Row about what?"

"Oh, a death certificate or a post-mortem or something."

"Good old Toliver."

"They went into the office and closed the door but

you could still hear them. Toliver was shouting about how important he was and he'd take the whole matter to the board of governors. I heard him say that he was doing this for 'a certain department of state that shall remain nameless.' Pompous old fool. Trying to pretend he was something to do with the Secret Service or something."

"He's been watching late-night television," I said.

"He's been watching the world through the bottoms of empty glasses," said Marjorie. "That's his problem, and everyone knows it."

"You're right," I said. "But just out of vulgar curiosity, could you find out exactly what Toliver wanted?"

"Why?"

"I'm just curious. He wants Ferdy to go into business with him—a new clinic or something—I'd like to know what he gets up to." It was a feeble improvisation, but Marjorie said she'd try to find out. I suppose she was curious about it too.

"You haven't forgotten that tomorrow we're having lunch, darling."

"How could I, you've reminded me every hour on the hour."

"Poor darling. We don't have to talk—we can just eat." She hugged me. "You make me feel like a terrible shrew, Patrick, and I'm not. I'm really not. I can't help being possessive. I love you."

"We'll talk," I said.

Chapter 9

Chess. A pejorative term used of inexperienced players who assume that both sides make rational decisions when in full possession of the facts. Any history book provides evidence that this is a fallacy and wargaming exists only because of this fallacy.

GLOSSARY. "NOTES FOR WARGAMERS." STUDIES CENTRE. LONDON

If the phone rings in the middle of the night it's always for Marjorie. That's why we keep it on that side of the bed. That night, full of wine and cognac and Dawlish, I came only half awake, snorted and turned over. "It's for you," said Marjorie.

"It's me. Ferdy. I'm in my car."

"I've had this one fitted in the bed—pretty wild, eh?"

"Yes, I know. I'm awfully sorry but I've got to talk with you. Will you come down and open the front door?"

"And it couldn't wait until morning?" I asked.

"Don't be a pig," said Marjorie. "Go down and let him in." She yawned and pulled the bedclothes up over her face. I couldn't blame her, she seldcm had the luxury of seeing me turned out in the middle of the night.

"It's life and death."

"It had better be," I said, and hung up.

"You talk to him as though he's a child," said Marjorie. "He's much older than you are."

"He's older, richer and better-looking. And he smokes."

"You haven't started again? I'm proud of you, darling. It's nearly two months, isn't it?"

"Sixty-one days, five hours, and thirty-two minutes."

"It's not even fifty days."

"Must you ruin my best lines?" I shook the token box of matches on my bedside table and put it back unused. There wasn't a pack in the house or I might have succumbed. I'd even refused the cigars at Ferdy's. It was sometimes difficult not to feel very proud of myself. I pulled on some clothes: evening-dress trousers and a turtle-neck sweater. "I'll talk with him in the sitting-room," I said, switching off the bedside lights.

There was no answer. Marjorie had acquired the knack of instant sleep. I yawned.

I let Ferdy in and sat him down in the sitting-room. There was last night's cocoa in the saucepan. I lit a flame under it and set up cups in the kitchen so that I had an excuse for waking up in easy stages. Ferdy paced the sitting-room carpet in enough agitation to make his hands shake as he lit the inevitable cigar.

"Just don't offer me one," I said.

He stirred the cocoa dutifully but did not even sip it. "Now perhaps you will believe me," he said. He fixed me with a beady stare but revised his opening each time he opened his mouth. "I don't know where to begin," he said.

"For God's sake, sit down, Ferdy."

He was wearing his impressario's overcoat: black loden with a collar of curly astrakhan. Ten years ago it would have been old-fashioned. He sat down and slipped it back off his shoulders in a matronly gesture. "This is a rum district."

"It's a lousy neighbourhood," I agreed. He looked round the dust-covered room, at the wad of paper that levelled the clock, the stains on the sofa, the burned carpet and the books that all had bargain prices pencilled on the flyleaf. "You could do better than this over my way."

"I was thinking that, Ferdy. Why don't you legally adopt me?"

"You don't know what happened tonight."

"Schlegel kicked Boudin?"

"What? Oh, I see." He scowled and then gave a perfunctory smile to acknowledge that it was a joke. "They've attacked poor old Tolly."

"Who?"

"Toliver. Ben Toliver the M.P. You were with him tonight."

"Who attacked him?"

"It's a long story, Patrick."

"We've got all night," I yawned.

"The bloody Russians attacked him. That's who."

"You'd better start at the beginning."

"The phone went tonight just before you left. Toliver was followed. He has a phone in his car so he called me on his way back. When you'd gone, I took Teresa's car and went to meet him."

"You sound pretty bloody calm about it. Why didn't you phone the police?"

"Yes, I've started at the wrong place. I should have

told you that Toliver works for the Secret Service . . .
now, don't pull a face. I'm telling the absolute truth,
and you can ask anyone . . ."

"What do you mean, I can ask anyone? How the
hell would anyone know?"

"Anyone who is anyone knows," said Ferdy primly.

"O.K., Ferdy, that puts me down. But this no one
remains unconvinced."

"Just for a moment suspend your hatred of Toliver . . ."

"I don't hate Toliver . . . It's just his teeth."

"Yes, you do, and I understand why you do, but if
you really knew him, you'd like him."

"On account of him being in the Secret Service."

"Do you want me to tell you?"

"I'm not desperate about it, Ferdy. I was asleep
when all this car-telephoning started."

"Forget the car-telephoning," said Ferdy. "I know
that irritates you, too."

"For God's sake get on with it." From the next
room Marjorie shouted for us to make less noise. I
whispered, "Toliver runs the Secret Service and was
being followed while he phoned you from his Bentley.
Let's move on to where you arrived. What sort of car
was following him?"

"It wasn't exactly a car," said Ferdy doubtfully. "It
was an enormous eight-wheeled lorry. I know you
won't believe me but I saw it."

"And he was in the Bentley? He could do a ton in
that job without putting his foot on the floor."

"At first there was an old Humber Estate behind
him. He realized that it was following him, so he slowed
right down trying to make it overtake. It was then that

the big ten-ton job overtook both cars. He was sand-
wiched. The lorry was doing fifty or more; while the
Humber pushed him close, the lorry swung out to prevent him overtaking."

"Nice fellows."

"The Humber was hitting the back bumper. Tolly
was scared stiff."

"You could hear him on the phone?"

"Yes, he'd put it on the seat but he was shouting.
Then the truck slammed on the brakes. It was a wonder that they didn't kill Tolly."

"They weren't trying to do that."

"How can you be so sure?"

"I can't be sure, Ferdy, but people who'd go to all
that trouble and expense . . . well, it would be easier
to make it a fatal accident than a non-fatal one."

"Tolly always has his seat belt on."

"Where were you all this time?"

"I came up behind the Humber right at the end.
They were too busy to notice."

"What happened when they stopped?"

"I stopped too, well ahead, and ran back. They still
didn't see me. They had opened the doors of Tolly's
car and were trying to drag him out."

"He was fighting them?"

"No," said Ferdy. "Tolly was unconscious. He still
is. That's why I came to you. If Tolly had been well
enough I would have asked him what to do. They were
speaking Russian. You think I'm joking but they were
speaking good Russian: regional accents of some sort
but only slight. They were townspeople—some Polish
vowels in there somewhere—forced to guess I might
say Lvov."

"Never mind the Professor Higgins stuff, Ferdy. What happened then?"

"Yes, I should have told you. The ten-tonner clipped the Bentley close as he pulled ahead trying to make him stop. Ripped Tolly's offside wing off . . . shook Tolly, I should think."

"It would gain anyone's attention."

"A police car came past just after we all stopped. They thought it was an accident. The whole side of the Bentley was dented and torn . . . the wing bent back. No one could have missed seeing it."

"And what did the Russians do when the police arrived?"

"So now you're beginning to see they are Russians—good."

"What did they *do?*"

"You know what they do—licences, insurance, breathalyser tests."

"But Toliver was unconscious."

"They let me take him home. The others were all with the police when I left. I pretended that I'd arrived at the same time as the police. None of them realized I knew what it was all about."

"Drink your cocoa."

I know you think I treat him badly, but I knew Ferdy Foxwell of old. I'm telling you, we could well be talking about a perfectly normal traffic shunt: two drivers with powerful scouse accents arguing with a drunken Toliver who'd nearly killed them going through a red light.

"I got the resignation numbers for both the Albion lorry and the Humber Estate. Will you find out about it? And see what the police did with the Russians?"

"I'll do what I can."

"Tomorrow?"

"Very well."

"And, Patrick. You must remember that Toliver really is working for the British Secret Service."

"What difference will that make?"

"What I mean is . . . don't let your prejudice mislead you."

"Look, Ferdy. Toliver is a drunk. They kicked him out of that Cabinet Office job he had, because he was a drunk. And they have put up with some very drunk people in the past."

"He's still an M.P.," said Ferdy.

"The chances of him remaining one after the next election are very slim. But the point I was going to make was that Toliver was a member of the Party back in 'forty-five and 'forty-six. He'd never be considered for a high security clearance, let alone a job in the Service."

"How do you know? About him being a communist, I mean."

I'd read it in Toliver's file many years ago but I could hardly tell Ferdy that. "It's an open secret. Ask anyone."

He smiled. "He was at Oxford a year ahead of me, another college, but our paths crossed now and again. He had a rough time there. His father gave him only a very tiny allowance. We all had cars and a little spending money but poor old Tolly did some lousy job in the evening to make ends meet. Never saw him at parties. The trouble was that he wasn't all that bright. Of course, it's no crime being average, no crime at all, but it meant he had to get his nose into the books whenever he wasn't washing dishes or whatever he did. It's enough to make anyone join the communists, isn't it?"

"You're breaking my heart. What about the poor bastards who didn't even get as far as grammar school. And some of them a lot more intelligent than Toliver at his brightest and most sober."

"You don't like him, I know. It's difficult to see the situation when there are personal feelings involved."

"Ferdy, you're in no position to pronounce judgment on people who are less than bright. Or those who let personal feelings warp their judgment. Toliver is not a part of any intelligence service and I'll bet everything I own on that."

"Do you still want the registration number?"

"O.K. But just get it clear in your mind that Toliver is nothing to do with the British Secret Service and that these men were not Russians. Or at least not Russian spies."

"Then who were they?"

"I don't know who they were, Ferdy. Maybe they were claret salesmen or a delegation of well-wishers from the *Good Food Guide*. But they were not Russian spies. Now do me a favour, and go home and forget it."

"But you'll check the registration?"

"I'll check the registration."

"I'd go, but with the TACGAME Schlegel would—"

"—kill you with his bare hands. You're right."

"You think it's funny, but did it occur to you that Schlegel might be behind this whole thing?"

"Because he crossed swords with Toliver tonight? If that's enough reason, why couldn't I be behind the whole thing?"

"I had to take a chance on someone," said Ferdy, and I realized that he had given that possibility a lot of thought.

"I'll send a message to Schlegel that I'll be late." Ferdy bit his lip at the thought of it. "He won't like it."

"No, but I won't be around to hear, you will."

Outside, the traffic lights had changed: a sports car with a broken silencer accelerated past a milk truck that rattled noisily as it went over a newly repaired patch in the road.

"I'd never get used to that traffic all night," said Ferdy.

"We can't all live in two acres of Campden Hill, Ferdy," I said. "It would get so damned crowded."

"Oh dear. No offence. I just mean, I don't know how you ever get to sleep."

"No? Well buzz off and I'll let you know."

"Yes, right-ho. Was there anything else then?"

That's what I like about the Foxwells of the world— was there anything else then, as if he'd already done me one favour.

Chapter 10

The actions of the civil power will not be included in the TACWARGAME.

RULES. "TACWARGAME." STUDIES CENTRE. LONDON

The new security badges that Schlegel had arranged for us seemed a suitable device for impressing detective-sergeants of the Met. I pushed mine across the debris-laden desk of Sergeant Davis. He read it, one word at a time, looking for spelling mistakes, tried to prise the plastic facing off it, put some tension on the safety pin fixed to the back and bowed it between his fingers. Having passed the forensic tests it was tossed back onto the desk. It slipped down between files marked "Life Saving (Cadets)" and "Community Relations." He watched me as I fished it out and put it back in my pocket.

"So?" he said. "So?" As if he'd found on it some affront: an insulting anagram or a sneer on the mouth of my identity photo.

"So nothing," I said, but he was unappeased. He pushed aside heaps of dead paperwork, reshuffling bits of it almost without noticing. "The Bentley." He found a sheet of paper and read from it. "Two forty-five ack emma?" He was that kind of policeman. Not only ack

emma, but skull-close haircut, and shoes polished on
the sole.

"That's it."

"And you are acting . . . ?"

"For the driver—Toliver."

"Unconscious."

"Yes."

He read his papers carefully and looked up. "All
that . . ." he screwed up his face trying to think of a
word. "All that . . . spy-now-pay-later, credit cards . . ."
he flicked a finger at my pocket where I'd put the card.
"That cuts no ice with me. Nor does it being a Bentley."
He waved a hand, to tell me he hadn't finished. "I'll
tell you as much as I'd tell the kid on the local rag.
No more, no less."

A policewoman came into the room. She brought
two mugs of tepid tea. His mug had a coloured photo
of the Queen, mine had Peter Rabbit. "Thanks, Mary."
He shuffled the papers again, hiding behind them coyly,
like a flirtatious Edwardian opera-goer. "Container
lorry in collision with green Bentley . . ." He stopped
reading and looked up. "There's no mystery story.
Traffic signals, hydraulic brakes, car driving too close—
it happens a dozen times a day, and night."

"You are not making it a police job?"

He looked at his watch. "You people really earn
your money, don't you. It's only ten past eight. I
thought coppers and burglars were the only people up
this early."

"Are you?"

His voice rose a fraction. "A police job? How could
we? The breathalyser was O.K., licence, insurance,
hours on duty, all O.K. The lorry was halted at the

red light, the damage to the Bentley was the offside *front* wing. Front wing speaks for itself, doesn't it? If your boss Toliver sent you down here to save his no-claim bonus he's unlucky, forget it."

"Toliver is unconscious."

"That's right, I forgot. Well, the answer's still the same." He read a little more from his script and broke it down into baby-talk for me. "The constable took the names of the lorry drivers but you can tell your boss he's wasting his time. The court will always take the policemen's evidence in a case like this, and they'll say your boy was following too close. If there was a care-less driving charge to be made, *he'd* get it."

"This could be more serious than just a traffic accident," I said.

He whistled softly—to feign amazement. "Are you trying to tell us something, Mr. Armstrong?" The way he said "us," it meant the police forces of the Western world.

"I'm trying to ask you something."

"And I'm not getting it. Yes, I'm very dense this early on a Thursday morning."

"But this is Tuesday."

"No, it's not, it's . . . ah, I thought you'd turn out to be a comedian."

"Sergeant, a ten-ton truck stopping hard in front of a car would be a good way of killing a man, wouldn't it?"

"It would be a risky way of killing a man, Mr. Armstrong, for a number of reasons. Motive, for a start: a fatality like that attracts enough paperwork for the connection to be noticed. Hell, we get enough allega-tions from *strangers* in collision." He grabbed his thumb to tell me that was his first lesson. "I won't mention the traffic lights again but I will remind you that your boss is not dead . . ."

"He's not my boss."

"Whoever he is, he's not dead. That's what proves it wasn't some maniac trying to kill him. They must have put the brakes on carefully enough or he would have been buried somewhere inside the mesh of the lorry's differential. So don't tell me murder."

Davis had mentioned the same flaw in Ferdy's allegation that I'd seen. There was no arguing it. Attempted murder was a possibility but a damned slim one. "There was a Humber Estate just behind him."

"Yes a whole procession of people driving up and down . . . Half the bloody world drives round London all night, didn't you know that? Beats me why they don't want to go home and get some sleep, but there they are every night. Anyway, all this lot arrived too late to see anything."

"Did they?"

"What am I supposed to do, give them the water torture?"

"But if anything new turns up, you'll phone me?"

"O.K., Philip Marlowe, leave your name and phone number with the desk sergeant."

"You are going to make it a traffic statistic, come what may, aren't you?" I said.

He looked through all his pockets for a cigarette but I failed to respond to my cue. Finally he had to walk across the room and get his own packet from his raincoat. He didn't offer them. He took one out and lit it carefully, held up his gold-plated Dunhill and snapped the top closed at arm's length. Then he sat down and almost smiled. "We have a witness, that's why, Mr. Armstrong. Fair enough? Can I get on with my work now?"

"What witness?"

"There was a lady in the car with Toliver. She signed a statement for us before the doctor gave her a sedative. It was an accident—no panic, no murder, just one of those traffic statistics you mentioned."

"Who?"

He took out a little black book. "Miss Sara Shaw, The Terrine du Chef—a French restaurant, sounds like, eh? You go and put your foot in her door but watch out that she doesn't send for the police." He smiled. "Put your foot in it but don't put your foot in it, if you see what I mean."

I got to my feet and waved goodbye. "You didn't finish your tea,'" he said.

He'd pulled that damned witness out of his helmet and now he was very pleased with himself. I said, "Can I have the name and addresses of the lorry drivers?"

"Now, you know I'm not supposed to do that," but he turned the sheets of paper over to find it. Then he twisted the page round so that it faced my side of the desk and got up and walked away so that I could read it.

"They were catching the boat," he said from behind me. "You wouldn't think it would pay a Polish meat-canning firm to send truck drivers all the way here and return empty, but I suppose they know what they are doing."

"Maybe it's a nationalized industry," I said. It was a long Polish name with an address in London Wall.

"You didn't drink the tea," he said again.

"I'm trying to give it up," I said.

"Stick with the tea," he advised. "Give up playing copper."

Chapter 11

Intelligence and espionage (in plus and minus categories) are programmed according to Section 9 of the STUCEN Programming Manual. Commanders are solely responsible for information, false or otherwise, collected outside game time, i.e. in off-duty hours.

RULES. ALL GAMES. STUDIES CENTRE. LONDON

I was half inclined to give the sedated Miss Shaw a miss, but it would only give Ferdy another excuse for a long whine. The Terrine du Chef was a converted shop in Marylebone. "Restaurant Française" had been gilt-lettered across the old shop window and the interior obscured with a large net curtain.

A menu was jammed into an illuminated holder in the doorway. It was handwritten, in the crabbed calligraphy that the English believe to be a hallmark of the French restaurateur. There was a "Closed" sign behind the glass panel in the door but I pushed and the door swung open. I reached up to catch the sprung bell before it announced my arrival.

It was a cramped place. An odd collection of bentwood chairs was dancing on the table-tops. The dining-room had been dressed to look like a Paris bistro of

the 'thirties, with enamel Suze adverts, marble-topped
tables and fancy mirrors on every wall. A debris of
corks, paper napkins and cigarette ends had been swept
to a neat pile in the corner under the serving hatch.
On the counter there was an array of cutlery, a line-up
of old bottles stuck with coloured candles and a pile
of freshly laundered red check tablecloths. There was
a smell of burned garlic, ancient cigars and freshly
peeled potatoes. I walked through to the kitchen. From
a tiny dark yard beyond it I could hear a young man's
voice singing softly and the noises of buckets and
metal lids.

Down two stone steps from the kitchen there was a
large pantry. A freezer was humming to a tin hip-
bath, full of peeled potatoes. Alongside there was a
large plastic sack containing dry ice, its smoke moving
around inside the clear plastic like a restless grey cobra
trying to escape. A scrubbed table had been cleared to
provide room for an electric sewing machine plugged
into the overhead light socket. Hanging over the back
of the kitchen chair there was a man's dark jacket. But
it wasn't the jacket that caught my attention: it was a
manilla file. It had been pushed under a folded length
of lining material, but not pushed far enough to conceal it completely. I pulled it clear and flipped it open.
On top there was a drawing of a splay-armed figure,
its measurements noted in neat red ink. The rest of the
contents were photographs.

There were a dozen photos, and this time they shook
me more than the ones in my flat. It was the same man
that I'd seen pictured with my car, and with my parents,
but these were better photographs and I could see his
face in greater detail than before. He was more than

five, perhaps even fifteen, years older than me, a barrel-chested man with a full mop of hair and large stubby-fingered hands.

There were no other papers in the file, nothing to tell me about his job or his family or what he liked for lunch. Nothing to tell me why someone had chosen to sit him in my car wearing my clothes, or pose him with my parents or frame the prints and position them carefully in my old flat. But these pictures revealed something about the people who had arranged this business. For the first time I realized that I was up against someone of considerable power and wealth. And it had all the clumsy power of a security department: a Russian security department for example. For reasons that I was unable to fathom, they had gone to all the trouble of dressing my *Doppelgänger* in the uniform of a rear-admiral of the Soviet Navy before having these photos taken. In the background on one of them there was a blurred but unmistakable flush-deck profile of a Tallinn Class destroyer. Was the photo taken on a sunny day at some British port, or could I recognize the water-front of Alexandria or Malta's Grand Harbour?

There were footsteps on the creaking wooden stairs. The sound of a cold room door and the clatter of footsteps on tiles. I closed the file and pushed it back under the lining material where I'd found it. Then I stepped quickly back through the door but grasped the edge, and peek-a-booed round it in what I hoped was the manner of a salesman.

"Who are you?" She was standing in the other doorway. Beyond her there was a food store. Through the open door I could see the entrance to the cold room. There was a rack of vegetables and a marble slab upon which some charcuterie had been sliced and arranged on plates and garnished with twigs of parsley. The movement of air activated the cold room thermostat, and the refrigeration system started. It was a loud vibrating sound. She closed the door.

"Who are you?" I said. It was the unsedated, fully dressed Miss Shaw, and I had made the right decision. She was a shapely blonde in her middle twenties. Her long hair was parted in the middle so that it fell forward framing her face. Her skin was tanned, and she needed no makeup and knew it.

She was so unexpected that I hesitated for a moment while I looked at her in detail. "It's about the accident," I said.

"Who let you in?"

"The door was open," I told her. A willowy man in flared denims came to the top of the stairs and paused for a moment. He was out of her sight but she knew he was there. "Did you leave the door open, Sylvester?"

"No, Miss Shaw. The fellow with the frozen pork loins."

"That explains it," I said. "These guys with frozen loins . . ." I gave her a smile that I'd kept unused for a year or more.

"The accident." She nodded. "Go and make sure it's closed now, Sylvester." A yellow tape measure hung around her neck and in her hand there was the dark-blue sleeve of a uniform jacket. She rolled the sleeve into a ball.

"Yes, the police sergeant phoned," she said. She was slim, but not so slim that she'd slip through your fingers, and she had this incredible pale-blue cashmere sweater that exactly matched her eyes. She wore a carefully fitted dark tweed skirt, and strap-across low-heeled shoes that were suitable for long walks in the country. "He said to throw you out, if you were a nuisance." I was expecting a high voice but it was soft and gentle.

"He spoke to *you* like that?"

"Policemen are so much younger these days."

"And stronger, too."

"I don't seem to get many chances to find out," she sighed. Then she put the blue uniform sleeve aside with far too much casualness, and she raised a hand to shoo me back into the kitchen. All the time she was giving me back my super smile, returning it tooth for tooth, chewed thirty times just like nanny had told her.

In the kitchen she took two chairs and placed them to face each other. She sat in the one that faced the door. I sat down. She smiled, crossed her legs and smoothed the hem of her skirt, just to be sure that I didn't get a glimpse of her knickers. "And you are from the insurance?" She embraced herself as if suddenly cold.

I reached for a small black notebook and creased the pages open with my thumb as I'd seen my insurance man do.

"And that's the little book in which you write it all down?"

"It's really the one I use for pressing wild flowers, but my wristwatch tape recorder is on the blink."

"How amusing," she said.

The blond man came back into the kitchen. From a hook behind the door he took a bright pink apron and put it on carefully, so as not to disarrange his hair. He began to place pieces of limp lettuce in wooden bowls. "Leave that for now, Sylvester. We're talking. Do the wine."

"I'll need warm water."

"Just get the bottles up from the cellar. We won't be long." Reluctantly he went out. His denims had bright red patches sewn on the behind. He went down the stairs slowly.

I said, "What's he going to do with the hot water? Put Mouton Rothschild labels on the Algerian?"

"What a good idea," she said, in a voice calculated to prove that the cashmere had been chosen to match her blood.

"You were with Mr. Toliver when the accident happened?"

"I was."

"And you and he were . . . ?"

"I am a friend."

"A friend, yes."

"One more wisecrack like that and you will leave." But she gave me the inscrutable Snow-queen smile to keep me guessing.

"You'd been out to dinner?"

"With friends—business associates I should say— we were on the way back to my apartment. It was the North Circular Road where the accident happened—or so they told me later."

I nodded. She wasn't the sort of girl who'd recognize the North Circular Road and admit it.

"The lorry driver pulled over too soon. He misjudged the distance."

"The police said the lorry was stopped at the lights."

"Sergeant Davis is driving me down to collect the Bentley this afternoon. I'll clear it up then. He said it's only a routine thing—thirty minutes or so and he'll bring me back."

Lucky old Sergeant Davis. If she'd been an old-age pensioner maybe he would have let her go down to collect the Bentley by bus.

"What colour was the lorry?"

"Maroon and beige."

"And there were two lorry drivers?"

"Two, yes. Would you like some coffee?"

"That would be great, Miss Shaw."

"Sara will do," She unplugged a machine and poured two bowls of coffee. Then she put the jug under a large cosy. The kitchen was a narrow place with many machines. All the dish towels were printed with coloured pictures and recipes. On the wall there was a cross-reference chart that I thought was an analysis of the hydrogen atom but on closer inspection became herbs. She put croissants, butter and jam on the table beside me. Her hands were elegant, but not so well cared for that she might not have done her own washing-up and sweeping. I bit into one of the croissants while she warmed the milk and checked through a spikeful of bills. I couldn't decide whether she was wearing a bra.

"You don't seem too upset," I said.

"Does that offend you? Ben was a friend of my father's. I saw him only two or three times a year. He felt it was a duty to see me eat a meal but we had very little to talk about except my parents." She flicked some crumbs off her sweater, and gave a sigh of irritation. "Messy sluts like me should always wear aprons." She turned to me and held her hands up. "Look at me, I've only been in the kitchen two minutes." I looked at her. "You don't have to look at me like that," she said. A buzzer on the electric oven sounded and a red light switched on. "You're not really in insurance, are you, Mr. . . ." She put some ready-cooked pizzas into the oven and reset the timer.

"Armstrong. No, I'm a leg-man for Sergeant Davis." She shook her head; she didn't believe that either.

"It was an accident, Mr. Armstrong. And quite frankly it was Ben's fault. He was driving very slowly, he thought he could hear a whining noise in the engine."

"People with Bentleys get that way about engines."

She didn't encourage my generalizations about people with Bentleys. She probably knew more of them than I did.

She reached over me for a croissant. I watched her in that way she hadn't liked.

"The street was dry and the lighting good?"

She swallowed some coffee before answering. "Yes to both." She paused before adding, "Do you always look so worried?"

"What worries me, Miss Shaw, is the way you are so certain about everything. Usually witnesses are full of maybes, thinks and abouts, but even in that sodium arc lighting you can tell that the truck was maroon. That's almost psychic."

"I am psychic, Mr. Armstrong."

"Then you'll know that I was at dinner last night with Mr. Toliver. And unless you were hiding under the jelly, he seemed to be unaccompanied."

She picked up her coffee and became very busy with the spoon, deciding how much sugar she needed.

Without looking up she said, "I hope you didn't tell the police that."

I continued breakfast with a second croissant. She said, "It's a complicated situation—oh, nothing like that. But Ben collected me last night from a friend of mine—a girl friend—I didn't want to get into all that with the police. I can't believe there's any need, is there?"

From time to time she would embrace herself as though she was cold, or needed love or just to make sure her arms were still there. She did it now.

"There's probably no need," I said.

"I knew you were nice," she said. She took the silk cosy from the silver coffee pot and poured some for me. "Things like that . . . I knew I'd be found out. Even when I was a child I could never tell a lie and get away with it."

"What did you do *after* the car stopped?"

"Oh, must we go into that?"

"I think we should, Miss Shaw." This time she didn't tell me to call her Sara.

"I knew he was in a coma—he wasn't just dazed or semiconscious. We'd done first aid at school. He had almost no pulse, and there was the blood."

"You sound pretty calm about it."

"You feel happier with girls who jump on the table and pull their skirts up—"

"You bet!" I said tonelessly.

"—at the sight of a mouse." I was hoping that if she got just a little more angry she'd tell me something worth hearing. She sat back on the seat, kicked off her shoes and tucked her feet under her chair. She smiled. "You push your way in here with some nonsense about insurance companies. You all but call me a liar. You tell me I'm not upset enough, and you litter the place with your second-rate jokes. And all the time I'm not expected to ask you who the hell you are and send you packing."

"Ask me."

"One of Mr. Toliver's secret little helpers. I know who you are all right."

I nodded.

"It's not as though you are good at it. No wonder it's all such a mess."

"What's all a mess?"

"No matter." She gave a world-weary sigh.

From the cellar the blond man called, "I can't find the rosé."

"Bloody fairies," she said. Then she regretted the lapse of composure. "I'm coming, Sylvester. I'll just show my guest to the door."

I poured a little more coffee for myself. "Your coffee is so good," I said. "I just can't resist it."

Her brow furrowed. It must be terrible to be so wellbred that you can't order a stranger out of your own restaurant.

"Isn't it on the bench?" she called.

"I've looked everywhere," the boy insisted.

She got to her feet and hurried down the creaking steps. I heard her speak to the boy as I stepped across to the pantry door. I reached for the dark blue jacket and spread it open on the table. It was an officer's high-button working uniform. On the breast there was a large slab of ribbons and on its cuffs the rings that denote a kontr-admiral of the Soviet Navy. I flipped the jacket over and bundled it back into the corner.

It took only a moment to be back in my seat again but the beautiful Miss Shaw was at the open door.

"You found it?" I asked politely.

"Yes," she said. Her eyes bored into me and I remembered her little joke about being psychic. "I almost forgot," she said, "will you buy a couple of tickets for our play?"

"What play?"

"We're all amateurs but the two leads are awfully good. It will only cost you fifty pence a ticket."

"What are you doing?"

"I can't remember the title. It's about the Russian revolution—the battleship *Potemkin*—you must have seen the film. The play's less political—a love story, really." She stood up to hint that I should go away now.

And when this girl hinted she did it with her every last gene at the ready. She stood arms akimbo and tossed her head to throw back her loose blonde hair and provide for me the final proof that she was braless. "I know you think I'm being evasive," she said in a soft, gentle, sexy voice.

"You could say that," I agreed.

"You're wrong," she said, and ran her hand through her hair in a manner more that of a model than the proprietor of a restaurant. Her voice dropped even more as she said, "It's just that I'm not used to being interrogated." She came round close behind me but I didn't turn my head.

"You do very well for an amateur," I said. I didn't move from my chair.

She smiled and put her hand on my shoulder. I could feel her body as she moved against me. "Please," she said. How can I convey the sound of the word in her mouth?

"What are you thinking?" she said.

"You want to get me arrested?"

It wasn't simply her perfume that I could smell now, it was a whole pattern of events, the potatoes she'd peeled, the talc she'd used, the tweed skirt and her body under it. Some other time, some other motive, I might have proved a walkover for her.

I said, "I went to a Paris fashion show once. You get in through a scrum of sharp-elbowed lady fashion experts, and they sit you on these toy-sized gilded chairs. From behind the velvet curtains we could all hear the screaming of the fashion models. They were swearing and fighting about mirrors, zips and hairbrushes. Suddenly the lights were lowered to the level of candlelight. There was the muted music of violins and someone pumped Chanel into the air. From the old biddies came only the refined sound made by petite hands in silken gloves."

"I don't get you," said Miss Shaw. She moved again.

"Well, it's mutual," I said. "And no one regrets it more than I do."

"I mean the fashion show."

"It taught me all I ever learned about women."

"What's that?"

"I'm not sure."

From the cellar Sylvester called, "Will the Chablis do, Sara?"

"No it won't do, you bloody fairy queen," she screamed. Sylvester was chalked on the casing, but the bomb-sight was set on me.

I said, "I've still a lot more questions, I'm afraid."

"It will have to wait. I must start the lunches."

"Better get it over with."

She looked at her watch and sighed. "You couldn't have chosen a worse time of day."

"I can wait."

"Oh Lord! Look, come back for lunch—on the house. We'll do your questions after."

"I have a lunch appointment."

"Bring her with you."

I raised an eyebrow.

"I told you; I'm psychic." She consulted a large book. *"Deux couverts*—one o'clock? It will give you time for a drink." She uncapped a gold pen. "What was the name again?"

"You make it hard to refuse."

"Excellent," she said, and fidgeted with the pen.

"Armstrong."

"And I'll give you your tickets for the play." She went to the door. "Sylvester!" she called, "what the bloody hell are you doing down there! We've got the devil of a lot to do before lunch."

Chapter 12

At the discretion of CONTROL game time can be speeded, halted or reversed so that bounds can be replayed with the advantage of hindsight. No appeal can be made except on the grounds that notice in writing was not received before CONTROL's action.

RULES. ALL GAMES. STUDIES CENTRE. LONDON

I went up to the Control Balcony when I got back. Schlegel was on the phone. It was still early; I hoped that he hadn't missed me. "Sonofabitch," he shouted, and slammed the phone down. I wasn't dismayed; it was just his manner. He used too much energy for everything he did: I'd seen such activity before in small thickset men like Schlegel. He smacked a fist into his open palm. "For Christ's sake, Patrick. You said an hour."

"You know how it is."

"Never mind the goddamned apologies. Not content with flying boats, your friend is putting ice-breakers on a converging pattern along the Murmanskiy Bereg. Ice-breakers with sonar buoys . . . get it? He'll plot both the subs by taking bearings."

"That's not bad," I said admiringly. "No one's

thought of that before. Maybe that's why the Russians keep those two nuclear breakers so far west."

Schlegel had a lot of hands, and now he threw them at me, so that the index fingers bounced off my shirt. "I've got two admirals and selected staff from Norfolk running the Blue Control." He walked over to the tele-printer, fed out some paper, tore it off, screwed it up and threw it across the room. I said nothing. "And your friend Foxwell chooses *this* moment to demon-strate how well the commies can shaft us."

He pointed down at the War Table. Plastic discs marked those spots where Ferdy had wiped out nuclear subs. The two replacement subs coming from Iceland and Scotland were moving along the Murmansk coast and would be detected by Ferdy's buoys.

"They should have dog-legged those subs nearer to the Pole," I said.

"Where were you when we needed you?" said Schlegel sarcastically. He picked up his jacket and stood there in his shirtsleeves, his thumb hooking the jacket of his blue chalk-stripe, over his shoulder, his fingers grasping his bright red braces. He climbed into his jacket and smoothed the sleeves. That suit was Saville Row, from label to lining, but on Schlegel it was Little Caesar.

"How do we know that in a real war the Russians wouldn't be just as nutty?" I said.

"And leave the Kara Sea wide open?" He tightened the knot of his tie.

"It's working out O.K." I looked at the Game Clock, which moved according to the computer-calculated re-sult of each bound. I picked up the pink flimsies that

Blue Control had issued, trying to call the destroyed submarines.

"They just won't buy it," said Schlegel. I noticed that on the electric lights of the tote board they were still shown as undestroyed and in action.

I looked at the Master Status Report. I said, "We should programme Ferdy's ideas, using every last ice-breaker available to the Russians. And we should do it again, giving every ice-breaker sub-killing capability."

"It's all right for you," muttered Schlegel. "You won't have to go to the post-mortem with these guys this weekend. When they get back to Norfolk the shit will hit the fan, mark my words."

"Aren't we supposed to be putting up the best defense of the Russian mainland that we can devise?"

"Where did you get that idea?" said Schlegel. He had a habit of running his index finger and thumb down his face, as if to wipe away the lines of worry and age. He did it now. "The navy comes here for one reason only: they want a print-out that they can take to the Pentagon and make sure the trash haulers don't steal their appropriations budget."

"I suppose," I said. Schlegel despised the men of Strategic Air Command, and gladly allied himself with the navy to fight them at any chance he got.

"You suppose! Ever wonder what a flying gyrene like me is doing over here, running this toy-box? I was the nearest they could get to having a submarine admiral." He worked his jaw as though getting ready to spit but he didn't. He switched on the intercom again. "Phase Eight." He watched the Game Clock hands spin round to fourteen thirty hours.

"Now they'll *have* to write off their two subs," I said.

"They'll tell themselves it's pack-ice affecting the radio for another Phase yet."

I said, "Well they'll have one missile-submarine close enough to fire."

Schlegel said, "Can they retarget the MIRVs before launching?"

I said, "No, but they can make the independently targeted warheads fall as a cluster."

"So it becomes a Multiple Re-entry Vehicle but not independently targeted?"

"That's what they call it."

"That's like making a Poseidon back into a horse-and-buggy Polaris."

"Not really," I said.

"It's name rank and number time again, is it?" said Schlegel. "Not really? How much not really? Jesus, I really have to drag information out of you guys."

"There's far more bang per megaton for one thing. Also the clusters are more useful against dispersed targets."

"Like silos?"

"Like silos," I said.

"How does the computer answer that? Against a ten-missile silo, for instance?"

I said, "Providing there are no 'climate specials' or 'programming errors' it usually comes out as one hundred per cent destruction."

Schlegel smiled. It was all Blue Suite needed to defeat Ferdy, given average luck. And Schlegel in Master Control could provide that.

"Dandy," said Schlegel. I was Schlegel's assistant and it was my job to brief him with anything he wanted to know. But I had the feeling he had his thumb in the scale for the admirals in Blue Suite, and that made me feel I was letting Ferdy down.

"I'll give Ferdy the air reconnaissance of the drift-ice and the water temperatures, shall I?"

Schlegel came close. "A word of advice, Patrick. Your friend is under surveillance."

"What are you talking about?"

He looked over his shoulder to be sure the door was closed. "I mean he's under surveillance. Security, right?"

"Aren't we all? Why are you telling me?"

"For your own good. I mean . . . if you are with the guy . . . well, I mean . . . don't take him to your favourite whore-house unless you want the address on my desk next morning. Right?"

"I'll try and remember."

I took the weather reports and the air analysis down to Ferdy in the basement.

Ferdy switched off the console when I entered. It was dark in Red Ops. Around us the edge-lit transparent sheets showed a changing series of patterns as the coloured lines drew closer. "What did you find out?" he asked anxiously.

"Nothing much," I admitted. I told him about Detective-Sergeant Davis, and the girl. He smiled. "Didn't I tell you: Schlegel has set it all up."

"Schlegel!"

"He was sent here to set it up. Don't you see?"

I shrugged it off. I went out through the light trap into the corridor. I closed the door noisily. When I got back upstairs in the Main Control Balcony the plotters were putting flying boats on a square-search along the coast as far as the Norwegian border. Out of Archangel, more were patrolling the narrowest part of the White Sea. Not that there were any seas. The coastlines on that map meant nothing in the Arctic, where you could walk across the pack-ice of the world's roof, all the way from Canada to the U.S.S.R., and where the drift-ice comes down nearly to Scotland. There wasn't much moving on that great white nothing, where the blizzards roared, and wind turned a man to ice, scattered the fragments and screamed on hardly noticing. Nothing moved on that—but under it. Under it the war never stopped.

"Phase eight, section one," whispered the loudspeaker on Schlegel's console. The plotters moved the subs and the ice-breakers. The phone from Red Suite flashed.

"Challenge," said Ferdy. He had obviously expected it to be Schlegel on the phone and he changed his voice when he discovered it was me.

"What can I do for you, Admiral?"

"The ice-limit on these weather reports you brought down. They are for an earlier part of the season."

"I don't think so, Ferdy."

"Patrick. I don't want to argue but the drift-ice goes solid all along the estuary and links the islands at this time of year. You've been there, you know what it's like."

"They are machine compiled from earth satellite photos."

"Patrick, let me see the whole season, and I'll show you you are wrong. They have probably jumbled the cards in the machine."

I was sure that he was wrong but I didn't argue. "I'll get them," I said, and put down the phone. Schlegel was watching me. "Mr. Foxwell challenges the ice-limits," I said.

"Just keep him off my neck, Patrick. That's the fourth challenge of the game. Blue Suite haven't challenged me once."

I phoned down to the geography room where they kept the ice maps. They said they would take nearly an hour to get the whole lot together. I phoned the duty processor to tell him he'd be needed. Then I phoned Ferdy and told him the challenge would be allowed.

"Could you come down here again?" Ferdy said.

"I'm up and down like a yo-yo," I complained.

"It's important, Patrick," he said.

"Very well." I went down to the basement again. As I was going into the darkened Ops Room, the young submariner who had elected to be Ferdy's assistant passed me on his way out. I had a feeling that Ferdy had found him an errand to be rid of him. "War is hell," the boy said, "don't let anyone tell you different."

Ferdy confessed that it wasn't really important even before I was through the door. "But I really needed a chat. You can't talk with that American boy."

"Schlegel will go crazy if he finds out we've sent a processor to code those instructions, and used computer time, just to give you a chance for a chat."

"I'm allowed a few challenges."

"The other side have made none so far."

"Amateurs," said Ferdy. "Patrick, I was thinking about what you told me . . . about the girl."

"Go on," I said. But Ferdy didn't go on. He didn't want a conversation so much as an audience. He'd placed his counters across the neck of the White Sea.

On his small War Table it looked like the Serpentine Lake but it was well over twenty miles of frozen water with ice-breakers keeping two shipping lanes clear all through the winter.

The teleprinter clerk read off the computer material as it came on the print-out. "Hunter-killer submarines searching square fifteen . . ."

"What have I got in hunter-killer subs?" Ferdy asked the operator.

"Only the Fleet Alerted ones at Poliarnyi, and the ones at Dikson."

"Damn," said Ferdy.

"You must have known what would happen, Ferdy," I said. "You've had your fun but you must have realized what would happen."

"There's still time," said Ferdy.

But there wasn't time. Ferdy should have stuck to the usual procedure of hitting the electronic surveillance submarine first. They were the subs that we used for our listening posts to set up the game in the first place. Ferdy knew better than anyone in Blue Suite what they could do, and why the rest of the U.S. missile fleet depended upon them. There were two of them now, positioning the others for the missile attacks on Moscow, Leningrad and Murmansk, while the subs with the more sophisticated MIRV knocked out the missile silos, to lessen the retaliation upon our Western cities.

"Are you going to play it out for Doomsday?" I said. But if Ferdy intended to go for maximum destruction without caring about winning the war, he didn't intend to confide in me about it.

"Bugger off," said Ferdy. If he could find which of

the U.S. subs had the MIRVs, he might still pull off a freakish win. For the Polaris subs firing from the seabed up through the ocean or the ice aren't accurate enough for targets smaller than a town. The MIRV was Ferdy's real danger.

"It's all over bar the shouting, Ferdy. You can fiddle around for a week of game-days but you'll need uncanny luck to win."

"Bugger off, I said," said Ferdy.

"Keep your hair on," I told him. "It's only a game."

"That Schlegel is out to get me," said Ferdy. He got to his feet. His giant frame could only just squeeze between console and the game array panels.

"It's only a game, Ferdy," I said again. Reluctantly he gave a little grin to acknowledge the feeble standing joke of the War Studies Centre. If they ever give us a badge or a coat of arms that will be on the scroll beneath it.

I watched Ferdy as he ran his fingertips over the Arctic map. "There is another trip scheduled for us next month."

"So I hear," I said.

"With Schlegel," said Ferdy archly.

"He's never been to the Arctic. He wants to see it all working."

"We will have only been back a month by then."

"I thought you liked the long trips."

"Not with bloody Schlegel, I don't."

"What now?"

"I've waited a week to have my library permit renewed."

"I waited a month last year. That's just old English bureaucracy. That's not Schlegel."

"You always make excuses for him."

"Sometimes, Ferdy, you can be a little wearing."

He nodded repentantly.

"Hang on a minute," said Ferdy. He was a curiously lonely man, educated to feel at home only with the tiny world of men who identified his obscure Latin tags, tacitly completed his half-remembered Shelley and Keats and shared his taste for both the food and jokes of schooldays. I was not one of them, but I would do. "Hang on for five minutes."

The Tote—the computer's visual display—changed rapidly as he fingered the keyboard.

We were playing a modified number five scenario: the Russian A.S.W. (Northern Fleet) had twenty-four hours of 'war imminent' to neutralize the Anglo-American subs on Arctic station. In this case the scenario opened with a MIRV sub one hundred miles north of Spitzbergen. If Blue Suite got that—or any of their missile subs—much closer to Murmansk, Ferdy would not be able to attack them without a risk that the resulting explosion would wipe out his own town. This was the basic tactic of the twenty-four-hour game: getting the Blue Suite subs close to the Russian towns. Ferdy playing what Schlegel called "madman's checkers" could never pay off.

"They think it's all over down there, do they?" Ferdy said.

I said nothing.

"We'll see," said Ferdy.

There was a double long flash on the phone. I picked it up.

"Schlegel here. Did you bring the Mediterranean Fleet analysis?"

"It wasn't ready. They said they'd put it in the satchel with the stuff for the library. It's probably there now. I'll get it."

"You don't have to carry books over here from the Evaluation Block. We got messengers do that."

"A walk will do me good."

"Suit yourself."

"I have to go," I told Ferdy. "We'll have that chat later on."

"If your master allows."

"That's right, Ferdy," I said with a little irritation ~~and though~~ if my master allows."

The Evaluation Building was three hundred yards down the road. There would be no important movements in the war game before the noon bound. I put on my hat, coat and scarf and took a walk through the brisk Hampstead winter. The air smelled good. After the Centre, any air would smell good. I wondered how much longer I could go on working in a project that swatted warships like flies and measured wins in 'taken-out' cities.

Chapter 13

Conclusions reached by any member of STUCEN staff concerning the play are deemed to be secret, whether or not such conclusions were based upon play.

STANDING ROUTINE ORDERS. STU████ ████
    LONDON

Evaluation looked like a converted office block but once you got inside the front door it was not at all like a converted office block. There were two uniformed Ministry of Defence policemen in a glass box, and a time clock, and a wall full of punch cards that the two men spent all day every day inspecting very closely before placing them in different racks.

The policeman at the door took my security card. "Armstrong, Patrick," he announced to the other man, and spelled it, not too fast. The other man searched through the cards on the wall. "Did you just come out?" said the first cop.

"Me?" I said.

"Did you?"

"Come out?"

"Yes."

"No, of course not. I'm just going in."

"They've muddled the cards up again this morning. Sit down a moment would you?"

"I don't want to sit down a minute," I said patiently. "I don't want to sit down even for a second. I want to go in."

"Your card is not in the rack," he explained.

"What happens to the cards is strictly your job," I said. "Don't try and make me feel guilty about it."

"He's looking as fast as he can look," said the gate man. The other man was bending and stretching to look at the entry cards on the wall. As he did it he repeated "H I J K L M N O P" over and over again to remind himself of the sequence.

"I'm only going up to the library," I explained.

"Ah," said the gate-man, smiling as if he'd heard this same explanation from any number of foreign spies. "It's all the same in'it? The library is on the third floor."

"You come with me, then," I said.

He shook his head to show that it was a good try for a foreigner. He wiped his large white moustache with the back of his hand and then reached inside his uniform jacket for a spectacle case. He put his glasses on and read my security card again. Before we had the security cards, there had been no delays. I was a victim of some Parkinson's law of proliferating security. He noted the department number and looked that up in a greasy loose-leaf folder. He wrote down the phone extension and then went into the glass booth to phone. He turned to see me watching him, and then slid the glass panel completely shut, in case I should overhear him.

I lip-read him saying, "This card has been used once this morning and there is no exit time against the entry. This holder is . . ." he turned for a better view of me, ". . . late thirties, spectacles, clean shaven, dark hair, about six foot . . ." He stopped as I heard Schlegel's rasping voice even through the glass panel. The gateman opened it. "Your office wants to speak with you."

"Hello," I said.

"That you, Pat?"

"Yes, sir."

"What are you playing at, sweetheart?"

I didn't answer. I just gave the phone back to the gate man. I suppose Schlegel got my message because the gate man had no time to close the panel before Schlegel's voice spilled over, cursing him for all kinds of a fool. The old man's face went bright pink and he subdued Schlegel with a barrage of placatory noises. "Your boss says to go ahead," said the man.

"My boss says that, does he. And what do you say?"

"We'll sort out the cards. Someone has probably walked out with the card still in his pocket. It happens sometimes."

"Am I going to have the same trouble getting out of here?"

"No, sir," said the gate man. "I'll make sure about that. You'll never have trouble getting *out* of here."

He smiled and brushed his moustache with his hand. I didn't try to cap it.

* * *

There was not one library but many, like strata of ancient Troy. Deepest were foxy leather spines and tattered jackets of the original Trust donations, and then box-files and austerity bindings of the war years, and then, in layers above that, the complete Official Histories of both world wars. Only the new metal shelving held the latest additions, and much of that was stored as microfilm, and could be read only in the tiny cubicles from which came a steady clatter and the smell of warm projector bulbs.

I started with the Northern Fleet but I would have found him even had I selected all the rear-admirals, and worked my way through them alphabetically. None of the microfilm up-datings were of much interest but there were new pictures. This was the man who wanted to be me.

Remoziva, Vanya Mikhail (1924–   ) Kontr-
   Admiral,
Commander: Anti-Submarine Warfare Command,
Northern Fleet, Murmansk.

The Remoziva family provided a fine example of revolutionary zeal. His father was a metal worker from Orel, his mother a peasant from Kharkov who'd moved farther east when the Germans occupied vast areas of Russia from the Bolsheviks, by the Treaty of Brest-Litovsk. Of their family of seven children, two daughters and three sons survived. And what children they were: not only a rear-admiral, but Piotr, a professor of zoology; Evgeni, a sociologist; Lisaveta, a political analyst; and Katerina, the second daughter, who had been an assistant to Madame Furtseva, the

first woman to reach the Presidium of the Central
Ferdy Foxwells of the workers' soviets.
Committee. The Remoziva family sounded like the

The compiler had done a thorough job—even if most
of his data were cross-referenced to Central Registry
—and he had included the sociologist's order of Alex-
ander Nevsky, the three amputated fingers of the
zoologist—yes, I wondered that, too—and the kidney
trouble that was likely to cost the Rear-Admiral his
promotion to the First Deputy's office.

I went through the sheet on which was listed Remoziva's career. He owed much to Admiral Rickover,
U.S. Navy, for the American decision to build nuclear
submarines—armed with Polaris missiles—was the best
thing that could have happened to Remoziva. It was
a nuclear rags to riches story. When the keel of the
Nautilus went down, in 1954, he was a Starshii Leiten-
ant, sitting around in the Coast Defence Department
of Northern Fleet, desperate for even a staff appointment with Naval Artillery. Suddenly his anti-submarine
work in the war is taken out and dusted off. He immediately regains his wartime rank. Northern Fleet
A.S.W. trumps even Baltic Fleet A.S.W., now that the
U.S. Navy is sailing under the Arctic ice. Remoziva gets
a senior staff job. Khruschev pushes for a nuclear submarine fleet, and by 1962 the *Leninskii Komsomol*
has also been to the North Pole under the ice. From
being a forgotten bywater in a neglected arm, Northern
Fleet's A.S.W. staff are the élite of the Russian armed
services. No wonder it was difficult to find a photo in
which Remoziva wasn't smiling.

I returned the material, and picked up the analysis
that Schlegel wanted. I checked out past the smiling

men in the glass box, and took the papers back to the Centre. I dumped them into the reception guard and then strolled through to Saddler's Walk to have a quiet cup of coffee.

There, a Georgian façade had been newly adorned with red and black stripes, and its name, "The Anarchist," painted in gold letters. It was another of those art, coffee and non-chemical coleslaw hang-outs that sprout, bloom and die. Or worse, survive: a crippled commercial travesty of the original dream.

Che and Elvis shared the walls. The coffee cups were folk-art and the potato salad cut with loving care. It was a bright dry day, the streets were filled with woolly-hatted Australians, and delicate men with nervous dogs. Some of them were sitting around here drinking coffee. Behind the counter there was a girl anarchist. She had heavy-rimmed spectacles and a pony-tail tight enough to make her squint.

"This is our first week," she said. "There is a nut cutlet free for everyone."

"The coffee will do."

"There is no charge for the nut cutlet. It's a way of getting customers to see how delicious a vegetarian diet can be." She picked up a slice of the pale-grey mixture, using plastic tongs like an obstetrician. "I'll put it on the tray—I'm sure you'll like it." She poured out the coffee.

"With milk—if that's allowed."

"Sugar is on the table," she said. "Natural brown sugar—it's better for you."

I sipped the coffee. From my table near the window I watched two parking wardens clobber a delivery van and a Renault with French plates. It made me feel much better. I brought out my notebook and wrote down that biographical note on the Rear-Admiral. And then I listed all the things that puzzled me about the changes to my old flat. I drew an outline picture of Rear-Admiral Remoziva. Then I drew a plan of the old flat and included the secret ante-room with the medical machinery. When I was a kid I'd wanted to be an artist. Sometimes I thought Ferdy Foxwell only tolerated me because I could pronounce Pollaiuolo, and tell a Giotto from a Francesca. Perhaps I was more than a little envious of the half-baked painters and hairy bohemians that were always in evidence up here in Hampstead. I wondered if I might have been one of them under different circumstances. It was while I was doodling, and thinking about nothing of any consequence, that some subconscious segment of my brain was dealing with the mix-up at the entrance to the Evaluation Block that morning.

I put down my pen and sipped the coffee. I sniffed it. Perhaps it was acorns. Behind the soy sauce was propped a pamphlet advertising "Six lectures in modern Marxism." I turned it over, on the back someone had pencilled, "Don't complain about the coffee, you might be old and weak yourself some day."

Suppose that the two gate men had not been so far wrong. Suppose that I had been in the Evaluation Block once already that morning. Ridiculous, but I pursued the notion. Suppose I had been drugged or hypnotized. I decided to discount both those possibilities for the time being. Suppose my exact double had been there. I rejected that idea too because the men on the door would have remembered: or would they? The card. Those gate men seldom bothered to look at faces. They checked the card numbers against the rack and against the time-book. It wasn't my *Doppelgänger* that had been through the gate: it was my security card.

Before I got to the door another thought occurred to me. I sat down at the table and took out my wallet. I removed the security card from its plastic cover and looked at it closely. It was exactly the right shape, size and springiness for sliding up the door catch of my locker. I'd used it to force the lock dozens of times. But this card had never been used for that purpose. Its edges were sharp, white and pristine. This wasn't the security card I'd been given, someone else had that. *I was using the forgery!*

That disturbing conclusion got me nowhere. It just made me lonely. My world wasn't peopled by charming, wise and influential elders as Ferdy's world was. My friends all had real worries: like who can you get to service a new Mercedes properly, should the au pair have colour TV, and is Greece warmer than Yugoslavia in July. Yeah, well maybe it was.

I looked at my watch. This was Thursday and I'd promised to take Marjorie to lunch and be lectured about my responsibilities.

I got to my feet and went to the counter. "Ten pence," she said.

I paid.

"I said you'd eat the nut cutlet," she said. She pushed her spectacles up on her forehead to see the cash register better. Damn, I'd eaten the wretched thing without even tasting it.

"You didn't like the coffee?" she asked.

"Is this anarchist's coffee?" I asked the girl.

"Grounds enough for arrest," she said. I suppose

someone had said the same thing before. Or maybe they thought of the joke and then built the coffee shop around it.

She passed me the change. Alongside the cash register there were half a dozen collection boxes. Oxfam, World-Wildlife and Shelter. One of the tins had a hand-written label with a Polaroid photo fixed alongside it. "Kidney Machine Fund. Give generously for Hampstead Sick and Elderly." I picked up the tin and looked closely at the photo of a kidney machine.

"That's my pet charity," said the girl. "Our target is four machines by Christmas. Going all the way to the hospital every week or so is too much for some of the old ones. They can have those machines in their own home."

"Yes, I know." I put my change into the tin.

The girl smiled. "People with kidney trouble would do almost anything for one of those machines," she said.

"I'm beginning to believe you're right," I said.

Chapter 14

Attacker. *For the purposes of the assessment the "phasing" player, who brings his unit into range, is called the attacker. The player against whom the unit is brought is called the defender.*

GLOSSARY. "NOTES FOR WARGAMERS." STUDIES CENTRE. LONDON

The loneliest place in the world is the entrance hall of a big hospital. The huge and elaborate Victorian palace in which Marjorie worked was a maze of cast-iron staircases, stone arches and decorated paving. From these pitiless materials, whispers echoed back like the endless thrash of a furious sea. The staff were inured to it. They clattered past in white coats, smelling of ether and hauling trolleys which I did not dare examine. By the time Marjorie arrived I needed medical reassurance.

"Then you should wait outside in the car."

"I haven't brought the car."

"In my car." She was wearing a pink jersey shirt-dress instead of one of the dark suits she usually wore when on duty. She tied a black silk scarf and put on her belted raincoat.

I said, "I haven't got the key of your car."

161

"Wait near my car."

"You didn't bring it today remember?"

"The real answer," said Marjorie, "is that you like the frisson of hypochondria." We stepped through the portal. The sun was high in a clear blue sky. It was hard to believe it was almost Christmas.

She was always like this when she was on duty: trimmer, younger, more independent. More like a doctor, in fact. It was difficult to escape the thought that the scatterbrained little girl that she became when with me was not the person she wanted to be. And yet we were happy together, and just waiting for her I rediscovered all the excitements and anxieties of adolescent love. We took one of the taxi cabs from the hospital cab rank. I gave him the address of The Terrine du Chef.

"I bought you a present."

"Oh, Pat. You remembered."

She unwrapped it hastily. It was a wristwatch. "It must have cost a fortune."

"They'll exchange it for a desk barometer."

She held the watch tight, and put her closed fist inside her other hand, and pressed it to her heart, as though frightened that I might take it from her. "You said repapering the sitting-room would be for my birthday."

"We'll probably be able to afford that as well," I said. "And I thought . . . well, if you do go to Los Angeles, you wouldn't be able to take the wallpaper."

"And it's got a sweep second-hand." Tears welled up in her eyes.

"It's only steel," I said. "Gold isn't so waterproof or dustproof . . . but if you want gold . . ."

There was a lot of the little girl in her. And there was no denying that that was what attracted me. I leaned forward to kiss the tip of her nose.

"Los Angeles . . ." she said. She sniffed, and smiled. "It would mean working in a research lab . . . like a factory, almost . . . I like being part of a hospital . . . it's what makes it worth while."

The cab swerved and threw her gently into my arms. "I do love you, Patrick," she said.

"You don't have to cry," I told her. Her hair came unclipped and fell across her face as I tried to kiss her again.

"We just don't get on together," she said. She held me tight enough to disprove it.

She drew back from me and looked at my face as if seeing it for the first time. She put out a hand and touched my cheek with the tips of her fingers. "Before we try again, let's find somewhere else to live." She put her hand lightly across my lips. "There's nothing wrong with your flat, but it is your flat, Patrick. I feel I'm only a lodger there, it makes me insecure."

"I have another trip scheduled. While I'm away, you could speak with one of the less crooked house-agents."

"Please! Do let us look. I don't mean in the suburbs or anything. I won't look at anything farther out than Highgate."

"It's a deal."

"And I'll try for a position in whatever hospital is local."

"Good," I said. As long as she worked in the same hospital as her husband there would always be this distance between us, even if—as she insisted—it was solely of my creation. I'd seen her with her husband. It was bloody disconcerting when they got on to the topic of medicine: it was as if they had their own culture, and their own language in which to discuss its finer nuances.

For a few minutes neither of us spoke. As we passed Lords Cricket Ground I saw a newspaper seller with a placard: RUSSIAN MYSTERY WOMAN CHAIRS GERMAN UNITY TALKS. That's the way it is with newspapers. The car strike had already become ANGRY CAR PICKETS: VIOLENCE FLARES after some name-calling outside the factory that morning.

"Have you got a game in progress?" It was Marjorie's attempt to account for my moodiness.

"I left just as Ferdy was deciding whether to atomize a sub outside Murmansk and risk contaminating the shipping and ship yards in the fjord. Or whether to wait until its multiple clusters leave him without nukes for retaliation—or with the random target selection of the surviving silos."

"And you ask me how I can work in the Pathology Lab."

"It's comparable in a way . . . disease and war. Perhaps it's better to pick them to the bone and see what they are made of than to sit around and wait for the worst to happen."

The cab stopped outside The Terrine. "I must be back by two thirty at the latest."

"We don't have to eat here," I said. "We can have a beer and a sandwich and get you back ten minutes early."

"I'm sorry. I didn't mean that," she said. "It was a lovely idea."

I paid the taxi off. Marjorie said. "How did you find this little place—it's sweet."

I was cupping my hands and peering close to the window. There were no lights on and no customers, just the neatly arranged place settings, polished glasses and starched napkins. I tried the door and rang the bell. Marjorie tried the door too. She laughed. "That's typical of you, darling," she said.

"Just cool it for a minute," I told her. I went down the narrow alley at the side of the restaurant. It gave access to back entrances of houses above The Terrine. There was a wooden gate in the wall. I put my arm over the top of it, and by balancing a toe on a ledge in the wall I reached far enough to release the catch. Marjorie followed me through the gate. There was a tiny cobbled yard, with an outside toilet and a drain blocked with potato peelings.

"You shouldn't."

"I said cool it." There seemed to be no one looking down from the windows, or from the iron balcony crammed with potted plants, now skeletal and bare in the wintry sun. I tried the back door. The net curtains were drawn. I went to the window but its lacy-edged yellow blind was down, and I couldn't see in. Marjorie said, "Rich gifts wax poor when givers prove unkind."

I tried to lever the spring bolt open with the edge of my security card but it must have been one of those double turn movements with a dead-bolt. "That's women," I said. "Give them presents and they complain they're not getting enough kindness." I gave her another tiny kiss on the nose.

The lock wouldn't give. I leaned my back against

the glass panel in the door to deaden the sound, then I pressed against it until I heard the glass snap.

"Have you gone mad?" said Marjorie.

I put a finger in the crack and widened it enough to pull a large piece of broken glass away from the putty. "O.K., Ophelia," I said. "You're the only one I love; stop complaining."

I put my hand through the broken glass panel and found the key, still in the old-fashioned mortice lock. It turned with a screech of its rusty tumblers. Glancing round to be sure there was no one coming down the alley, I opened the door and went in.

"This is burglary," said Marjorie, but she followed me.

"House-breaking, you mean. Burglary only at night, remember what I told you for that crossword?"

The sun came through the holland blind; thick yellow light, viscous, almost, like a roomful of pale treacle. I released the blind and it sprang up with a deafening clatter. If no one heard that, I thought, the place is empty.

"But you could go to prison," said Marjorie.

"We'd be together," I said, "and that's what matters." I leaned forward to kiss her but she pushed me away. We were in the pantry. Lined up along the servery there were wooden bowls, each with a limp piece of lettuce and a segment of pale-pink tomato. There were desserts, too: platoons of caramels and battalions of babas, deployed under muslin and awaiting the word to attack.

I helped myself from a tray of sausages. They were still warm. "Have a sausage, Marjorie." She shook her head. I bit into one. "Entirely bread," I said. "Be all right toasted, with butter and marmalade." I walked into the next room; Marjorie followed.

"A really long lease is what we should go for," said Marjorie. "And with both of us working . . ."

The sewing machine was still there but the uniform had gone and so had the dossier of measurements and photos. I went down the worn stone steps to the room into which the refrigeration chamber had been built. It switched itself on and made us both jump. "Especially with me being a doctor," said Marjorie. "The bank manager told me that."

There was a tall cupboard built into one wall. Its door was fastened with a massive padlock A hairpin had no effect on it.

I opened the kitchen drawers, one by one, until I found the sharpening steel. I put that through the padlock and put my weight behind it, but, as always, it was the hasp that gave way: its screws slid out of the dead woodwork and fell on the floor.

"It's against the law," said Marjorie. "I don't care what you say."

"A shop, or a restaurant? Implied right of access— a tricky point of law. It's probably not even trespass." I opened the cupboard.

"It's better than paying rent," said Marjorie. "You've paid for your old place three times over, I've always said that."

"I know you have, Marjorie." There was nothing inside the cupboard except dead flies and a packet of account-overdue stickers.

"We might get it all from the bank—not even have to go to a building society," said Marjorie.

The door of the cold room had two large swing clips

holding it. Outside, on the wall, there were light switches and a fuse box marked "Danger." I put the light switch on and a small red neon indicator came alight. I put my weight upon the swing clips and without effort opened up the giant door.

"That would be wonderful," I said.

"You're not listening," said Marjorie.

"Building society," I said. "Wonderful idea."

"*Not* have to go to one," said Marjorie.

"Well, there you are," I said, "you've answered your own question."

Score nothing for guessing that this was an ordinary room disguised as a cold chamber. The frozen air came out to meet me. I stepped inside. It was a normal refrigerated room, about eight feet square, with slatted shelving from floor to ceiling on all sides, except for the part of the rear wall that was occupied by the refrigeration machinery. The displacement of the air tripped the thermostat. The motor clicked on and built up the revolutions until it was wobbling gently on the sprung mounts. It was cold and I buttoned my jacket and turned up the collar. Marjorie came inside. "Like the mortuary," she pronounced. Her voice echoed in the tiny space. I did my monster walk towards her, my hands raised like claws.

"Stop it," she said. She shivered.

Five sides of mutton were lined up along one side. Frozen fillets—fifty according to the label on the box —had been piled up on the top shelf, and crammed alongside them were three large bags of ready peeled frozen sauté potatoes and three cardboard boxes of mixed vegetables.

"One gross individual portions: *Coq au vin, su-*

prêmes de volaille, suprêmes de chasseur. Mixed." A large tin of "Curry anything" and a shelf crammed with frozen lamb chops. Just inside the door there were three bottles of champagne being cooled the hard way. No hollow walls, no secret compartments, no trapdoors.

We came out of the refrigerated room and I closed the door again. I went back into the kitchen and sniffed at the saucepans in the *bain marie*. They were all empty. I cut a slice of bread. "Bread?"

She shook her head. "Where could they all be?" said Marjorie. "It's not early closing."

"There you've got me," I admitted, "but I'll look down in the wine cellar. They could just be hiding."

"It's nearly half past."

"You'd better have a sausage. By the time we've finished this burglary, there won't be time for lunch." I took another one myself and squashed it between a folded slice of bread.

She grabbed my arm. "Have you done this sort of thing before?" she asked.

"Not with a partner. Sausage sandwich?"

I thought she was going to cry again. "Oh, Patrick!" She didn't stamp her foot exactly, but she would have done in her other shoes.

"I was only joking," I said. "You didn't think I was serious?"

"I don't even think you are serious about the house," she said.

There was no one in the cellar. No one in the toilet. No one in the store room upstairs.

An hour or so ago this had been a flourishing restaurant, now it was not just deserted: it was abandoned.

There was something in the atmosphere, perhaps the sound that our voices and footsteps made with all the windows and doors closed, or perhaps there really is something that happens to houses that are forsaken.

It had been hastily done and yet it was systematic and disciplined. No attempt had been made to save the valuables. There was an expensive Sony cassette player, a cellar full of wine and spirits, and two or three boxes of cigars and cigarettes in a cupboard over the serving hatch. And yet not one scrap of paper remained: no bills, receipts or invoices, not even a menu. Even the grocery order that I'd seen wedged down behind the knife rack had been carefully retrieved and taken away.

"There's sliced ham: you like that."

"Do stop it," she said.

I walked into the restaurant. The light came through the net curtains and reflected upon the marble table-tops and the bentwood chairs arranged around them. It was all as shadowy and still as a Victorian photograph. Antique mirrors, gold-lettered with advertisements for cigarettes and apéritifs, were fixed to every wall. Mirrored there were seemingly endless other diningrooms, where red-eyed pretty girls stretched ringless hands towards tall shabby furtive men.

Reflected there, too, was a bright-red milk float, and I heard it whine to a halt outside in the street. I pulled back the bolts on the front door and let Marjorie pass me. The milkman was putting two crates of milk on the doorstep. He was a young man with a battered United Dairy cap, and a brown warehouse coat. He smiled and spent a moment or two recovering his breath. "You've only just missed them," he said.

"How long ago?"

"Best part of half an hour, bit more perhaps."

"It was the traffic," I said.

"Poor fellow," said the milkman. "How did it happen?"

"How do any of these things happen?" I said.

"Ah, you're right there," he said. He took off his hat and scratched his head.

"Looked bad, eh?" I said.

"All drawn up—knees against his chest."

"Conscious?"

"I was right down the end of the street. I saw them putting him in. They had to open both doors to get him through."

"What was it: Ambulance Service?"

"No, a fancy job—painted cream with lettering and a red cross."

"If only I knew where they'd taken him," I said. "This lady is a doctor, you see."

He smiled at Marjorie and was glad to rest a moment. He put a boot on the crate, plucking at his trouser leg to reveal a section of yellow sock and some hairy leg. He took out a cigarette case, selected one and lit it with a gold lighter. He nodded his head as he thought about the ambulance. "It came right past me," he admitted. "A clinic, it was."

"The rest of them went with him, I suppose?"

"No, in a bloomin' great Bentley."

"Did they!"

"A Bentley Model T. That's like the Rolls Silver Shadow, except for the Bentley radiator. Nice job. Green, it was."

"You don't miss much, do you."

"I made one, didn't I? Plastic—two hundred separate

parts—took me months. It's on the tele, you should see it: my missus is afraid to dust it."

"Green?"

"Front offside wing bent to buggery. A recent shunt, not even rusted."

"And the ambulance was from a clinic?"

"It's gone right out of my mind. Sorry, Doctor," he said to Marjorie. He touched the peak of his cap, "I've got a terrible memory these days. You'd be National Health, I suppose?"

"Yes," I said. "I suppose they can afford a private place."

"Oh, yes," said the milkman. "Little goldmine, that place is."

"I'd better run," Marjorie said to me.

"No one here today," I said.

"No, well they don't do lunches," said the milkman. He picked up two crates of empty milk bottles and staggered away.

"How did you know about the ambulance?" Marjorie asked me.

"Ah," I said, feeling rather clever.

"But who was it?" insisted Marjorie. "What happened here?"

"A Russian admiral with kidney trouble," I said.

Marjorie became angry. She stepped out into the road and hailed a cab. It stopped with a squeal of brakes. She opened the door and got in. "The incredible amount of trouble you will go to to avoid a serious talk! It's sick, Patrick! Can't you see that?"

The cab pulled away before I could answer.

I waited on the pavement, watching the milkman as he staggered under the weight of more crates of milk.

Sometimes he put them down and caught his breath for a moment. He was a quick-witted, energetic fellow, whom any dairy would be well advised to employ, but milkmen who lavish hand-made crocodile boots upon themselves do not wear them on their rounds, especially when the boots are new and unbroken. Footwear is always the difficulty in a hasty change of dress but the gold lighter was pure carelessness. It was obvious that The Terrine was staked out, but as the bogus milkman moved down the street I wondered why he should have told me so much, unless a course of action had already been prepared for me.

I crossed the street to an upturned crate from which an old man was selling newspapers. I looked at the crate with its placard on the front, and the tin tray of loose change. I wondered if by kicking it over I might damage a few hundred pounds-worth of two-way radio. Oh yes, The Terrine was staked out all right, and they weren't bothering about the subtleties.

"The latest," I said automatically. It started to rain again and he pulled a plastic sheet over his papers. "Sports edition?"

"I'm not sure I can tell the difference," I said, but I took the early news, and for a few moments stood there reading it.

The woman leading the Russian delegation to the German reunification talks was fast becoming a cult figure in the West. Women's Liberation supported her nomination for chairman above any claim by British, French or American male delegates. Her brief appearance on TV news was helping the media to sell this otherwise dull conference to a public who didn't give a damn about Germany's eastern border. Now here was

Katerina Remoziva in a three-column photo on the front page. She was a thin elderly spinster with an engaging smile, her hair in a bun, her hand raised in a gesture somewhere between workers' solidarity and papal blessing.

The caption said, "For Madame Katerina Remoziva, the Copenhagen talks represent repayment for six years behind-the-scenes work, and nearly a hundred semi-official meetings. Next Monday we begin to tell the story of this amazing woman and her hopes for permanent European peace and prosperity."

Nice work, comrades, a propaganda triumph in the making. It was raining faster now and I put the paper over my head.

Chapter 15

If you measure power and success by the time taken to move in comfort to or from a city centre—and many use that criterion—then the next couple of hours was the pace-setter by which all London's tycoons and politicians must measure themselves.

The police car stopped outside The Terrine at one forty-five. "Mr Armstrong?" He was a man of about forty. His coat was unbuttoned and revealed a police uniform that had been tailored to put the top button high. His shirt was white linen, its collar fastened with a gold pin. Whoever he was, he didn't have to line up on parade each morning and be checked by the station sergeant. The driver also was wearing a civilian coat, and only his blue shirt and black tie suggested that he was a constable.

"Perhaps," I said. I held the newspaper over me to keep the rain off.

"Colonel Schlegel's compliments, and we are to take you to Battersea. There is a helicopter waiting to connect with the airport." He didn't get out of the car.

"Do you come with a book of instructions?"

"I beg your pardon, sir?"

"Why would I want to go to London airport . . . Why would anyone?"

"It's something to do with this restaurant, sir," he said. "It's a Special Branch matter. I was just the nearest available spare bod."

"And if I don't want to go with you?"

"The helicopter has been there an hour, sir. It must be urgent." He looked up at the sky. The rain continued.

"Suppose I was afraid of heights?"

He began to understand. He said, "We were just told to bring you the message, and give you a lift if you wanted it. As long as you identify yourself, that will get me out of trouble . . ." He lifted a hand awkwardly to show that he had no instructions about collaring me.

"O.K.," I said. "Let's go." He smiled and unlocked the passenger door for me.

The helicopter was a museum piece: a Westland Dragonfly painted in the Royal Navy livery of dark steel blue. There were no roundels on it, and no lettering except for a civil registration number painted no larger than the "Beware of the Rotor" sign at the back.

The pilot's appearance was similarly discreet. He wore military flyer's overalls, with maggots of cotton outlining clean patches from which the badges had been removed. He was in the left-hand seat by the time the car was parked, and as I climbed aboard the main rotor was spinning. The noise of the blades, and the old piston engine, inhibited conversation. I contented myself with looking out at the tall chimneys of Fulham making billowing white gauze curtains that closed across the river behind us. We passed over Wandsworth Bridge, keeping to the course of the river, as the safety regulations specify for everyone except royalty.

From the private aircraft park at London Heathrow, the same pilot took a Beagle Pup. Within an hour of leaving Marjorie outside The Terrine I was over Rugby at eight thousand feet and still climbing. We were heading north-west and, according to the gauges, sufficiently fuelled to get to the last landfall of the Outer Hebrides. The map on the pilot's knee bore an ancient wax pencil mark that continued in that direction and ended only on the margin. Now and again he smiled and stabbed a finger at the map and at the plexiglass, to show me the M1 Motorway, or the dark grey smear on the horizon behind which Coventry coughed. He offered me a cigarette but I declined. I asked him where we were going. He slid his headset back off his head and cupped his ear. I asked again but he shrugged and smiled as if I'd asked him to predict the outcome of the next general election.

A winter's sun was a carelessly sprayed yellow patch

on the hard cumulus clouds that were building up over Ireland. Liverpool—and a Mersey crowded with ships —slid beneath our starboard wing, and ahead the Irish Sea glittered like a cheap brass tray. Flying over the ocean in single-engined light planes could never become a pleasure for me but the pilot smiled, pleased to get clear of the Control Zone and reporting areas, and off the confluence of airways through which came traffic jams of commercial jets. He climbed again, now that he was no longer forced down under the lanes, and that comforted me.

I studied the map. This aircraft's electronics were primitive. Flying V.F.R. meant he'd have to put it down before dark. The huge shape of the Isle of Man was not going there, nor to the airport at Blackpool, which we'd already passed. The fuel needles were was only just visible in the gloomy ocean to port. He flickering and still we maintained the same course that we'd steered since Castle Donington. It would be the chin of Scotland, or beyond that its nose, drooped down into the Western Isles. After the peninsula of Kintyre our track would be past the Scottish mainland. Then there were just the Islands and the Atlantic and eventually, long after the last drip of fuel had sounded the final beat of the little engine, Iceland. It had to be an island or a piece of peninsula. I just hoped that it would come over the horizon soon.

*　　*　　*

"The only way to guarantee privacy, old chap," said Toliver. He replenished my tumbler from a decanter of malt whisky. "The grass strip and the landing stage were built in 1941. This peninsula and the neighbouring islands were taken over by the military. Some were used for testing biological warfare stuff. Anthrax was the most persistent . . . won't be safe for a hundred years, they say. Ours was used for training secret agents: the big manor house, the high cliffs, the ruined villages—there was a good sampling of landscape."

Toliver smiled. Once, many years before, in the sort of electioneering invective that endears politicians to all of us, his opponent had called Toliver a "talking potato." It was a cruel taunt, for it made one notice the small black eyes, receding hair and oval face that were part of his otherwise boyish features.

He smiled now. "What I'm about to tell you comes under the contract. You understand me?"

I understood him well enough. Every time I signed that damned Official Secrets Act I read the fine print. I nodded and turned to look out of the window. It was dark but there remained a watery pink sky in the west, with a pattern of trees drawn on it. Beyond them, I knew the aircraft was pegged down tightly against the chance of winds that came off the Atlantic with a sudden and terrible fury. But I could see more reflected in the leaded window than I could see through it. The flames flickered in the open hearth behind me, and men were seated around it drinking and speaking softly so that they could half listen to the words that Toliver spoke to me.

"It's too late to leave," I said. "You'd have to be damned inhospitable for me to want to face a take-off in this . . . and positively hostile before I'd brave the water."

"Splendid," said Toliver. "That's all we ask. Take

a look at what we're doing—no less, no more. Should you want no part of it—no hard feelings."

I turned away from the window. This sober Toliver was a different man from the one I'd seen the other night at Ferdy's. It had become understood between us that the dinner party was not mentioned, nor the traffic accident that might, or might not, have come after it. "It will make a change," I said.

"Exactly. Nice of Colonel Schlegel to let us steal one of his best people . . . even for a couple of days." Toliver touched my elbow and turned me to face the other men in the room.

Among them I recognized Mason. I also saw the tall policeman who had been at number eighteen that night. The others called him Commander Wheeler. They were all talking softly together but the words flared up a little in good-natured argument.

". . . worse in a way—more insidious—pop music and nancy-boy actors."

"And most of the big international concerns are American-based."

"No doubt about it."

"You can't separate them." It was the tall man speaking. "Ecology—as they persist in calling it, God knows why—trade unions, big business: all in league, even if unwittingly so."

"Growth," said Mason, as if they'd had this argument before and each knew his lines.

"The unions want money for the workers, this forces a policy of growth on the government, so industry pollutes the earth. It's a vicious circle and all of them too stupid to break it."

"It all comes back to the voter."

"Yes, it does," said Mason regretfully.

They were robust types, with quiet voices that here and there retained a trace of Yorkshire or Scotland. I looked for some strong common denominator in the group and was irritated with myself for finding none. Their clothes were well-fitting tweeds and cords, with the leather patches and frayed cuffs so often affected by prosperous Englishmen. The group suggested to me some provincial dining club, where ambitious young men drank too much wine, and agreed that the workers would be better off without trade unions.

"You get these damned Huns reunified and you'll start to see what's what," said Wheeler.

"Who will?" said Mason.

"Everyone," said Toliver. He couldn't resist joining their conversation, even though he'd been about to introduce me. "East Germany is largely agricultural. It will knock agriculture for six, and their shipbuilding will close the rest of our yards, mark my words."

"It's going to turn Europe upside down," said another man.

"The Yanks are behind it," said Wheeler. "God knows what kind of a deal they are cooking up behind the scenes with the Russians."

"This is Pat," Toliver announced. "Pat Armstrong —works at the Studies Centre and . . ." Toliver appraised me with a quick glance up and down, ". . . a man who knows how to look after himself if I'm any judge. What?" He looked at me quizzically.

"I play a dangerous game of billiards," I said.

There were half a dozen of them, aged from middle twenties up to Toliver. Their common interest could have been anything from chess to yachting. I was unsure whether Whitehall was behind them, or just turning a blind eye their way.

"Commander Wheeler," said Toliver putting an arm around Wheeler's shoulder. "Our guest would probably like to be put into the picture."

"And he's cleared for Top Secret stuff, is he?" said Wheeler. He was a tall man, with the kind of ruddy face that comes with those duel benefits of sea-faring: open air and duty-free drink. He had this deep flag-officer voice, and he bit down hard on his Latin roots. "You probably know as much about Rear-Admiral Remoziva as we do," he said.

Toliver smiled at me and patted my shouldr. "I think Armstrong would agree that the Rear-Admiral would be a strategic asset for us," he said.

"He's not here then?" I said.

"Not yet," said Toliver. "But very, very soon."

Wheeler said, "The simple fact is, if the Admiral doesn't get a kidney transplant within the next eighteen months, he'll be dead a year after."

"And he can't get that in the Soviet Union?" I asked.

"The Admiral is an able statistician," said Toliver. "They started a kidney unit in Leningrad a year ago last July. They are capable of it, yes. But in London we've done thousands of such operations. Ask yourself what you'd prefer."

"And he'd defect?"

"To live?" said Wheeler. "A man will go to great lengths to live, Mr Armstrong."

I suppose I sniffed, or grunted, or made some other noise that fell short of the enthusiasm that Toliver expected. "Tell me why not," said Commander Wheeler.

"It's possible," I agreed. "But peasant family to Soviet nobility in one generation is quite a jump. They've plenty to be grateful for. One brother is planning a new town near Kiev, the elder sister chairing the Copenhagen talks, and getting more publicity than Vanessa Redgrave . . ."

"The Admiral is not yet fifty," said Wheeler. "He has a lot of life ahead of him if he's wise."

"We were also sceptical at first," said Toliver. "If the emphasis hadn't been placed upon proving death . . ." He stopped and looked apologetically at Wheeler. "But I'm getting too far ahead."

Wheeler said, "We divided the problem into three separate tasks. The safest place for the transfer was obvious from the start. There's only one place where we can guarantee security. He can fly a helicopter. We will rendezvous with him at a prearranged place on the pack-ice of the Barents Sea and bring him back by submarine."

"British submarine," said Mason.

"A Royal Navy nuclear submarine," said Toliver. "If the Yanks got wind of it they'd spirit him away to America and that's the last we'd see of him."

"Next," said Wheeler, "there is the problem of holding him for debriefing . . ."

"And you thought of the War Studies Centre," I said.

"Well, it's bloody marvellous, isn't it?" said Wheeler. "War-game his debriefing, and put NATO resources against him."

"And programme the computer to his reactions," said Toliver.

"Dangerous," I said.

"Not as a war plan—just into the data bank," said Toliver.

"And what about Schlegel?" I asked.

Wheeler frowned. "That's set us back a month or more—but he'll be posted elsewhere. It was finally fixed today."

"And the Rear-Admiral will become Pat Armstrong?" I said.

"Sorry about that," said Toliver, "but you are about the right build and you'd just vacated the flat. We never guessed for a moment that you might go back there."

"It's quite good," I admitted.

"Only for a few weeks," said Mason. "The tenancy of the flat and all the necessary personal documentation is in your name. There will be no trace of a new person at the Studies Centre. We've gone to a lot of trouble. Getting that damned kidney machine up those stairs and into the flat next door to your old one . . . I damned near got a hernia. And then when they told us you'd gone back there, and you still had your old key. We got chewed out for that, I'll tell you."

"And what happens to me?" I asked. "Do I go back and take over Northern Fleet?"

"I say," said Wheeler, pretending to take it seriously, "that would really be a coup, wouldn't it?" They all laughed.

"We should have told you right at the beginning," said Toliver. "But our rule is to check out security before information is passed. Foxwell swore on a stack of bibles that you were a sound proposition. But a rule is a rule. Am I right?"

"And the restaurant and the girl—Miss Shaw—how

does that fit in? I thought you were holding the Rear-Admiral there at one time."

"We know you did," said Wheeler. "You're quite a bloodhound."

"Miss Shaw is the daughter of one of my oldest friends," said Toliver, "and she's turned out first class. It's been beastly for her . . ."

Mason said, "We needed a body—a dead body—to leave at the rendezvous, to make the helicopter crash look right."

Toliver said, "And it has to be a body with a diseased kidney. It gave us problems, I can tell you."

"Hence the cold room at The Terrine," I said. I didn't tell him that Marjorie had recognized him at the mortuary.

"And damned tricky," said Mason. "Must be in a sitting position so that we can leave it in the wrecked helicopter."

"Ever tried to dress and undress a stiff?" one of the others said.

"You try and get a pair of trousers on a sitting corpse," said Wheeler. "And you might agree that it's the next most difficult thing to doing it standing up in a hammock." They smiled.

Toliver said, "Sara stitched every bit of that uniform together on the frozen body. She's quite a girl."

"And where is the body now?" I asked. There was only a moment of hesitation, then Toliver said, "It's here, frozen. We have to be careful of what the post-mortem johnnies call adipocere. That's what the flesh becomes when immersed in water. It's got to look right for the Russkies when they find it."

"What about the hand stitching?" I said.

"A calculated risk," said Toliver.

"And the uniform will be burned in the crash," said Mason.

I looked from Wheeler to Toliver and then at Mason. They appeared to be serious. You didn't have to be living with a beautiful doctor to know that post-death discoloration was going to reveal to those same Russkies the fact that the body died full-length in a hospital bed, but I said nothing.

Toliver came round with the gin bottle. He topped up their glasses with Plymouth and put a dash of bitters into each one. Pink gins made with Plymouth. That was the common denominator, or the nearest thing they had to one: they were all ex-Royal Navy, or adopting wardroom manners with careful enthusiasm.

A message came late that night. I was told that Schlegel did not want me back in London. I was to remain with Toliver's people on Blackstone until I was ordered to the submarine base for the Arctic trip.

I didn't believe the message. Schlegel was not the sort of man who sent vague verbal messages via men not known to both of us. But I took great care to show no sign of my disbelief. I reacted only by attempting to establish my love of the great outdoors. If I was going to get out of this place against their wishes I'd need the few hours start that only a habit of long country walks could provide.

So I hiked alone across the moorland, feeling the springy turf underfoot. I found grouse, and startled hares, and I tried the tail of Great Crag that was no more than a steep slope. I went past the pines and climbed through the hazel and birch and then bare rock, all the way up to the summit. A couple of hours of such walking gave even a vertigo-prone stumbler like me a chance to look down through the holes in the cloud. I saw the black terraces and crevices of the rock face, and beyond the gully to the loch: shining like freshly tempered blue steel. And I could see where the valley was an amphitheatre upholstered in yellow deer grass and curtained with remnants of white sea mist. I took cheese and Marmite sandwiches up with me, and found a mossy ledge amongst the ice ridges. There I could shelter and blow on my hands, and pretend I'd got there by way of the chimney and three pinnacles, of which the others spoke so proudly.

I polished the salt spray from my spectacles and looked seaward. It was one of the wildest and most desolate landscapes that Britain offers. A stiff wind was striking the snow-clad peak, and snow crystals came from the summit, like white smoke from a chimney.

A mile out in the ocean, a small boat made slow progress in the choppy sea. Toliver had warned that unless the boat came today there would be no fuel for the generator and no meat, either.

And from here I could see many miles inland, to where the peninsula narrowed and dead heather gave place to rock, chewed unceasingly by the sharp white teeth of the breakers. It was a place where a natural fault of the Central Highlands had crumbled under the battering of the Atlantic Ocean, so that now a moat of rough water divided Blackstone from the mainland. There, two vast bodies of water raced headlong into collision, and turned the rock-lined gap into a pit of foam.

Neither did the far bank offer a welcoming prospect

From the water, the strata tilted up to where a copse of beeches bent almost double under the prevailing winds. The slope was scotched with the black courses of mountain streams, and a drystone wall had scattered its rubble entrails down the steep incline to the seashore, where a dead sheep, rusty tins and some bright plastic jetsam had been beached by the high tide.

For those indifferent to a north wind that numbs the ears, and damp mists that roll in from the sea like a tidal wave, the Western Isles are a magic kingdom where anything is possible. After outdoor exercise and an evening beside the open fire—a glass of malt whisky in my hand—I was beginning to believe that even the curious fantasies of my fellow guests had a logic in proportion to their enthusiasm.

That night, sitting round the scrubbed refectory table, waiting while Toliver carved the boiled pork into paper-thin slices and arrayed them upon a serving platter, there was an extra guest. He was a tall, dour-faced man of about forty-five with close-cropped blond hair, going white. He wore steel-rimmed spectacles and had a harsh accent that completed the caricature of a German general, circa 1941. He offered only a few bits of phrase-book English. He'd been introduced over predinner pink gins as Mr Erikson, but his home was farther east than that, if I was any judge. His suit was dark blue gaberdine, of a cut that tended to confirm my reasoning.

Erikson's presence was not explained, and the officers' mess atmosphere clearly forbade direct questioning, unless Toliver initiated it. There was only small-talk round the dinner table, and apart from thanking Toliver for the promise of some sea fishing the next day, the stranger was silent.

"Did you have a good walk?" said Wheeler.

"To the lower ledges."

"You can see a long way from there," said Toliver.

"When you're not blowing on your hands," I said.

"We lose sheep up there sometimes," said Wheeler, and gave me a nasty smile.

Erikson took the port decanter from Mason. He removed the stopper and sniffed at it. The men round the table watched him expectantly. Erikson pulled a disapproving face and instead of pouring a measure for himself he poured some for me. I nodded my thanks. I too sniffed at it before sipping some. But it wasn't the aroma of the port-wine that I smelled but the pervasive and entirely unique smell that some say comes from the nuclear reactor, and others say is that of the CO_2 scrubber that cleans the air in an atomic submarine before recirculating it. This is a smell that goes home with you, stays on your skin for days, and remains for ever in your clothes, triggering memories of those big floating gin palaces.

But this wasn't the suit I'd worn on any of my trips on the nuclear subs. I looked at Erikson. The small boat I'd seen from the crag had been coming from the west—the Atlantic Ocean—not from the Scottish mainland, and it had brought this taciturn East European, smelling of atomic submarine.

Toliver was telling a story about a TV producer friend doing a documentary on rural poverty. The ending came . . . ". . . never go hungry, sir, bless your heart, we can always find a few quails' eggs."

"Ha, ha, ha," Mason laughed louder than any of

the others, and looked at me, as if trying to will me to join in.

Wheeler said, "Just like my chaps saying they didn't like the jam—it tasted of fish. I told you that story, didn't I?"

"Yes, you did," said Toliver.

"Caviare, of course," said Wheeler determined at least to get the punch line in.

"Jolly good," said Mason. "Caviare! Jam that tasted of fish. That's a good one, Commander."

"The meat came today, but no petrol," said Toliver.

"Whose turn to get the new gas bottle?" said someone, and they all laughed. It was as if they were all working to a script that I didn't have.

I sipped at my port and took a long look at Mr Erikson. There was something unusual in his manner and at first I did not recognize what it was, for he smiled at the jokes, accepted a cigar with a polite bow of the head, and met the eyes of the other guests with the confident gaze of any man at a dinner table with friends. I reached for the matches and struck one to provide him with a light for his cigar. He murmured his thanks and, pretending to have difficulty getting his cigar going, he turned in his chair. I was sure that he'd chosen a seat next to me because he feared I would recognize his face across the table. Now I became quite certain that he'd been landed from a submarine, a Russian submarine.

"Until the fuel boat comes we'll have to ration the generator," said Toliver. He got to his feet and fetched one of the paraffin lamps. "Plenty of oil for the lamps, though." He lit the lamp and adjusted the wick carefully.

"Cold-water shaving in the morning, chaps," said Wheeler. "Unless there's a volunteer to boil up a few kettles before reveille."

"I'll be glad to do that, sir." Of course it was Mason, apple-polishing himself into a state of nervous exhaustion. "I'll set the alarm for five. That should do it, I think."

"Good show, Mason," said Commander Wheeler. "That's damned sporting of you."

They weren't satisfied just to create a self-congratulatory, and exclusively masculine, society, they were attempting to re-create one that existed only in their wishful thoughts. The I've-been-here-before feeling that all this was giving me had come undiluted from old British war films, especially those about Colditz.

"Good show, Mason," I said, but they all glared at me. I suppose they didn't like the way I told them.

The quietness of the house, the mysterious way in which food and drink seemed to arrive without human agency, added to the mysteries of what these men called "The Club." In spite of the grandeur of the house itself, and of the quality of the badly worn Persian carpets and panelled doors, there was little evidence of its less spartan days. The leather sofas, the stair-carpet and the rugs had all been repaired with the same coarse grey sailcloth, and with the sort of stitches that sailors call "dogs' teeth." The flagstones, worn by the feet of countless ages into curious ring-like depressions, had here and there been carelessly filled with concrete. The bedrooms were cold and damp, in spite of the cheap electric fire that glowed bright only when the generator started. The blankets were thin and grey, and the sheets were clean, but threadbare and rough-dried.

There was in the house no trace of femininity: no flowers, cushions, domestic animals, perfumed soaps, and virtually no pictures or ornaments.

I was not a prisoner in the house. That had been explained to me several times. I merely had to wait until the plane returned. I had the idea that any suggestion about taking the one and only bicycle or walking due east would be met with pleasant smiling affirmative-ridden explanations that meant no. So I didn't make any suggestions like that. I tried to act like a happy healthy well-adjusted human, who likes playing secret agents in an unheated Scottish castle, but who occasionally needs a nice long walk. They understood that all right: they were nice long walk sort of people.

Chapter 16

The "retreat before combat option" is only available to land forces with intact flanking units. The "retreat before combat option" is available to all naval units at sea at all times.

RULES. "TACWARGAME." STUDIES CENTRE. LONDON

I had been given cramped rooms, almost circular in shape, at the top of the north tower. Above me, in the conical roof, there was the endless gurgling of the water tanks. Before it was properly light I heard Mason's peremptory rap upon the bathroom door. "Hot water," he called.

"Leave it there."

"I need the kettle for the others."

Outside the night was still dark enough to see the stars. I sighed and went down the iron stairs to the bathroom. There was no electricity, a fact I confirmed by clicking the light switch half a dozen times. Mason knocked at the door again. "Coming," I said, "coming." A dog began to howl from the courtyard.

The light from the glazed slit window was just sufficient for me to see white rectangle on the floor near the door. I picked it up. Mason rapped again and I put the folded sheet of paper on the washstand while I unlocked the door.

"Locked doors?" said Mason. His manner conveyed all the condescension of a man who had been working while others slept. "Who are you frightened of?"

"The fairies," I said.

"Where do you want it?" Mason said, but before I could decide he'd poured the hot water into the wash-basin.

"Thanks."

"If you want more, you'll have to come down to the kitchen. The cold's working." He turned the tap to show me what cold water was, and then closed it off again. Mason was like that.

He looked around the room to see how untidy it was. Toliver had put shaving kit, pajamas and shirts and underwear in the chest, but now these items were distributed around the bathroom. Mason sniffed. He looked for a moment at the folded sheet of paper, too, but he made no remark.

When he'd gone, I again locked the door. I unfolded the sheet of paper. It had been torn from a school exercise book by the look of it. The message had been typewritten on a machine that badly needed a new ribbon. Some of the characters were little more than indentations:

You're making our newly arrived friend very uneasy. I don't have to tell you he's Remoziva's A.D.C., but he insists that everyone be coy about it. Hence the charades this evening. Did you meet him? It sounds as if it was some time when you worked for us—late 'fifties?—a conference he thinks.

Someone should tell the old man about this. I

don't think he'll like it. I can't go, and using the phone here would be too risky. But if you took your usual long walk and got a bit lost you could get as far as the phone box at Croma village. Just tell them about Erikson and say that SARACEN confirms it. If they give you instructions for me, wait till we're all together and then ask Toliver or Mason where you can buy some French cigarettes. I will then offer you a packet with three cigarettes in it, so you'll know who I am. You might think this is all going a bit far, but I know these boys and I'm staying covert—even to you.

They're all touchy now while Erikson is here, so leave by the kitchen garden and the paddock and keep to the south side of the big rocks. Skip breakfast, I've left some sandwiches for you in the old greenhouse. You could always say you made them last night. Keep to the south of the peninsula, there's a footbridge on that side of Angel Gap. It looks rickety but it will hold you. Head for the cottage with the collapsed roof, you can see the bridge from there. The road is four miles beyond (running north/south). The post office is on that road. Turn right on the road and it's the first house you come to. The box is on the far side—take coins with you. Keep moving, I can't guarantee these boy scouts won't follow.

And if you think they would hesitate to knock you off to make their plan work, think again. They are dangerous. Burn this right away. I'll be around if you run into problems getting away this morning.

I didn't remember the Russian skinhead. But if he was from Russian Naval Staff (Security Directorate) he could have been at any one of a dozen Joint Security conferences I'd attended in the 'fifties. If he was from the G.R.U., the chances we'd met were considerably greater. It was all getting too rich for my blood, and I wasn't any longer on salary for this kind of action. If Soviet General Staff Directorate were joining Toliver's troop, they'd put his boy scouts into long trousers and tell them about girls. And I didn't want to be around when it happened.

I read the note again, very carefully, and then tore it into small pieces. In a remote country house like this flushing it down the toilet was not good enough—it needs only one man-hole cover lifted between here and the septic tank.

I burned the paper in the sink when I'd finished washing and shaving but it left scorch marks that I could not completely erase with soap. I started to shave while the water was still warm. To say I didn't like it was an understatement. If they were going to get rid of me, a secret note—that I must destroy—advising me to take a chance on a rickety footbridge in a snowstorm . . . that might be the perfect way to arrange it.

But doctors can't pass a street accident, nor dips an open handbag, coppers can't pass a door with a broken lock, Jesuits can't pass sin in the making, everyone falls prey to their training. The idea of Erikson coming off a submarine weighed heavily upon me. And it would stay that way until I contacted Dawlish's office via the local engineers, as he'd so thoughtfully explained the latest system. I knew that even if I spent all morning thinking about it I would eventually try to find that damned post office phone, but I couldn't help thinking that if Toliver had failed to bring that line of communication under his control or surveillance he was a darn sight less efficient than he'd so far shown himself to be.

Perhaps I should have passed up the post office, and the sandwiches too, and evolved a completely different plan of action, but I couldn't think of anything better.

I went down into the hall. It was a gloomy place with amputated pieces of game adorning the walls: lions, tigers, leopards and cheetahs joined in a concerted yawn. An elephant's foot was artfully adapted to hold walking-sticks and umbrellas. There were fishing-rods and gun cases, too. I was tempted to go armed but it would slow me down. I contented myself with borrowing a donkey jacket and a scarf and went through the servants' corridor into the pantry. There was a smell of wet dogs and the sound of them barking. I could hear the others at breakfast. I recognized the voices of Toliver, Wheeler and Mason and I waited to hear the voice of Erikson before moving on.

I welcomed the blizzard. The wind roared against the back of the house, and made the windows kaleidoscopes of scurrying white patterns. It would take me two hours, perhaps more, to Angel Gap. I buttoned up tight.

The south of the peninsula was the high side. It was the best route if I did not stumble over the cliff edge in the snow storm. The other coastline was a ragged edge of deep gullies, inlets and bog that would provide endless detours for someone like me who didn't know the geography, and no problems for pursuers who did.

I didn't go directly into the kitchen garden, for I

would have been in full view of anyone at the stove. I went down the corridor into the laundry room and from there across the yard to the barn. Using that as cover, I made my way along the garden path behind the raspberry canes and along the high wall of the kitchen garden. I stopped behind the shed to have a look round. The wind was blowing at gale force and already the house was only a grey shape in the flying snow.

The greenhouse was not one of those shiny aluminum and polished-glass affairs you see outside the garden shops on the by-pass. This was an ancient, wooden-framed monster nearly fifty feet long. Its glass was dark grey with greasy dirt and it was difficult to see into it. I pushed the door open. It creaked, and I saw my sandwiches on the potting bench, conspicuously near the door. It was a shambles inside: old and broken flower pots, dead plants and a false ceiling of spiders' webs entrapping a thousand dead flies. Outside, the wind howled and thumped the loose panes, while whirling snow pressed little white noses against the glass. I didn't reach for the sandwiches, I froze, suddenly aware that I was not alone. There was someone in the greenhouse, someone standing unnaturally still.

"Mr. Armstrong!" It was a mocking voice.

A figure in a dirty white riding mac stepped out from behind a stack of old wooden boxes. My eyes went to the shotgun carried casually under arm, and only then up to the eyes of Sara Shaw.

"Miss Shaw."

"Life is full of surprises, darling. Have you come for your sandwiches?" Her coat shoulders were quite dry, she'd been waiting a long time for me.

"Yes," I said.

"Last night's pork, and one round of cheese."

"I didn't know you were here, even."

"That building worker's coat suits you, you know." The smile froze on her face, and I turned to see someone coming from the kitchen door. "Mason, the little bastard must have seen me," she said.

It was Mason. He was bent into the wind, hurrying after us as fast as his little legs could carry him. She had her left hand under the shotgun's wooden foregrip and raised it level.

Mason came into the greenhouse like there was no door. In his fist he had one of those little Astra automatics with a two-inch barrel extender. It was just the sort of gun I would have expected Mason to choose: about thirteen ounces total weight, and small enough to go into a top pocket.

"Where did you get that?" said Sara. She laughed. "Have you discovered the Christmas crackers already?"

But no one who has seen a .22 fired at close range will smile into its barrel. Except maybe Mickey Spillane. I didn't laugh and neither did Mason. He pointed the gun at Sara and reached out for her shotgun.

"Give it to him," I said. "Don't make headlines."

Mason took the gun and, using one hand, he undid the catch and broke it open. He gripped the stock under his arm while he removed the shotgun cartridges, and then let it drop to the floor. He kicked it under the potting bench with enough energy to break some flower pots. The cartridges he put into his pocket. Having disarmed Sara he turned to me. He ran a quick hand over me but he knew I wasn't armed, they'd searched me immediately after I'd landed in the plane.

"O.K.," he said. "Let's move back up to the house."

He prodded me in the arm with his automatic and I moved along the bench towards the door, looking at the potting bench in the hope of spotting a suitable weapon.

Mason was too near. Once outside the greenhouse he'd keep me at a distance and my chance to clobber him would be gone. Lesson one of unarmed combat is that a man with a gun muzzle touching him can knock the barrel aside before the armed man can pull the trigger. I slowed and waited until I felt the muzzle again. I spun round to my left, chopping at his gun with my left hand and punching at where his head should have been with my right fist. I connected only with the side of his head but he stepped back and put an elbow through a panel of glass. The noise of it was amplified by the enclosed space. Again I punched at him. He stumbled. Another panel of glass went and I didn't dare look round to see if it had alarmed those still at breakfast. The dogs in the courtyard began barking furiously.

The girl shrank away from us as Mason struggled to bring his gun hand up again. I seized his wrist with my right hand and the gun with my left. I pulled, but Mason had his finger on the trigger. There was a bang. I felt the hot draught as the slug passed my ear and crashed out through the glass roof. I swung my elbow round far enough to hit his face. It must have made his eyes water. He let go and fell to the floor amongst the rusty gardening tools. He rolled away rubbing his nose.

Sara was already reaching for the shotgun. "Good girl," I said. I pushed the little Astra gun into my pocket and ran out into the blizzard. The path was slippery, and I cut off it into the cabbages. There was a rubbish heap against the wall at the bottom of the garden. That would be my best place for climbing over it.

I was halfway down the garden when there was the deafening bang of a twelve bore and a crash of shattering glass that seemed to go on for hours.

Even before the last few pieces broke there was a second blast that took out another large section of the glass-house. She hit me with the second shot. It knocked me full length into a row of brussels sprouts and I felt a burning pain in the arm and side.

I had no doubt that more cartridges were going into the breech. In spite of the damaged arm, I set a new world record for the kitchen garden free-style, and went over the wall in a mad scramble. As I fell down the other side of it, another shot hit the weeds along the top of the wall and showered me with finely chopped vegetation. The ground sloped steeply behind the house but my feet didn't touch the ground for the first half mile. I hoped that she'd have trouble getting over the wall, but with women like that, you can't be sure they'll have trouble with anything.

By the time I reached the stream I realized that Mason—not the girl—was Dawlish's contact and the author of the note. He'd pressed the gun against me reasoning that I'd know how to break free. It was the best he could do, if he was to have any chance of talking his way out of that one. I felt sorry for him but I was glad I'd hit him hard. He was going to need some corroborative evidence to show Toliver. Sara Shaw must have followed him when he took the sandwiches there for me. Then she'd waited to see who turned up and why. I hoped that she could not guess, for now I suddenly found it easier to believe Mason's contention that they were a dangerous mob.

My arm was bleeding enough to leave a trail behind me. I changed course for enough time to make it look as though I might be going to the bridle path. There I slipped the donkey jacket off, bound the silk scarf around the bloody part of my sleeve, and pushed my arm down into the donkey-jacket sleeve to jam it tight. It hurt like hell but there was not time to do anything more. I hoped the pressure would stop the bleeding. A shotgun spreads an inch per yard of range. I'd been far enough to get only the edge of it. My clothes were torn but the bleeding was not serious. I kept repeating that to myself as I hurried on.

I made good progress, avoiding the outcrops of rock upon which the flailing snow had settled to make a glaze of ice. But losing the use of my arm made keeping my balance more difficult, and twice I fell, yelping with pain and leaving a dull red mark in the snow.

In spite of the low visibility in the snowstorm, I felt sure that I could find the tail of Great Crag. After that, it was merely a matter of keeping close to the edge without falling over. But everything is more difficult in a blizzard. I even had trouble finding the big clump of conifers that marked the stepping-stones over the burn. When I did get there I became entangled in the brambles and undergrowth and had to kick hard to get out of it.

I didn't curse the weather. As soon as it cleared I would become visible to anyone with the sense to ascend to the Crag's first terrace. And there were plenty of people back there with enough sense for that. And more, much more.

The clifftop path required care. I had not walked it before, though I had seen the course of it from my solitary picnics on the heights of Great Crag. The path was an old one. Here and there along its course there were metal markers. They were simple rectangles of tin, nailed to stakes that had almost rotted. The paint had long since flaked away and the metal was rusty but there was no mistaking their military origin. There is something common to all artifacts of all armed forces, from tanks to latrines. I hurried along faster whenever I had the rusty patches to guide me. I feared that the snowstorm was passing over. The dark clouds were almost close enough to touch. They sped over me, mingling with flurries of snow and allowing me sudden glimpses of the rocky seashore nearly a hundred feet below.

Not only the markers, but the path itself, had in places eroded. I stopped for a moment and made sure that my arm was no longer leaving a blood trail. It wasn't, but there were ugly retching noises from inside my sleeve and I guessed that I was still bleeding. I was looking forward to that period of numbness that doctors say happens after wounding but I was beginning to suspect that that was just their rationalization for prodding the painful bits. Both my side and my arm were throbbing and hurting like hell.

I looked at the tiny footpath where the metal tabs led. It was no better than a man-made ledge along the windy cliff face. Not at all the sort of place I ever visited, outside of nightmares. But ahead of me there was an acre of underbrush, so I took the cliff path, edging along it carefully, but dislodging pieces that spun off into space and fell somewhere that I dared not look.

After a quarter of a mile the blazed path narrowed suddenly. I stepped even more gingerly now, edging forward a step at a time, cautioned by large sections of path edge that crumbled under the touch of my toe. The ledge continued round a gently curving section of cliff. Soon I reached the point at which I could see below me a tiny bay. Through the driving sleet I studied the path ahead. I had hoped it would soon rejoin the clifftop but it continued to be a ledge. The section at the far side of the bay was especially worrying. The sharp edge of cliff resembled the prow of some gigantic ship far out over the fierce green sea. The curved profile of the cliff continued above the path. It looked as though a man would have to bend almost double to pass along it.

Standing still, in order to see through the whirling snow, brought a resurgence of doubts and fears. I decided to retrace my steps. I would go back to the bridle path and continue up over the higher part of the cliff. But as I studied the face of the promontory I saw that there was a thick tangle of thorn dangling over the cliff, like a lace tablecloth. The men who'd made the path had not laboured on it without good reason. If it was easier to make a path along the cliff face than along the clifftop then surely I would find it easier to follow it.

The overhang was not such a severe test as I feared. It's true that I spread my arms and flattened my body against the cliff face in a fearful embrace, leaving a ghost of blood there, but I edged along crablike and gave up the testing probes of the path ahead.

"No atheists in a foxhole," they say. And none on a narrow cliff path around a headland either, if my journey was anything to go by. Spreadeagled close against the cold wall of stone, I felt a gust of wind batter against it hard enough to make the prow-like cliff shake as if about to fall. The same wind was provoking the ocean into great white-tops that thumped the shingle far below. Again and again the wind tried to prise me away from the cliff and carry me with it, but I stayed motionless until its brunt was gone. Vertigo, as all its victims know, is not a fear of falling but an atavistic desire to fly, which is why so many of its sufferers are aviators.

I rounded the headland, and breathed a sigh of relief before seeing another bay and another headland. Worse, this section of the path was blocked. It looked at first like a fall of rubble but the boulders were too evenly matched in colour and size; balanced precariously upon the smallest of toeholds they shimmered as a gust of wind thumped the cliff face, roaring upwards and scooping in its draft both snowflakes and fragments of cliff.

Alone on this extreme edge of the peninsula I tried to comfort myself with the thought that I could not be seen from anywhere on Blackstone. I released my grasp on the rock and, moving my arm very slowly, I bared my wrist to see the time. Would they by now have mustered their full manpower to form a line across the peninsula's waist? I shivered with cold, fear and indecision, except that there was no real decision to make. I had to go on, as fast as possible.

The ledge widened. It was enough for me to quicken my progress to something like walking pace, if I pressed a shoulder to the rock. Still I could not discern the nature of the blobs that covered the cliff face like pox upon an ashen face. Even when I was only ten yards away I still could not see what was waiting in my path. It was then that an extra large breaker, a gust of air, or just my approach seemed to cause the cliff itself to explode into whirling fragments. The grey blobs were all over me: a vast colony of sea-birds, sheltering from the storm. They raised up their enormous wings, and climbed into the blizzard to meet me. Blurred grey shapes circled the intruder who had invaded these ledges to which they returned each year to nest. They dived upon me, screaming, croaking and clawing and beating their giant wings, in the hope that I might fall, or fly away.

By now I was climbing through the colony itself, my hands lacerated and bloody as I groped through the ancient nests of mud, spittle and bleached vegetation. My feet were crunching them and sliding in the dust and filth of a thousand years of stinking bird droppings.

I closed my eyes. I was afraid to turn my head as I felt the wings striking my shoulders and felt the fabric tear under their beaks and claws. I still didn't slacken my speed, even when I found enough courage to look back to where the sea-birds wheeled and jeered and fidgeted in the crevices. The wind had continued the work of destruction and now the brittle nests were shattered by the air current that roared up the cliff face, like a great flame licks a chimney, taking the colony with it and grinding all to dust.

Ahead of me I saw a bent piece of rusty tin and

persuaded myself with all kinds of twisted rationalizations that the path would be easy going from this point onwards. There was still another headland to negotiate, but it was easy only compared with the journey I had already made. After that, the path sloped gently upwards until it regained the cliff edge. I sat down, hardly noticing the thorns and mud. For the first time I became aware of the fast shallow breathing that my anxiety had produced and of the thumping of my heart, as loud as the breakers on the shingle a hundred feet below me.

From here I was able to look north-west across the width of the peninsula, and I didn't like what I could see. The blizzard, which was still driving hard against the cliffs at sea level, had thinned enough for visibility to increase to a mile or more in between the flurries. If they were after me, a dozen of them could put me up like a frightened partridge. I stood up and started off again. I forced myself to increase the pace, although my tortuous cliffside journey had left me in no state to attempt records.

From this place on the clifftop, my path was mostly downhill. This world was white and a thousand differing shades of brown: bracken, heather, bilberries and, lowest of all, the peat bogs. All of it dead, and all of it daubed with great drifts of snow that had filled the gullies and followed the curious pattern of the wind. There were red grouse, too. Disturbed, they took to the air, calling, "Go-back, go-back," a sound that I remembered from my childhood.

Already I fancied I could see the dark patch that would be the pines at the little croft. I promised myself cubes of chocolate that I never did eat. I walked as soldiers march, placing one foot before the other, with hardly a thought for the length of the journey, or the surrounding landscape. "All my soldiers saw of Russia was the pack of the man in front of them," said Napoleon, as though the ignorant rabble were declining his offers of side trips to St. Petersburg and the Black Sea resorts. Now I bent my head to the turf.

A shaft of sunlight found a way through the clouds so that a couple of acres of hillside shone yellow. The patch ran madly up and down the slopes and raced out to sea like a huge blue raft until, a mile or more offshore, it disappeared as if sunk without trace. The clouds closed tight and the wind roared its triumph.

Once I knew where to look, there was no difficulty in finding the footbridge. It was a good example of Victorian ingenuity and wrought iron. Two chains across the Gap were held apart by ornamented sections of iron, into which fitted timber flooring. Shaped like stylized dolphins, smaller interlocking pieces had tails supporting two steel cables anchored into the ground at each end as supplementary supports. That, at any rate, must have been how the engraving looked in the catalogue. Now a handrail was hanging in the gully and one chain had slackened enough to let the frame twist. It groaned and swayed in the wind that came through its broken flooring, singing like the music of a giant flute.

Adapted into a fairground ride it might have earned a fortune at Coney Island, but suspended above the demented waters of Angel Gap only the cliff path behind me was less welcoming.

There was no going back now. I thought of that trigger-happy girl—custom tailoring for cadavers, and *cuisine française* while you wait—and I shuddered. If she'd not been so keen to kill me that she'd fired from inside the greenhouse, I'd have been a statistic in one of those warning pamphlets that the Scottish travel and holidays department give people going grouse shooting.

Any kind of bridge was better than going back.

The off-sea wind had kept the cliffs virtually free of ice, but the bridge was precarious. There was only one handrail, a rusty cable. It sagged alarmingly as I applied my weight to it and slid through the eyes of the remaining posts so that I fancied it was going to drop me into the ocean below. But it took my weight, although as I passed each handrail post it paid the slack cable to me with an agonizing whinny. Without a handrail I could not have crossed, for at some places the floor of the bridge had warped to a dangerous angle. I had to use both hands and by the time I reached the other side my wounded arm was bleeding again.

I hurried up the hill so that I could get out of sight. Only when I was hidden in the copse did I stop. I looked back, at the ocean roaring through the gap, and at as much of the peninsula of Blackstone as was visible through the storm. I saw no pursuers, and I was truly thankful for that, for I could see no simple way of wrecking the bridge.

I took off the short overcoat and with some difficulty pulled my jacket off too. I'd lost a lot of blood.

It took me over an hour to do the four miles to the road. The clouds broke enough to allow a few samples of sunlight to be passed around among the trees. There were sunbeams on the road when I finally caught sight of it. Perhaps by that time I was beginning to expect a four-lane highway with refreshment areas, gift shops and clover-leaf crossings, but it was what they call in Scotland a "narrow class one" which means they'd filled the ditch every two hundred yards in case you met something coming the other way.

I saw the two soldiers sitting at the roadside when I was still a couple of hundred yards away. They were sheltering under a camouflage cape upon which the snow was settling fast. I thought they were waiting for a lift, until I saw that they were dressed in Fighting Order. They both had L1 A1 automatic rifles and one of them had a two-way radio too.

They played it cool, remaining seated until I was almost upon them. I knew they'd put me on the air, because only after I'd passed him did I notice another soldier covering me from fifty yards along the road. He had a Lee Enfield with a sniper-sight. It was no ordinary exercise.

"Could you wait here a moment, sir?" He was a paratroop corporal.

"What's going on?"

"There will be someone along in a minute."

We waited. Over the brow of the next hill there came a large car, towing a caravan of the sort advertised as "a carefree holiday home on wheels." It was a bulbous contraption, painted cream, with a green plastic door and tinted windows. I knew who it was as soon as I saw huge polished brass headlights. But I didn't expect that it would be Schlegel sitting alongside him. Dawlish applied the brakes and came to a standstill alongside me and the soldiers. I heard him saying to Schlegel ". . . and let me surprise you: these brakes are really hydraulic, actually powered by water. Although I must confess to putting methylated spirit in for this trip, on account of the cold."

Schlegel nodded but gave no sign of the promised surprise. I suspected that he'd acquired a thorough understanding of Dawlish's brakes on the way up here. "I thought it would be you, Pat."

It was typically Dawlish. He would have died had anyone accused him of showmanship, but given a chance like this he came on like Montgomery. "Are you chaps brewing up, by any chance?" he asked the soldiers.

"They send a van, sir. Eleven thirty, they said.".

Dawlish said, "I think we'll make some tea now: hot sweet tea is just the ticket for a chap in a state of shock."

I knew he was trying to provoke the very reaction I made, but I made it just the same. "I've lost a lot of blood," I said.

"Not *lost* it exactly," said Dawlish, as if noticing my arm for the first time. "It's soaking into your coat."

"How silly of me," I said.

"Corporal," said Dawlish. "Would you see if you can get your medical orderly up here. Tell him to bring some sticking plaster and all that kind of thing." He turned to me. "We'll go into the caravan. It's awfully useful for this kind of business."

He got out of the car, and ushered me and Schlegel into the cramped sitting-room of the caravan. All it needed was Snow White: it was filled with little plastic candelabra, chintz cushion-covers and an early Queen Anne cocktail cabinet. I knew that Dawlish had hired the most hideously furnished one available, and was energetically pretending that he'd hand-picked every item. He was a sadist, but Schlegel had it coming to him.

"Useful for what kind of business?" I said.

Schlegel smiled a greeting but didn't speak. He sat down on the sofa at the rear, and began smoking one of his favourite little cheroots. Dawlish went to his gas ring and lit it. He held up a tiny camper's kettle and demonstrated the hinged handle. "A folding kettle! Who would have believed they had such gadgets?"

"That's very common," said Schlegel.

Dawlish waggled a finger. "In America, yes," he said. He started the kettle and then he turned to me. "This business. Useful for this business. We watched you on our little Doppler radar set. Couldn't be sure it was you, of course, but I guessed."

"There's a submarine out there in the Sound," I said. I sniffed at Schlegel's cigar smoke enviously but I was now counting my abstinence in months.

Dawlish tutted. "It's naughty, isn't it? We've just come down from watching him on the A.S.W. screen at H.M.S. *Viking*. He's moved south now. Picked up someone, did he?"

I didn't answer.

Dawlish continued, "We are going in there, but very gently. The story is that we've lost a ballistic missile with a dummy head. Sounds all right to you, does it?"

"Yes," I said.

Dawlish said to Schlegel, "Well if he can't fault it, it must be all right. I thought that was rather good myself."

"There's only a broken-down footbridge," I warned. "You'll lose some soldiers."

"Not at all," said Dawlish

"How?" I said.

"Centurion bridge layer will span the gap in one hundred seconds, the R.E. officer told me. The Land Rovers will follow."

"And the tea van," said Schlegel, not without sarcasm.

"Yes, and the NAAFI," said Dawlish.

"Takes the glitter off your story about looking for a lost missile warhead," I said.

"I don't like Russians landing from submarines," said Dawlish. "I'm not that concerned to keep our voices down." I knew that anything concerning submarines made Dawlish light up and say tilt. The best part of Russian effort, and most of their espionage successes over a decade, had been concerned with underwater weaponry.

"You're damned right," said Schlegel. I realized—as I was supposed to realize—that Schlegel was from some transatlantic security branch.

"Who are these people that Toliver has over there?" I asked. "Is that some kind of official set-up?"

Schlegel and Dawlish both made noises of distress and I knew I'd touched a nerve.

Dawlish said, "A Member of Parliament can button-hole the Home Secretary or the Foreign Secretary, slap them on the back and have a drink with them while I'm still waiting for an appointment that is a week over-due. Toliver has beguiled the old man with this Remoziva business, and no one will listen to my words of warning."

The kettle boiled and he made the tea. Dawlish must have slipped since I worked under him, for in those days he ate M.P.s for breakfast, and as for M.P.s with cloak and dagger ambitions—they didn't last beyond the monthly conference.

"They said the man who came ashore was Remoziva's A.D.C.," I said.

"But?"

"Could have been a very good friend of Liberace, for all I can tell: I don't know any of Remoziva's associates."

"But Russian?" asked Schlegel. The sun came through the window. Backlit, his cigar smoke became a great silver cloud in which his smiling face floated like an alien planet.

"Tall, thin, cropped-head, blond, steel spectacles. He traded a few bits of phrase-book Polish with a character who calls himself Wheeler. But if I was going to stake money, I'd put it on one of the Baltic states."

"Doesn't mean anything to me," said Dawlish.

"Not a thing," said Schlegel.

"Says he knows me, according to your Mason—Saracen—over there. I had to thump him by the way, I'm sorry but there was no other way."

"Poor old Mason," said Dawlish, with no emotion whatsoever. He looked me directly in the eye and made no apology for the lies he'd told me about Mason being charged with selling secrets. He poured out five cups of tea, topping them with a second lot of hot water. He gave me and Schlegel one each, and then tapped the window, called the soldiers over and gave a cup each to them. "Well let's assume he is Remoziva's A.D.C.," said Dawlish. "What now? Did they tell you?"

"You think it's all really on?" I said, with some surprise.

"I've known stranger things happen."

"Through some tin-pot little organization like that?"

"He's not altogether unaided," said Dawlish. Schlegel was watching him with close interest.

"I should think not," I said with some exasperation. "They are talking about diverting a nuclear submarine to pick him up in the Barents. Not altogether unaided is the understatement of the century."

Dawlish sipped his tea. He looked at me and said, "You think we should just sit on Toliver? You wouldn't advocate sending a submarine to their rendezvous point?"

"A nuclear submarine costs a lot of money," I said.

"And you think they might sink it. Surely that's not on? They could find nuclear subs easily enough, and sink them, too, if that's their ambition."

"The Arctic is a quiet place," I said.

"And they could find nuclear subs in other quiet places," said Dawlish.

"And we could find theirs," said Schlegel belligerently. "And don't let's forget it."

"Exactly," said Dawlish calmly. "It's what they call war, isn't it? No, they are not going to all this trouble just to start a war."

"You've made a firm contact with this Admiral?" I asked.

"Toliver. Toliver got the contact—a delegation in Leningrad, apparently—we've kept completely clear by top-level instructions."

I nodded. I could believe that. If it all went wrong they'd keep Toliver separate, all right: they'd feed him to the Russians in bite-sized pieces, sprinkled with tenderizer.

"So what do you think?" It was Schlegel asking the question this time.

I looked at him for a long time without replying. I said, "They talked as though it's all been arranged already: British submarine, they said. Toliver talks about the R.N. like it's available for charter, and he's the man doing the package tours."

Dawlish said, "If we went ahead, it would be with a U.S. submarine." He looked at Schlegel. "Until we can be quite sure who Toliver has got working with him, it would be safer using an American submarine."

"Uh-huh," I said. Hell, why would these two high-powered characters be conferring with me at this level of decision.

It was Schlegel who finally answered my unasked question.

"It's us that will have to go," he said. "Our trip: you and me, and that Foxwell character: right?"

"Oh, now I begin to see the daylight," I said.

"We'd consider it a favour," said Dawlish. "No order —but we'd consider it a favour, wouldn't we, Colonel?"

"Yes, sir!" said Schlegel.

"Very well," I said. They were obviously going to let me bleed to death until they got their way about it. My arm was throbbing badly by now and I found myself pressing it to still the pain. All I wanted was to see the army medical orderly. I wasn't cut out to be a wounded hero.

"We think it's worth a look," said Dawlish. He collected my empty cup. "Oh, for God's sake, Pat! You're dripping blood all over the carpet."

"It won't show," I said, "not in that lovely humming-bird pattern."

Chapter 17

Environment neutral. The environment neutral condition is one in which weather, radio reception, sonar operation and water temperatures remain constant throughout the game. This does not change the chance of accidents (naval units, merchant shipping, air), delays of material or communications or random machine operation.

GLOSSARY. "NOTES FOR WARGAMERS." STUDIES
CENTRE. LONDON

The sudden cry of an alarm clock was strangled at birth. For a moment there was complete silence. In the darkness there were only four grey rectangles that did not quite fit together. Rain dabbed them and the wind rattled the window frame.

I heard old MacGregor stamp his way into his old boots and cough as he went down the creaky stairs. I dressed. My clothes were damp and smelled of peat smoke. Even with the window and door tightly closed, the air was cold enough to condense my breath as I fought my way into almost every garment I possessed.

In the back parlour, old MacGregor knelt before the tiny grate of the stove and prayed for flame.

"Kindling," he said over his shoulder, as a surgeon might urgently call for a scalpel, determined not to take his eyes from the work in hand. "Dry kindling, man, from the box under the sink."

The bundle of dead wood was dry, as much as anything was dry at The Bonnet. MacGregor took the Agatha Christie paperback I'd left in the armchair, and ripped from it a few pages to feed the flame. I noticed for the first time that many other pages had already been sacrificed on that same altar. Now perhaps I would never know whether Miss Marple would pin it on the Archdeacon.

MacGregor breathed lustily upon the tiny flames. Perhaps it was the alcoholic content of his breath that made the fire flicker and start to devour the firewood. He moved the kettle over to the hob.

"I'll look at the arm," he said.

It had become a ritual. He undid the bandage with studied care and then ripped away the dressing so that I gave a cry of pain. "That's done," said MacGregor. He always said that.

"You're healing well, man." He cleaned the wound with antiseptic spirit and said, "Plaster will do you now —you'll not need a bandage today."

The kettle began to hum.

He applied the sticking plaster and then treated the graze on my back with the same care. He applied the sticking plaster there too and then stood back to admire his work, while I shivered.

"Some tea will warm you," he said.

Grey streaks of dawn were smeared across the windows, and outside the birds began to croak and argue— there was nothing to sing about.

"Stay in the parlour today," said MacGregor. "You don't want it to break open again." He poured two strong cups of tea, and wrapped a moth-eaten cosy round the pot. He stabbed a tin of milk with the poker and slid it across the table to me.

I pressed the raw places on my arm.

"They are beginning to itch," said MacGregor, "and that is good. You'll stay inside today—and read. I have no use for you." He smiled, sipped some tea and then reached for the entire resources in reading matter. *Garden Shrubs for the Amateur, With the Flag to Pretoria*, volume three, and three paperback Agatha Christies, partly plundered for their combustibility.

He put the books alongside me, poured me more tea and added peat to the fire. "Your friends will be coming today or tomorrow," he said.

"When do we go on the trip—did they tell you?"

"Your friends will be coming," he said. He was not a garrulous man.

MacGregor spent most of that morning in the shed, with the power-saw reduced to its components and arranged on the stone floor round him. Many times he fitted the parts together. Many times he snatched at the starter-string so that the engine turned. But it did not fire. Sometimes he swore at it but he did not give up until noon. Then he came into the parlour and threw himself into the battered leather armchair that I never used, realizing that he had a prior claim. "Bah!" said MacGregor. I'd learned to interpret it as his way of complaining of the cold. I prodded at the fire.

"Your porridge is on," he said. He called all the food porridge. It was his way of mocking Sassenachs.

"It smells good."

"I'll have none of your caustic London irony," said MacGregor. "If you do not fancy a sup—you can run down to the wood shed and wrestle that damned wood-saw." He clapped his hands together and massaged the red calloused fingers to bring the blood back into them. "Bah," he said again.

Behind him, the view from the tiny window, deepset into the thick stone wall, was partly obscured by two half-dead potted begonias. I could just see sunlight picking up traces of snow on the distant peaks, except when a gust of wind brought the chimney smoke into the yard, or worse, brought it down into the parlour. MacGregor coughed. "It needs a new cowl," he explained. "The east wind gets under the eaves and lifts the slats too."

He followed my gaze out the window. "That will be a London car," he said.

"How do you know?"

"Hereabouts folks have vans and lorries—we don't go much on cars—but when we do buy them we choose something that will get us up the Hammer or over the high road in winter. We'd not choose a smart London car like that one."

At first I thought it might turn off at the lower road, go through the village and along the coast. But the car continued on the road. It meandered along the slopes on the other side of the valley, so that we could see it climbing each hairpin for the first two or three miles. "They'll want dinner," said MacGregor.

"Or at least a drink," I said. I knew that it was a gruelling run for the last few miles. The road was not good at any time of the year but with the pot holes concealed by snow, the driver would have to pick his way past the worst bits. He'd need a drink and a moment by the fire.

"I'll see that the bar room fire is alive," he said. It was only the constant replenishment of fires, at back and front, that kept the house habitable. Even then he needed an oil heater near his feet in the bar, and the bedrooms were cold enough to strike the lungs like a stiletto. I tucked Agatha Christie behind the striking clock.

The car turned in on the gravel. It was a DBS, dark blue with matching upholstery. But the Aston was dented and spattered with mud and filthy snow. The windscreen was caked with dirt except for the two bright eyes made by the wipers. Only when the door opened did I see the driver. It was Ferdy Foxwell wearing his famous impresario's overcoat, its astrakhan collar buttoned up over his ears, and a crazy little fur hat tilted askew on his head.

I went out to see him. "Ferdy! Are we off?"

"Tomorrow. Schlegel is on his way. I thought with this I'd be here ahead of him. Give us a chance to chat."

"Nice car, Ferdy," I said.

"I treated myself for Christmas," he said. "You disapprove?"

The car cost more than my father earned from the railway for ten years' conscientious service, but Ferdy buying a small Ford wasn't going to help my father. "Spend, Ferdy, spend. Be the first kid on the block with an executive jet."

He smiled shyly, but I meant it. I'd been around long enough to find out that it wasn't the proprietors of three-star restaurants, designers of custom jewellery or the manufacturers of hand-made sports cars who were sitting in the sun in Bermuda. It was the shrewdies who did tinned beans, frozen fish and fizzy drinks.

Ferdy sniffed at MacGregor's stew. "What the devil are you boiling up there, MacGregor, you hairy Scotch bastard?"

"It's your chance to taste Highland haggis, fatty," said MacGregor.

"One of these days you'll say that, and it really will be a haggis," said Ferdy.

"Never," said MacGregor, "can't stand the filthy muck. I would no' have the stench of it in my house."

"You can put a gill of your home-made ginger wine into a double measure of your malt," said Ferdy.

I said, "Make it two of them."

"Finest ginger wine I ever tasted," said Ferdy. He grinned at me. MacGregor deplored the idea of mixing anything with his precious malts but he was vulnerable to compliments about his ginger wine. Reluctantly he took his time before he poured the measures into the glasses, hoping the while that we'd change our minds.

"The Colonel is coming?"

"The new Colonel is coming, MacGregor, my friend." It was declared now, that we all had the same employer, and yet even during my two days with him he'd not admitted it.

The wind was backing. No longer was smoke coming down into the back yard but the radio aerial gave a gentle moan. It was an uncommonly tall radio aerial, if intended only to bring in the B.B.C. programmes.

"I must have the power-saw ready for morning," said MacGregor diplomatically, for he guessed that the contents of Ferdy's document case were only for me to see.

Ferdy had the schoolboy intensity that I never ceased to admire. He'd brought all the right documents and codes and radio procedure charts marked up for the dates of the changes. No matter how much he complained, no matter, in fact, how anyone treated him, Ferdy saw himself as Mr Reliable, and he worked hard to keep his own esteem.

He hurried through the papers. "I suppose Schlegel poked you away up here because he didn't want us talking together." He said it casually, while giving the edges of the pages too much attention. It was a girl's response, if I can say that about Ferdy without giving you a completely wrong idea about him.

"No," I said.

"He hates me," said Ferdy.

"You keep saying that."

"I keep saying it because it's true."

"Well, that's a good enough reason," I admitted.

"I mean, you know it's true, don't you." Again it was an adolescent's wish to be contradicted.

"Hell, Ferdy, I don't know."

"And don't care."

"And don't care, Ferdy. Right."

"I've been against the Americans taking over the Centre, right from the start." He paused. I said nothing. Ferdy said, "You haven't, I know."

"I'm not sure the Centre would still be functioning if the Americans hadn't pumped life into it."

"But is it recognizable? When was the last time we did a historical analysis?"

"You know when, Ferdy. You and I did the P.Q. 17 convoy in September. Before that, we did those Battle of Britain variable fuel load games. You wrote them up for the journal. I thought you were pleased with what we did?"

"Yes, those," said Ferdy, unable to conceal the irritation which my answers gave him. "I mean a historical game played right through the month—computer time and all—with full staff. Not just you and me doing all the donkey work. Not just the two of us scribbling notes, as if it was some new boxed game from Avalon Hill."

"Who pays the piper . . ."

"Well I don't like the tune. That's why I first started telling Toliver what was happening."

"What?"

"Only after they started the surveillance submarines."

"You mean . . ." I paused as I thought about it. "You mean you were reporting all that classified material back to Toliver?"

"He's one of the senior people in intelligence."

"For God's sake, Ferdy, even if he was, what's that got to do with it?"

Ferdy bit his lower lip. "I had to make sure *our* people knew."

"They knew, Ferdy. We are a combined services outfit. They knew. What good could it possibly do, telling Toliver?"

"You think I did wrong?"

"You can't be that stupid, Ferdy."

"Let Schlegel down?" Ferdy said angrily. He shook an errant curl off his forehead. "Is that what I did?"

"How could they . . ." I stopped.

"Yes," said Ferdy. "I'm waiting."

"Well, what makes you so sure that Toliver is not

working for the Russians? Or the Americans, come to
that. How do you know?"

Ferdy went ashen. He ran his splayed fingers through
his hair a couple of times. "You don't believe that,"
he said.

"I'm asking you," I said.

"You've never liked Toliver. I know you haven't."

"Is that why he deserved the analysis every month?"

Ferdy huffed and puffed, fidgeting with the curtain
to get more light in the room, and picking up my
Agatha Christie and reading a line or two. "You reading this?" he asked. I nodded. He put it back on the
mantelshelf, behind the broken jug in which MacGregor
kept the unpaid bills. "I wish I'd spoken with you
about this before, Patrick," said Ferdy. "I nearly did.
Lots of times I nearly told you." The blue jug was
safely positioned on the mantelpiece but Ferdy pushed
it close against the mirror, as though it might leap into
the fireplace and smash into a thousand fragments just
to spite and embarrass him. He smiled at me. "You
know about this sort of thing, Patrick. I've never been
awfully good at the public relations side of it."

"Thanks a lot, Ferdy," I said, without working hard
at making my appreciation shine through.

"No offence."

"And none taken, but if you think that is public
relations . . ."

"I didn't mean public relations exactly."

"Oh, good."

"You think old Mac would let us have some tea?"

"Now don't change the subject. Schlegel will be
here in a moment."

"Oh, he'll be chasing as fast as he can go. He won't relish the idea of us working against him."

"Then that makes two of us."

"Don't be odious, Pat. I can help you. I mean, these people are trying to get at both of us, you know."

"What do you mean?"

"Am I right in saying that you've seen this fellow before, for instance?" He unclipped the lining of his document case and produced a large envelope from which he took a photo. He passed it to me.

"Seen him before?"

I took the picture. It was a small print, rephotographed from another print, judging by the fuzzy quality and the reflection. I'd seen it before, all right, but I wasn't going to say so.

"No."

"Would you be surprised if I told you that he was Rear-Admiral Remoziva?"

"No."

"You know what I'm getting at?"

"Not a clue."

"Remoziva is Chief of Staff, Northern Fleet."

"A real, live Red Admiral."

"A real, live Red Admiral," said Ferdy.

He looked at me, trying to see what reaction his information had produced. "Murmansk," he added finally.

"Yes, I know where the Russians keep the Northern Fleet, Ferdy."

"One of the best submarine men they have. Rear-Admiral Remoziva is the favourite for the First Deputy's department next year. Did you know *that?*"

I walked across to where he was standing. He was

pretending to look out of the window to where Mac-Gregor's dog was sniffing along some invisible track that circled the coal store. The window had frosted, making the dog no more than a fluffy growl. Ferdy breathed upon the glass and cleared a small circle, through which he peered. Over the sea the sky looked like a bundle of tarry rope but there were strands of red and gold plaited into it. Tomorrow would be a fine day.

"Did you know it?" Ferdy asked again.

I put my hand on his shoulder. "No, Ferdy," I said, and I pulled him round to face me, then grabbed his coat collar in my hand and twisted it so that the cloth tightened against his throat. He was a bigger man than me. Or so he'd always seemed. "I didn't know that, Ferdy," I told him very quietly. "But," and I shook him gently, "if I find that you . . ."

"What?"

"Are anything to do with it."

"To do with what?" His voice was high, but who knows whether it was indignation, fear, or just bewilderment.

"What?" he said again. "What? What? What?" He was shouting by this time. Shouting so loud that I only just heard the door slam as MacGregor came back into the house.

"No matter." I pushed Ferdy angrily, and stepped back from him as MacGregor came into the room. Ferdy straightened his tie and coat.

"Did you want something?" said MacGregor.

"Ferdy was wondering if we could get some tea," I said.

MacGregor looked from one to the other of us.

"You can," he said. "I'll brew it when the kettle boils. It's on the fire."

Still he watched us both. And we watched each other, and in Ferdy's eyes I saw resentment and fear. "Another trip so soon," said Ferdy. "We deserved a longer break."

"You're right," I said. MacGregor turned and went back to the power-saw.

"So why does Schlegel want to come?"

"He wants to find out how the subs work. It's a new kind of department for him."

"Huh!" said Ferdy. "He doesn't give a damn about subs. He's from the C.I.A."

"How do you know?"

"Leave me alone," he said.

"Sent to harass you, you mean?"

"You're a hard bastard, Pat." He straightened his tie. "You know that, don't you? You're a hard bastard."

"But not hard enough," I said.

"And I'll tell you something else, Patrick. This business with this Russian—this is Schlegel's pet project. I keep my ears open and I can tell you, it's Schlegel's pet project." He smiled, anxious to be friends again— a schoolgirl quarrel, soon mended, soon forgotten.

MacGregor called from the bar. "Car coming."

We both turned to the window. Already it was getting dark, although the clock said it was not much past four in the afternoon.

"Schlegel," said Ferdy.

"In a space ship?" The bright yellow, futuristic car made me smile. What a character.

"It's his new sports car—you buy the kit and assemble it. You save a lot of tax."

"There had to be a reason," I said. Schlegel brought it into the park, and revved-up before switching off, in the way that racing motorists are reputed to do. The silence lasted only a few minutes. Even before Schlegel had the car door open, I heard MacGregor's power-saw stammer and then roar into action. Nothing dared not work, once Schlegel had arrived.

*   *   *

"Oh boy," said Schlegel. "When I choose, I choose a lulu."

"What?"

"Spare me the static."

"What are you talking about?"

"Why didn't you lay it on me, about working for the goddamn Brits?"

I said nothing.

Schlegel sighed. "I was bound to find out. You made me look like a creep, do you know that, Pat?"

"I'm sorry "

"Sure. You're sorry. You don't get the flak. You spent years working for the goddamn intelligence service, and you let me put a screening request to them just like you are a two-bit clerk, and now you say you're sorry."

"You didn't tell me you were screening me."

"Don't get smart with me, Patrick."

I raised the flat of my hand and lowered my eyes. I owed him an apology and there was no doubt about it. They'd make his face burn red for a couple of months, if I knew anything about those megalomaniacs at Joint Service Records. "I'm sorry," I said. "What do you want me to do: commit hari-kiri with a blunt screwdriver?"

"I might," said Schlegel, and he was still very mad.

Ferdy came outside then, so I knew the Colonel would drop it. He did, too, but clearly it would be a little time before he came around to being our happy laughing leader again.

"Both the bags?" said Ferdy.

"Jesus, don't fuss round me," said Schlegel, and Ferdy flinched like a whipped dog and gave me a look to tell me that it was no more and no less than he'd expected.

"Let's go. Let's go," said Schlegel. He picked up his baggage, including equipment for both golf and tennis, and strode into the bar parlour.

"And what will it be, Colonel, sir?" said MacGregor.

Schlegel looked him up and down. "Are you going to be another of these smart-arse Brits?" said Schlegel. "Because I don't need it, pal. I don't need it."

"I want to give you a drink, man," said MacGregor.

"Can you fix a Martini, American style?" asked Schlegel.

"I can," said MacGregor.

But Schlegel wasn't going to let him get away as easily as that. "I'm talking about a stem glass from the ice-box, really cold Beefeater and no more than seven per cent dry vermouth."

"I can," said MacGregor. He turned away to start fixing it.

"And I mean cold," said Schlegel.

"You can sit in the freezer and drink it, if you want to," said MacGregor.

"Listen," said Schlegel. "Make it a double Scotch will you. Less chance you'll screw up on that one."

It was after the second round of drinks that Mac-Gregor came into the back room laughing. "I've just seen a remarkable sight," he said. We turned to look at him, for he was not a man who was often surprised. And even less likely to admit it.

"A hearse—driving past like a mad feller."

"A hearse? Where was he going?" said Ferdy.

"Where was he going," said MacGregor. "Hah. I'd like to know the answer to that one myself. He was driving up over the high road. There's nothing along that way."

"Except the submarine base," I said.

"Aye, except the submarine base. It would be a detour of fifteen miles for him to go that way to the Glen, or any of the villages."

"Some kid stealing a ride home," said Schlegel. He had not even looked up from his drink.

"At this time of day?" said MacGregor. "Coming back from some local night club you mean?"

"Something like that," said Schlegel, unabashed at MacGregor's sarcasm. "What else, I'd like to know?"

"A burial at sea," I offered. MacGregor gave a great booming laugh as though I'd made a fine joke.

"Did it have a body in it?" asked the ever-practical Ferdy.

"Well, it had a coffin in it," said MacGregor.

We ate in the front bar that night. We sat on the stools and faced Mac across his highly polished bar counter. It was a good stew—a man's cooking: great chunks of beef with whole potatoes and beans, too.

And Mac's best beer to go with it. And as we finished eating, the sky threw a handful of snow at the window, and the wind rapped twice so that we couldn't fail to notice.

Chapter 18

... history does not prove games wrong, any-
more than games prove history so.

"NOTES FOR WARGAMERS." STUDIES CENTRE.
LONDON

The navies of the world have decreed that, although
submarines are called boats, nuclear submarines are
ships. To see one of these monsters, well over a hundred yards long, weigh anchor and creep out to sea, is to
understand why. Inch by inch we moved through the
anchorage, past pale-grey mother ships and the tiny
conventional submarines alongside them. We passed
through the anti-submarine booms, nets and anti-
frogman barrier, thankful for the brief snatches of
bright sun that shone from a cloudy sky and reminded
everyone aboard that we were heading into the continuous Arctic night.

The U.S. submarine *Paul Revere* was a huge vessel
by any standards, space to spare for laundry rooms,
cinema, library and a comfortable lounge. Just a
perfunctory tour of the ship took over an hour. No
sooner had we changed into U.S.N. khakis than
Schlegel was off, investigating every nook and cranny.
We heard his progress through the departments, mak-

ing jokes, poking fingers, shaking hands and introducing himself, "Colonel Chuck Schlegel, U.S. Marine Corps, buddy, and don't you forget you've got a gyrene on this tub. Ha, ha."

These intelligence submarines did not have the usual banks of sixteen missiles. Instead, the amidships section was crammed with electronic counter measures (E.C.M.) and radio monitoring and recording apparatus. Certain recorded intercepts were taken back to STUCEN and fed into the computer. Thus we could array on the Games Table up to date "dilemma assessment" which is the pre-game stage of each simulated conflict.

In a corner of the lounge, there was the ship's doctor, laying down the cards for a complicated bridge game that he claimed he could play all by himself.

"What's it like up there?" he said. He was a worn-out little man with balding head and heavy-lidded eyes.

"Bright sunshine, but we are running into sea mist."

"How about taking a bridge hand?"

I shook my head. "I promised my mother," I said.

The great submarine threaded its way out through the Sound. The Seal Beach lighthouse bellowed at us, and a sea mist clamped down upon the gap between the northern end of Ardvern and the tiny island of Lum, that sticks its black head out of the water like an inquiring seal, its neck garlanded with a ruff of white water.

It was radar weather after that. The skipper came down from the sail. Schlegel had been up there with him. When he came into the wardroom his face was blue with cold, in spite of the big U.S. Navy anorak he was wearing.

He slipped the anorak off his shoulders. "Oh boy!" said Schlegel.

The doctor looked up from his bridge game. Schlegel was wearing his old Marine Corps sun-tans: short sleeves, rank insignia and pilot's wings, and starched like a plank.

I was standing by the coffee machine and I poured him some.

"Jesus, it's pretty scary," Schlegel said. "We came past that damned reef so close I could have snatched a sea-gull off the fore-shore." He looked around to where Ferdy was sitting, feet on the table and half asleep, over a copy of *The Brothers Karamazov*.

"You guys haven't seen what's happening upstairs. That skipper slides this office block through the water like a dune buggy." He gulped the hot coffee. He pulled a face as it burned him.

"Be careful," said Ferdy. "That coffee is very hot."

"You should go up on the sail sometime," said Schlegel. He wiped his mouth with a handkerchief.

"Not me," said Ferdy. "Not after seeing what it's done to you, Colonel."

Schlegel put his anorak into a locker and poured himself some iced water.

"What was the skipper saying about oranges, Patrick?"

"We usually put a couple of crates aboard, Colonel. It's the first thing they run low on. And that way, we don't have to feel guilty about giving them three extra mouths."

"Now I've got to chip in on that," said Schlegel.

"Whatever you want to do," I said. I saw the Engineering Officer pass by the door on his way to the

Manoeuvring Room. There was a double blast on the
diving-klaxon. "Hold on to your ice water, Colonel,"
I told him.

The floor tilted suddenly. "Holy Moses," said
Schlegel. The floor's angle increased, and the ship
lunged forward as the bow wave, which had been
resting on us like a wall, streamed over the deck.
Schlegel nearly lost his balance, and put out a hand
to grasp the overhead piping. He smiled to show us
how much he was enjoying it. After we passed a
hundred feet the ship levelled off.

At a writing-desk in the corner of the lounge the
doctor slammed his hands on to the cards to stop them
sliding.

"Does that happen often?" Schlegel asked.

"It'll happen again within an hour," I said. "When
we're past Muck, Eigg and Rhum and into the Minches,
he'll take her down to four hundred feet. That's
cruising level. After that there's nothing to do except
watch Ferdy reading *Brothers Karamazov:* just as he's
been doing the last three trips."

"I can't remember their damned names," said Ferdy.

"I wouldn't get too settled in," said Schlegel. "This
trip is likely to be more active than usual."

Neither of us answered.

Schlegel said, "I'm going to the Control Room if
anybody wants me."

Ferdy chortled after Schlegel had gone. "If anybody
wants him," said Ferdy. "Where's he think he is, the
Playboy Club?"

I was wrong about the Captain waiting until we got
to the Minches. The klaxon sounded and the floor tilted
again. From the far end of the ship I heard a cry of

pain from Schlegel as he fell and slid across the polished deck.

"Good on the skipper," said Ferdy.

* * *

Conventional submarines make more speed on the surface than they can below it, but nuclear subs go faster submerged. Now, displacing four thousand tons of Atlantic Ocean, we were making better than twenty-five knots in the general direction of the Arctic. It was the literal end of the world: at this season the edge of the polar ice cap was as far south as it ever gets— locking Russia to the North Pole. To add to the fun, winter brings permanent night to the land of ice.

Apart from a bridge tournament that continued in the library, and the film show at 1400 hours and 2100 hours each day, there was little for us to do for the first three days. Even Schlegel simmered down enough to spend hours at a time reading *The Biography of von Richthofen.* Some of the corridor lights were dimmed from 2000 until 0700 hours in the morning. Apart from that, there was little difference between day or night, except that grapefruit segments and orange juice were on the chilled shelf for one meal in three. Once or twice we came up to periscope depth and let a blow of fresh air through the schnorkel. I suppose there was nothing wrong with the scrubbed air, but it was nice to smell the sea once in a while.

We had our own operators in the electronics rooms. When we surfaced they did the usual tests: tuning in to the Northern Fleet transmitters at Murmansk and the big Baltic Fleet radio at Baltiysk—on the Frisches

Haff. The submarine base at Kaliningrad—what used
to be Königsberg—and the C.-in-C. Baltic Naval Air
Force have heavy radio traffic. If London's reception
is poor, surfaced subs in transit monitor for them.

There was nothing special on the data collection log
except intercepts between a couple of conventional
subs steaming a parallel course north with us. They
were East Germans, from the submarine school at
Sassnitz, taking the boats up in the direction of Poliarnyi. We read them on the sonar and ranged them. A
nuclear power plant enables all the electronic equipment to give a performance superior to anything in a
conventional boat. The Conning Officer pleaded to do
mock attacks on them but the Captain wouldn't even
discuss it. The captains of these data collection subs
are given the full treatment at New London before
they take command. The idea of the Russians captur-
ing one of them was CINCLANT's constant nightmare.
That's why I was surprised that they'd chosen such a
sub to do Toliver's rendezvous for Remoziva.

The Norwegian Basin is a deep area of the Norwegian Sea that lies between Norway and Greenland.
Even on the rim of the Basin there are still a couple
of thousand metres of water. But before we were out
of the northern end of the Basin, the sonar picked up
the first of the drift-ice. Growlers, they call the grey
chunks that float off the pack. They don't remain flat
side up, as they were when they were part of the floe.
They tip over and look exactly like a submarine or a
trawler. And if they are big enough, a gust of wind can
catch them. Then they will sail off, leaving a wake behind them so that you start counting the seconds before a surface-to-surface hits you in the fanny.

We were having breakfast when the first growler was sighted. That morning there was cinnamon toast. Faintly, from the juke box in the crew's quarters, I could hear Neil Diamond singing "Cracklin' Rosie."

"The Captain says it's a long way south," said Schlegel.

"A north wind will bring them down a lot farther than this," said Ferdy. He turned to me. "What do you think he'll do?"

"Who?" asked Schlegel. He didn't like to be left out of things.

"The skipper," I said. "He'll go deep."

"Periscope depth," said Ferdy.

"A quid," I said.

"You're on," said Ferdy.

"Why do you think he'll go deep?" said Schlegel.

"He's a new kid. He's full of the marvels of science, but he'll want to convince himself that the sonar is perfect before we get into the rough stuff."

"And I've got a pound that says you're wrong," said Schlegel.

That's how I lost two quid. Mind you, Ferdy swore that Schlegel must have heard the Captain say what he intended to do beforehand. But hell, Schlegel isn't short of a quid.

He took us up to periscope level. He was a new kid —I was right about that—so why didn't I guess he'd be interested in seeing what the Arctic looked like.

It was an either/or situation. He could either take us down and rely on the machinery, or keep a sharp watch for ice on the surface. Ice is no softer than steel when you bump into it. Even a chunk no bigger than Ferdy could wreck the periscope vacuums.

"That's unkind," said Ferdy.

"No bigger than a Shetland pony," I offered.

"Shetland pony, I'll accept," said Ferdy, and giggled. "Do you want another serving of cinnamon toast?" He got to his feet to get it.

"And bacon," I said.

"You guys," said Schlegel. "That's the third helping of cinnamon toast! You get no exercise, you don't need all this chow."

Suddenly there was a thump. Crockery smashed in the dining-room and a dozen pairs of boots fell out of the rack in front of me and shot across the deck towards Ferdy's armchair.

"My God! What's that?" said Ferdy.

The deck tilted. The forward motion stopped, as the screws went into reverse and the ship heeled over. I hung onto the bulk-head as I clambered forward to the Control Room. We went into a violent up-angle.

"Hold it," said Schlegel when I got there. Already the Captain was at the sonar, hanging on to the operator to stop himself sliding across the floor.

"Contact fifty yards dead ahead," said the Conning Officer. He'd thrown her into the tightest turn she was capable of and now we were beginning to straighten slowly.

"What is it?" said the skipper. He was a baby-faced Commander with tailored khakis and soft brown leather high boots. He rubbed his eyes. There were no shadows, no shade, no escape from the fluorescent lights that glared in the glass dials.

"That goddamn Kraut sub," said the Conning Officer.

"Are you sure?" He looked not at the Conning Officer but to his Exec.

"We've been watching her," said the Exec. "She's been acting up . . . crossed our bow twice . . . then she dived ahead of us."

They were both watching the sonar screen. The shape moved just a flicker. It was still, and then slowly it turned. You could have cut the tension with a knife.

"Ten minds with but a single thought," said the skipper. Just the tiniest hint of a smile was on the corner of his lips but a bead of sweat on his forehead undid the cool he showed. He was right about this man's mind. I was waiting for her bow tubes to come round to us, and not liking it.

Suddenly there was bedlam in the Control Room. The air was filled with raucous noises: flutes up and down the scale, and a rasping noise from the P.A. system. I looked at the console. The radar screen was a snowstorm that dashed vertically and diagonally in a mad rhythm.

The Captain took the P.A. microphone and, raising his voice to make it heard above the interference, said, "This is the Captain. Stay loose, everybody. It's just their E.C.M."

The noise increased to a frenzy as the German submarine's counter measures jammed the electronics. Then it stopped and the instruments swung back to their rightful positions, the screen darkened and the P.A. speakers went silent.

"She's heading south—fast."

"Bastards!" said the Exec.

The Captain walked over to the screen and patted the operator on the back. "Not too many more like that, Al."

The boy smiled. "We'll come back the scenic route, sir."

"Do that for me. My old lady will never forgive you if you do something silly now," said the skipper. He ran the back of his hand across his brow.

The Exec took the con again. I felt the edge of vibration as the screws began to turn and a ripple of freshly disturbed water ran along the hull like a cautionary finger.

"Steer, Oh, three, five-er."

We were on the way again.

"Is this something I should try to get used to?" said Schlegel.

"They hassle us sometimes," said the Captain. "We displace four thousand tons. That East German skipper is in a tiny, thirteen-hundred-ton, W Class job . . ." The Captain wiped his hands on a silk handkerchief. That's the nuclear age, I thought; in the old days it would have been oily cotton waste.

"How do you know?"

"The size on the screen . . . and it's their most common sub. They copied it from the Krauts' old Type XXI, in the war. When he cuts my bow like that, he makes us slew round half the ocean to recover. We're damned heavy, Colonel, and the trouble with the high cruising speed is . . . well, you just saw what it was."

"It makes us jumpy seeing those little conventionals jazzing across us like that," said the Exec. "Those are the babies that have the hunter-killer gear. When the chips go down, it won't be the Reds' nukes that come after us, it will be their little conventionals. That's why they keep building them."

Schlegel nodded. "The East Germans are moving their hardware back to the Polish and Russian ports. They'll be pushing some of it up into the Northern Fleet, too. Watch out for it."

"What's their angle?" said the Captain.

"Don't you get past the funnies section? The Russians are sitting down to talk about German reunification. You don't imagine that they intend to let any of us capitalist reactionaries get our hands on it, before they complete an energetic asset-stripping operation, do you?"

"What kind of ships do the East Germans have?" the Captain asked. "And what kind of men?"

Schlegel waved to me. I said, "Frigates and coastal stuff. It took a long time before the Russians would let the D.D.R. have submarines. But all the People's Navy are ten-year men. Officer-training is a four-year stint and they have to do two years on the lower deck before they can even apply for it. So every officer's had six years' service."

The Captain said, "If they only let six-year officers go to sea in this man's navy, I guess we'd have me and Doc Harris. My Exec would be promised for next year."

The Executive Officer didn't smile. "Six years' training, eh? Did you ever see a flotilla of those bastards come steaming through a NATO exercise, or any other Western naval unit? Twice I've seen them come right through the middle of ships at sea. No signals, no lights, nothing. And not turning a fraction off course. Came within ten yards of one destroyer. They know our safety instructions make us avoid collision. It makes them feel like big men doing that . . .

six years! . . . seamen! Just bastards, that's what they are."

"They do that to discover our emergency wave-lengths," said the Captain. "There are always electronics boats with them when they do that."

"Bastards," said the Exec.

"The East German ships are well built, I guess," said the Captain.

"First class," I said. "That's the D.D.R.'s real value to the Eastern bloc—ship construction for satellite navies. And they have deep-buried oil supplies, submarine pens in cliffs, and yards well tucked away."

"Reunification, eh?" said the Captain, as though he was hearing about it for the first time. "Sounds like it would be good for us. It would push the Reds right back to Poland, wouldn't it?"

"That's it," I said. "Or bring them right up to Holland. Depends whether you are an optimist or a pessimist."

Chapter 19

Submarine units of any type surfaced within range of enemy Class A missiles will be considered destroyed.

RULES. "TACWARGAME." STUDIES CENTRE. LONDON

"Navigator to the Control Room."

I came awake suddenly. The door was not fully closed and there was a dull orange light from the corridor. I switched on the bunk light and looked at my watch. It was the middle of the night. Schlegel's bunk was empty and so was Ferdy's. I dressed hurriedly and went forward.

At first the drift-ice is no more than a few patches. Then the sonar starts picking up the big floes: as big as a car, as big as a house, as big as a city block. And is it seven-eighths, or nine-tenths, of an iceberg that remains submerged and invisible? Well, who cares how much. Enough submerged to shred us. Or, as Schlegel explained to the Captain, enough to cool every Martini from Portland to L.A.

But once you dive under the ice you are committed to the element of the water. And this was not the two-thousand-metre deeps of the Norwegian Basin. We were over the Jan Mayen Ridge and into the

Barents Sea to where your ocean is measured in feet. For eight hours under the Polar pack we could predict the ice thickness with a reasonable degree of certainty, but after that we were in the "brash and block" and some of those pieces could be any size at all. I'd heard about these deep winter trips but this was the first one I'd ever done, and now and again I found myself thinking of the ship they lost two winters before.

"Engineering Officer to the Control Room."

"Any sign of that goddamn Polack sub?"

"The two of them went off the screen south."

"Murmansk. Watch out for them on sonar."

"Yes, sir."

"Shoaling steeply, sir."

"Watch her, Charlie—even slower, I think." The skipper turned to Schlegel and me. "This chunk of ice above us is a mile wide."

"That big?" said Schlegel.

"The one beyond is nearer nine miles wide," said the Captain.

When the Captain wasn't looking, Schlegel pulled a face at me. He was right, what the hell are you supposed to say. Next the kid was going to be showing us his appendix scar.

"All hands. This is the Captain speaking. Complete silence throughout the ship."

The pings of the sonar were suddenly very loud. I looked round at the crowded Control Room. The duty watch were fully dressed in their khaki shirts and pants, but the Captain was in his shirt-sleeves and the Navigator was in striped pyjamas.

American submariners had been charting the beds of the Arctic seas for many years. They'd recorded the canyons and the peaks of the shallow northern seas, in thousand-mile highways that could be followed as a truck driver uses the motorways of Europe. But truck drivers do not have an unpredictable roof of solid ice above their head: great floes, with keels so deep that they'd scalp him unless he steered off the highway and bumped across uncharted routes trying to find a way through unscathed.

"Pressure ridge coming up, sir." Ferdy moved aside as the Captain pushed past him.

The needle of the sonar drew a picture of the ice above us. In winter, the newly formed ice presses against the older floes, forcing them down deep into the water. The pen inked a careful drawing of the ridges: up and down, up and down like a fever chart: each one a little farther down.

"I don't like it, Charlie."

"No, sir." The ship was unnaturally still: men held their breaths, left words unsaid, itches unscratched.

The log needle was on eight knots, the depth gauge needle on two hundred. The only sound was the hum of the machinery and the steady ping of the sonar. The ship edged forward. The sonar needle came lower this time. Each ice ridge had been thicker: eighty feet, then ninety feet, reaching down to us. A hundred and five! Now the needle passed the previous peak, and still kept coming. One hundred and ten, one hundred and fifteen!

"Jeeeesusss! Take her down!"

"Negative buoyancy." The planesmen had been ready for the order. The two sailors slammed the controls and the nose tilted. "To two hundred and fifty."

The world was tightening around us. The sonar

needle did not stop and turn back until one hundred and forty. If we'd stayed at our previous level the ice would have taken five feet off our sail top.

"Only just," said the Exec.

The skipper scratched his nose. He turned to Schlegel. "It's usually a bit hairy before we get to the ice-limits."

At the ice-limits the thickness is more predictable but the ocean is shallower, and after that we must turn to follow the Russian coastline towards the White Sea. There the shore-line ice starts building together. That's the worst section of all.

"That Polish sub has gone?" said Schlegel.

"Still on our sonar—she's turned almost parallel again."

"She's tailing us," said Schlegel. He looked at Ferdy.

"No," said the skipper. "She probably can't see us. She could be having the same ice problems we have. Her sonar range is nothing—she'd be rubbing noses with the Eskimos before they'd have a reading."

"She knows we're here?"

"She knows we're somewhere. They can hear our sonar hitting them. But they can't get us on their sonar."

"But she's making good speed," said Schlegel.

"They have better charts than we do for this area. Neither of us can guess the ice but she knows the soundings: it helps."

"I'd like to take a poke at it," said Schlegel.

"We both have plenty to occupy us at present," said the skipper.

"The history of the world," said Ferdy. "Overlooking

small enemies in the threat of greater ones—all history comes down to that finally."

Ferdy was wearing a black silk dressing-gown, its dark red kerchief fixed with a gold pin. The Captain looked at him as if noticing his attire for the first time. Finally he nodded. "I suppose."

"Still shoaling, sir."

It was the great silt deposits that made the sea bed flat, but beneath the silt, the bottom was hard enough to take the floor from under us. There was only eighty feet of water below us now, and above us another pressure ridge was building, under the nervous pen of the fathometer. Again the ink line faltered and turned back.

"Down another fifty," said the Captain.

We sank deeper. The pen line shrank away from the horizontal line that represented the top of our sail. I heard Ferdy sigh. We levelled off and the pen made a beautiful tall canopy above us.

"This is going to be a tough one," said the Captain. "Come left to north-east."

"Lagoon ahead," said the sonar operator.

"How far?"

"A mile, a bit more perhaps."

"Here she comes again."

This was a big ridge, the keel of an enormous floe. The drawing showed how it had been born out of corrugated ridges jammed so tight together that the whole floe tilted, so that the pen drew a mad inverted shape upon the thin white paper.

"Down thirty."

"Goddamn that packing." The Captain reached into his shirt collar to mop up the trickles of cold water that had been dripping from the periscope, increasing their rate of flow as the water became colder. The dribbling water had started off as a joke, but now the thought of icy water on the other side of the steel hull raised no laughs.

"Hold that," said the Captain.

Now there was just a swirl of silt beneath us. The fathometer was wobbling as it tried to register upon the soft bottom dislodged by our passing.

"Full astern—hold it, hold it."

The floor tilted as the propellers came to a standstill and then began slowly to turn the other way. For a moment the sub became unstable, like a dinghy riding out a long wave. Then the props picked up speed and the forward movement stopped us with a shudder and a loud rumble.

"Dead slow."

Now the needle made a series of corrugations over the dark horizontal line that was us. The Captain clamped his hand over his face as if he'd been hit, but I knew he was listening to the scrape of ice along the hull. It came scratching along the metal like predatory fingernails.

The ship had lost all forward speed now. "Negative buoyancy," said the Captain. There was a lurch and then a groan. The buoyancy chambers rang with a hollow sound as the ship sank to the ocean floor. I lost my balance as we heeled over ten degrees.

Everyone held on to a bulkhead, pipe or fitting. The Captain took the P.A. microphone. "Attention all hands. This is the Captain speaking. We are resting on the ocean bed while I take a good look at the sonar. There is no need for any alarm. Repeat: there

is no need for any alarm." The Captain replaced the
mike and beckoned Schlegel and me over to the control
console. He sat down and mopped his brow with a
paper tissue. "I think we'll have to try another way
through, Colonel."

"How?"

"We'll go south until we find the end of the rafted
ice."

"I don't know much about rafted ice, Captain, but
it sounds pretty unlikely that it's going to get better
that way. This stuff builds from the shore outwards.
Or that's what I hear."

"Or until we find one of the sea passages that the
ice breakers clear all the way to Murmansk."

"Nothing doing," said Schlegel. "That would prejudice my mission. I need a whip antenna in the air
inside the next sixty minutes."

"Impossible," said the Captain. He mopped his brow
with a fresh tissue and, taking careful aim at the
waste-bin, he threw it away with all the care and attention of an Olympics champion.

"You've got a lagoon a mile or so ahead. We're going
to squeeze this pig-boat through the mud and make it
by the time the big hand's on twelve. Got it?"

"I've got it all right," said the Captain. "But you
haven't. Prejudicing your mission is tough, but prejudicing my ship is not a contingency."

"The decision is mine," said Schlegel softly. He
glanced over his shoulder, but we weren't getting much
attention from the rest of them. "And the sealed orders
in your triple-lock safe will say so. Meanwhile glim
this." He passed the Captain an official-looking envelope. Inside it there was a sheet of paper headed

"Director of Undersea Warfare" and there was a Pentagon letterhead and lots of signatures.

"And if you find that impressive," warned Schlegel,
"let me tell you that the one in your safe is from
Joint Chiefs."

"There is no one can authorize me to risk my ship,"
said the Captain primly. He looked round at me. I
was the only person in earshot.

"Listen," said Schlegel in that Bogart voice with
which I'd seen him thrash champions. "You're not
speaking to some chicken-shit soldier-boy, Captain. I
was riding pig-boats before you were riding kiddie cars.
I say she'll go through and I'm not asking your advice."

"And I say . . ."

"Yes, and you say I'm wrong. Well, you prove I'm
wrong, sailor-boy. You prove I'm wrong by jamming
us under the goddamn ice-flow. Because if you turn us
around and toddle off home I'll make sure they kick
your ass from sun-up to sack-time. Because you can't
prove *your* contention without sinking us."

The Captain had spent a long time since last getting
that kind of treatment. He stood up, gasped and sat
down again to mop his brow. There were two or three
extra-long minutes of silence.

"Take her through, son," coaxed Schlegel. "It'll be
all right, you'll see." Schlegel mauled his face, as I'd
seen him do at other moments of stress.

The Captain said, "The floe over us is maybe as big
as the UN building; solid as concrete."

"Captain. There's some kid out there . . . driving
along the road that follows the Kola Fjord north from
Murmansk. He's in some lousy Russian automobile,
and the ice is getting under his wiper blades. He's been

watching the mirror for the last half hour, dreading to see the headlights of a prowl car. When he gets into position, on some desolate section of freezing cold headland, he's going to open up the boot and start fooling with the antenna of a radio transmitter to give us a message. He's doing all that—and risking his neck —because he believes that freedom is a beautiful thing, Captain. Now, are we—sitting here in this air-conditioned rinky-dink with a rare steak, corn-oysters and blueberry pie on the menu tonight—are we going to let that kid call us up and get no reply?"

"We'll maybe lose the periscope," said the Captain.

"Give it a whirl," said Schlegel.

Don't let me leave you with the idea that I personally was joining Schlegel's clamour for a chance to wriggle under the keel of that iceberg. Let that kid in the car keep right on driving if he's nervous.

"One more home-team try," said the Captain to his Executive, but no one gave the college cheer.

"Five knots is all I want."

The screws began to turn. As water flowed along the hull the deck lurched and slowly came level. I saw the Captain tell the Exec something and I guessed he was sending him off for the sealed orders before making the attempt to get through. That Captain didn't trust anyone. That was wise of him.

I heard the pen scrape again. "More head room, skipper."

He made a sound to show that he was unimpressed with the extra couple of feet clearance. But his eyes were on the sonar and the lagoon beyond the floe. "Close all watertight doors and bulkheads."

I heard the metal thump closed and the locks tight-

ened. A few of the crewmen exchanged blank stares.
The phone rang. The Captain took it. He listened to
the Exec for a moment. And then he looked at Schlegel.
"OK, Charlie. Then let's do that thing." He replaced
the phone. "Here we go, Colonel," he said to Schlegel.
Schlegel gave him a smile no thicker than a razor
blade.

There was another soft scraping noise on the hull.
We heard it clearly because everyone was holding their
breath. The ship wriggled as the contact slowed one
side of the hull and turned us a degree or two. The
revolutions thrashed a little as the prop lost its hold
and then gripped the water and went back to normal.
Again the same thing happened, but suddenly we
lurched forward and the pen scratched a near-vertical
line that represented fifty feet or more. The pen came
down again, but only made fifteen feet, and then was
a steady corrugation on the polar pack no more than
ten feet deep.

"Can't see the damned lagoon, Captain."

"If we don't pick up a suitable break in the ice inside thirty minutes I'm going to ask you to put a couple
of fish into the underside of that polar pack."

"That doesn't sound healthy," said the Captain.
"We'd be only three ship-lengths away."

"Ever hear of Polaris subs, Captain?" Schlegel asked.

The Captain said nothing.

"I don't know what kind of money that fleet of pig-
boats costs, but you don't think they built those con-
traptions without finding out how to knock a hole in
the ice, do you?"

"We've got thirty minutes yet," said the Captain.

"Right," said Schlegel, and he threw a finger at the Captain. "Cool your kids off a little, huh?"

"Attention all hands. This is the Captain. We're under the polar pack. Resume normal activity but keep the juke box off."

We found a suitably large polynya—which is the proper name for a lagoon in the ice—and, with careful attention to the sonar, the Captain began surfacing procedures.

We were all in the electronics room with the operators that were assigned to this watch. "I've got every permutation of message he can send on call in my head," said Schlegel.

"Maybe he won't call," said Ferdy.

"We'll give him two hours and then we'll send the negative contact."

"Will the Captain hold her on the surface for two hours?"

"He'll do what I tell him," said Schlegel, with one of his special scowl-like smiles. "Anyway, it'll take his deck party an hour or more to paint the sail white."

"That won't prevent us being picked up on the radar or MAD," said Ferdy.

"Do me a favour and don't tell that Captain," said Schlegel harshly. "He's scared gutless already."

"He probably knows that radar chain better than you do, Colonel," said Ferdy.

"That's why the Colonel's not scared," I added.

"You guys!" said Schlegel in disgust.

The radio call came through on time. It was coded in Norwegian, but any Russian monitoring crew would have to be unusually stupid to believe that there were a couple of Norwegian fishing trawlers out there in the deep freeze.

"Bring number four net," came through in morse as clear as a bell and was followed by four five-figure cipher groups.

Schlegel looked over the operator's shoulder as he deciphered and stabbed a group in the code book. He said, "Send that code for 'market steady on today's catches—no change expected tomorrow.' And then wait for them to close."

Our operator released the key after the signature and there was the bleat of an acknowledgment. Schlegel smiled.

When we were back in the lounge Ferdy sank into an armchair, but Schlegel fiddled with the writing-desk light over the doctor's one-man bridge game. "Our boy made it," Schlegel said.

"Our boy with the suitcase radio set came in five by five. A powerful signal, and clear enough to compare with the Northern Fleet operational transmitter," I said.

Schlegel bared his teeth in a way that most people do only for the dentist. I was beginning to recognize it as a sign that he was on the defensive. "It was an official transmitter," he admitted. "Confirming the rendezvous with the helicopter."

I stared at him. It seemed a lot of words for such a simple message, and why wasn't it in high speed morse? "A Russian transmitter?" I said. "So we are going bare-arse into a lagoon of their choosing?"

"You don't like the idea of it?"

"With a Russkie egg-beater overhead? They could come down with a feather and tickle us to death."

Schlegel nodded agreement and then studied the doc's bridge game. Schlegel looked at all the hands and then checked the dealer. He didn't cheat the cards; he just liked to know where they all were. Without looking up he said, "No sweat for the sub, Patrick. Save all your prayers for us. The sub won't be there: it will arrive early, deposit us and then make itself scarce until we bleep it up. For all we know the RV won't be a lagoon. We'll have to make it on foot."

"Make it on foot?" I said. "Across that big vanilla-flavoured ice-cream sundae? Are you out of your mind?"

"You'll do as you're told," said Schlegel in the same voice he'd used on the Captain.

"Or what? You'll tell weight-watchers anonymous about my extra cinnamon toast?"

"Ferdy!" said Schlegel.

Ferdy had been watching the exchange with interest but now he got to his feet hurriedly, murmured goodnights, and departed. When we were alone Schlegel moved round the lounge, switching lights on and off, and testing the fans.

"You don't think Rear-Admiral Remoziva will deliver?"

"I've been fed a rich diet of fairy stories all the way through this business," I complained. "But based upon the kind of lies I've heard, what I know, and a couple of far-out guesses, I'd say there isn't a chance in hell."

"Suppose I said I agree." He looked round anxiously to be sure we were not overheard. "Suppose I told you that that radio signal obliges us to continue with the pick-up, even if we were certain that it's phoney? What would you say to that?"

"I'd need a book of diagrams."

"And that's what I can't give you." He ran his open hand down his face, tugging at the corners of his mouth as if afraid he might give way to an hysterical bout of merriment. "I can only tell you that if we all get gunned down out there tomorrow, and there's no Remoziva, it will still be worth while."

"Not to me, it won't," I said. "Stay perplexed, feller," he said, "because if the Russkies pull something fancy out there tomorrow, it won't matter if they take you alive."

I smiled. I was trying to master that grim smile of Schlegel's. I am never too proud to learn, and I had a lot of uses for a smile like that.

"I'm serious, Pat. There are security aspects of this job that mean that I must be killed rather than captured alive. And the same with Ferdy."

"And are there security aspects of this job that cause you to run along now to Ferdy, and tell him that it doesn't matter if *he* goes into the bag but *I* mustn't get taken alive?"

"Your mind is like a sewer, pal. How do people get that way?" He shook his head to indicate disgust, but he didn't deny the allegation.

"By surviving, Colonel," I said. "It's what they call natural selection."

Chapter 20

It is in the nature of the war game that problems arise that cannot be resolved by the rules. For this reason CONTROL should be regarded as consultative. It is not recommended that CONTROL resolves such problems until adequate exploration of the problem has taken place between all players.

"NOTES FOR WARGAMERS." STUDIES CENTRE.
LONDON

We stood around in the Control Room, wearing kapok-lined white snow-suits, incongruous amongst the shirt-sleeved officers. Above us, the overhead sonar showed the open lagoon, but the Captain hesitated and held the ship level and still against the currents.

"Look at this, Colonel." The Captain was at the periscope. His tone was deferential. Whether this was due to Schlegel's blast, the letter from the Pentagon, or because the Captain expected us not to return from the mission, was not clear.

Schlegel needed the periscope lowered a fraction. It was sighted vertically. Schlegel looked for a moment, nodded, and then offered the place at the eyepieces to me. I could see only a blurred shape of pale blue.

"This is with the light intensifier?" I asked.

"That's without it," someone said, and the sight went almost black.

"I don't know," I said finally.

Ferdy looked too. "It's moonlight," he said. He laughed mockingly. "You think the Russians have rigged a battery of lights for us?"

It broke the tension and even Schlegel smiled.

"Is it ice?" said the Captain. "I don't give a damn about the light, but is it ice?"

"It's not on the sonar?" I asked.

"A thin sheet of ice might not show," said the Conning Officer.

"Take her up, skipper," Schlegel said.

The Captain nodded, "Down periscope. Flood negative."

The ship wobbled as the buoyancy control tank echoed, and the ascent began. The crash came like a sledgehammer pounded against the hollow steel of the pressure hull. The Captain bit his lip. All eyes were on him. Obviously some dire damage had been done to the submarine, and just as obviously there was no stopping the ascent just a few feet from the surface. We floated, rocking in the swirl of the disturbed water. Already the Captain was halfway up the ladder. I followed. Whatever was waiting up there, I wanted to see it.

After the bright glare of the submarine's fluorescent lighting, I'd half-expected a limitless landscape of gleaming ice. But we emerged into Arctic darkness, lit only by diffused moonlight and walled-around with grey mists. The icy wind cut into me like a rusty scalpel.

Only when my eyes became accustomed to the

gloom was I able to see the far side of the lagoon, where the dark waters became ash-coloured ridges of ice. The Captain was examining the dents in the periscope casing, and now he looked down and cursed the great sheet of ice that we'd broken into pieces and scattered on our waves.

"What are the chances, Dave?" the Captain asked the Engineering Officer, who was expected to know how to fix everything, from nuclear reactor to juke box.

"It's vacuum packed. It would be a long job, skipper."

"Take a look at it anyway."

"Sure thing."

Schlegel took the Captain by the arm. He said, "And since I've told you the authorized version, let's make sure you know what the score really is."

The Captain bent his head, as if to listen more attentively.

"Never mind your goddamned pig-boat, sonny. And never mind those orders. If you sail off into the sunset, leaving any one of us out there, I'll get back. Me, personally! I'll get back and tear your balls off. That's the real score, so just make sure you understand it."

"Just don't start anything the navy will have to finish," said the Captain. Schlegel grinned broadly. The Captain had taken less time to understand Schlegel than I had. Schlegel played noisy barbarian to examine the reactions of his fellow men. I wondered if I'd come out of it as well as the Captain had.

"Your boys ready to go, Colonel?"

"On our way, Captain." It was easier said than done. The high freeboard, and streamlined shape, of the nuclear subs, makes it difficult to land from them, except to a properly constructed jetty or mother boat. We clambered down the collapsible ladders, dirtied by the hull and breathless from the exertion.

There was the corpse too. We slid it out of the metal cylinder that breathed the grey smoke of dry ice. He was sitting on a crude wooden seat, which we took from the body and sent back to the sub. Then the body was clipped on two runners and we began to plod across the ice.

We had left the permanent fluorescent day of the submarine for the long winter of Arctic night. The cloud was low, but thin enough for moonlight to glow pale blue, like a TV left on in a deserted warehouse. The cold air and hard ground made the sound travel with unexpected clarity, so that even after we were a mile away from the lagoon we could hear the whispered conversation of the welders inspecting the damaged periscope.

Another mile saw all three of us beginning to feel the exertion. We stopped and deposited the radio bleeper that had been modified to operate on the Russian Fleet Emergency wavelength. We looked back to the submarine as the deck party disappeared back into the hull.

"Looks like they can't fix it," said Schlegel.

"That's what it looks like," I agreed.

For a moment it was very still and then, slowly, the black shiny hull slid down into the dark Arctic water. I've never felt so lonely.

We were alone on a continent composed solely of ice, floating on the northern waters

"Let's move over a little," I said. "They could home an antipersonnel missile on to that bleeper."

"Good thinking," said Schlegel. "And bring the incredible hulk." He pointed to the frozen corpse. It lay on its side, rolled into a ball as if someone had just floored it with a low punch. We moved two hundred yards and settled down to wait. There was still nearly an hour to go until RV time. We buttoned up the anoraks across the nose, and pulled down the snow goggles to stop the icicles forming on our lashes.

The low cloud, and the hard flat ice, trapped the sound and cast it back and forth between them so that the noise of the helicopter seemed to be everywhere at once. It was a Ka-26, with two coaxial rotors that beat the air loudly enough almost to eclipse the sound of its engines. It hovered over the radio bleeper, dipping its nose to improve the pilot's view. Still with its nose drooping, it slewed round, searching the land until it saw us.

"Search and Rescue livery," said Ferdy.

"Ship based," said Schlegel. "It could still work out."

"Remoziva, you mean?" Ferdy said.

Schlegel shot me a quick glance. "Yes, it could be," said Schlegel. "It could be."

The chopper settled in the great cloud of powdered snow that was lifted by its blades. Only when the snow settled could we see it, sitting a hundred yards from us. It was slab-sided, with twin-boom tailplane. The cabin was no more than a box, with two huge engine pods mounted high on each side. The exhausts glowed red in the darkness. The box-like design was emphasized by stripes of international-orange, calculated to make it conspicuous on either the ice or the dark ocean. There were dimension lights on every corner of it, and even after the blades came to a sticky halt —when the chopper's outlines were no longer easy to see—the lights continued to wink on and off like crazy fireflies on a summer's evening.

Schlegel put a hand on Ferdy's arm. "Let them come to us, let them come to us."

"Could that be Remoziva?" said Ferdy.

Schlegel only grunted. The man who had got out came from the door on the passenger side. He held on to the side of the airframe as he dropped to the ground. His breath hit the cold air like smoke-signals. He was clearly not a young man, and for the first time I began to believe that it might be on.

"You'd better go, Pat," Schlegel said.

"Why me?"

"You speak."

"Ferdy too."

"Ferdy knows what's happening here."

"You've got me there," I said. I got to my feet and walked towards the old fellow. He was easier to see than I was, for he was dressed in a dark-blue naval overcoat but without shoulderboards or insignia. Stok. It was Colonel Stok. He stopped forty yards from me and held up a flat hand to halt me too.

"We'll need the body," called Stok.

"It's here."

"The insignia? . . . Uniform? . . . Everything?"

"Everything," I said.

"Tell them to bring it to the aircraft."

"Your man," I said. "Where is your man?"

"He's with his assistant in the back seat. It's well. Go back and tell them, it is well."

I returned to the others. "What do you think?" said Schlegel. I was about to tell him that I didn't like anything about it, but we'd more or less agreed that I'd try to believe in fairies until they beat us over the head with exploding copies of *Izvestiia*. "He's a very wonderful human being, and you can quote me."

"Cut out the shit," said Schlegel. "What do you think?"

"He says Remoziva is in the back seat with his assistant. They want the body."

"I don't get it," said Ferdy. "If they wreck this helicopter with that corpse at the controls, how do they get back?"

"Do you know something, Ferdy, anytime now you're going to find out about Santa Claus."

"Hack it, you two! Help me with this goddamn stiff."

The Russians didn't help us. Stok watched us through light-intensifier glasses hooked up to the chopper's power unit. I suppose they needed such things for Arctic Search and Rescue, but that didn't help me feel any less conspicuous.

When we were about ten yards from the chopper I said to Schlegel, "Shouldn't one of us make a positive recognition of Remoziva?"

"What's the difference? What do we need the stiff for anyway?"

I stopped for a moment. "Nothing, but these people might want it as evidence against Remoziva. They might be security police holding your friend Remoziva in custody."

"Nice thinking, Pat," said Schlegel. "But if my Admiral friend is in custody, one uniformed body with kidney trouble is not going to matter much, one way or the other."

"You're the undertaker," I said, and we carried the corpse all the way to the doors of the chopper. From behind me I felt a hand grab my leather belt. Almost as if that was a signal, the Russian with Stok hit Ferdy on the face. Ferdy was bending to the body, to help get it feet first into the helicopter doors, and now he straightened. The punch had gone over his shoulder but Ferdy's retaliation landed. The Russian reeled back against the open door, which banged against the fuselage. The Russian's fur hat was knocked off and I recognized him as one of the men who'd been with Stok at my flat.

The pilot had jumped down at the other side of the plane. I stepped over the undercarriage rack but Schlegel pulled me back and then stepped clear. He held a hand above his head and fired a signal pistol. The shot sounded very loud and a great red light appeared high above us, and suffused the world in a soft pink glow.

The two men from the back seat were struggling in the door and they had Ferdy's arm while Stok wrestled with him. It was almost funny, for both Ferdy and the Russian gyrated and overbalanced like a couple of drunken ballet dancers.

The pilot must have climbed back into his seat after Schlegel's signal, for the clutch engaged and the contra-rotating rotors began with a fierce roar. Few helicopters have overhead rotors low enough to wound even the tallest of men, and yet few resist bending when in the vicinity of the blades. As the pilot revved up, Stok crouched away, and then, fearful that the machine would ascend without him, he stretched an arm to be helped inside. Now only one of the men had Ferdy's arm and the machine tottered into the air, swinging as the nervous pilot over-corrected. Ferdy was suspended under it, his legs thrashing trying to find the under-carriage rack.

"Help me, Pat. Help me."

I was very close. The corpse had already thudded back upon the ice. I threw my glove off and found Mason's little .22 gun in my pocket. I pulled it clear. Ferdy's feet were now well clear of the ground and I threw my arms round them in a flying tackle. Ferdy twisted one foot to lock under the sole of the other. It was that that enabled me to unwind my gun arm and raise it. The helicopter roared and lifted into the dark Arctic sky.

The helicopter yawed as it ascended. Then, perhaps in an effort to dislodge me, it slewed abruptly and tilted. I glimpsed Schlegel, standing alone on the grey ice, waving his arms frantically, in some vain attempt to keep me under his command. A puff of cloud smothered me and then, looking deceptively close as we roared across the ice, there was the submarine. She wallowed in water that was now grey: a sleek black whale, garlanded by chunks of surface ice, and on her foredeck, a party of seamen about to cut blubber.

Afterwards I realized that I should have fired through the thin alloy fuselage at the pilot, or even in the direction of the rotor linkage. But I could think only of the man gripping Ferdy's arm and I put all my shots in that direction. There was a scream of pain and then I felt myself falling. I hung tight to Ferdy's legs—and tighter still—but that didn't stop me falling.

*   *   *

There was no way to tell whether we'd been there for seconds, for minutes, or for hours. I must have stirred enough to move my arm, for it was the pain of that that brought me to consciousness.

"Ferdy. Ferdy."

There was no movement from him. There was blood on his face from a nose-bleed, and his boot was twisted enough for me to suspect that he'd fractured an ankle.

An ankle, it would have to be an ankle, wouldn't it. I didn't fancy my chances of carrying Ferdy more than twenty yards, even if I had known in which direction the submarine was, or whether it was still there.

Schlegel would be searching for us. I was sure of that. Whatever his shortcomings, he did not give up easily.

"Ferdy." He moved and groaned.

"The moon was north-easterly, right, Ferdy?"

Ferdy didn't exactly nod, but he contracted his face muscles as if he wanted to. I looked again at the sky. There was a glimpse of the moon now and again, as the low fast clouds parted. And there was a handful of stars too, but like any handful of stars I had no trouble converting them into a plough and making its handle point north any way I wanted. Ferdy was our only chance of heading in the right direction.

"The submarine, Ferdy."

Again there was that movement of his face.

"Would you say the submarine was thataway?"

He looked at the moonlight, and at the hand I held close to his face. The wind was howling so loudly that

I had to hold my head against his mouth to hear his words. "More," it sounded like. I held my hand above him, and turned it until his eyes moved to show me a sort of affirmative. Then I got to my feet very slowly, examined myself and Ferdy too. He was semi-conscious, but his ankle was the only damage I could see. Getting a fireman's lift on Ferdy was a long and difficult process but the pain of his ankle brought him almost back into the world again.

"Put me down," whispered Ferdy as I shuffled along, half-carrying him. His arms were clasped round my neck, and only infrequently did his good leg assist our progress.

"Put me down and let me die," said Ferdy.

"Listen, Ferdy," I said. "You'd better pull yourself together, or I'll do exactly that."

"Put me down," said Ferdy, and he gave a long groan of pain and weariness.

"Left, right, left, right, left, right," I called loudly. He couldn't do much about the rights, but with a bit more nagging I was able to persuade him to take his weight on his left foot now and again.

I was kidding myself, if I thought that I could get as far as we could see. And there was no submarine nearer than that. I stopped. But just holding Ferdy upright took more of my strength than I could spare.

"Schlegel will be searching for us," I said.

Ferdy groaned, as if to indicate that he'd rather be left there than rescued by the dreaded Schlegel.

"Left, right, left, right, left, right," I continued.

Sometimes the wet grey mist wrapped itself round us so completely that we had to stop and wait for the wind to find us a path through it.

"For God's sake, Ferdy, take some of your weight."

"Cinnamon toast," said Ferdy.

"Damn right," I said. "It's all that bloody cinnamon toast."

Sometimes I stopped even when the mist did not force us to. I stopped to recover my breath, and, as time went on, the stops became more and more frequent. But at least Ferdy was not demanding to be abandoned in the Arctic wastes. It was a good sign, I thought, perhaps not unconnected with thoughts of cinnamon toast.

It was getting darker and darker all the time and I was frightened of losing my sense of direction as already I had lost all track of time.

Once I thought I heard the sound of whistles. I stopped. "Listen Ferdy: whistles."

But it was just the shriek of the wind, playing the sharp fluted ice.

"Left, right, left, right."

By now I was croaking the time for myself, more than for Ferdy. I was commanding my own feet to crunch down into the unending snow. As it got darker I was more and more often blundering into ice ridges that came out of the mist at us, for all the world like ships steaming through a fog. "Here's another, Ferdy," I said. "Left, right, left, right, left, right. No slackening of pace. You're doing well, old son."

And so when I saw the bright-red flares ahead of me, it was just another ship in the convoy. "Left, right, right, left, right." And the whistles were just the wind. So Ferdy and I pressed on through them, even when the ice ridges steered two points or more to ram us, or those icy ships were tearing at our clothes. "Left, right, left, right. Pick your bloody feet up, Ferdy, you bastard, and take a bit of your two hundred pounds of cinnamon toast on your good ankle, for a change."

Slabs of up-tilted ice—as big as a man—were on every side of us. It was difficult to pick a way through them. I used an outstretched hand to steady myself, as in the half-light the ice seemed to place itself in our path.

"Not much farther now, Ferdy," I coaxed him. "I can almost smell that damned toast."

"Are they both crazy?" It was the Captain's voice.

"Left, right," I said, pushing my way past the ice, but snagged upon it, I felt myself stamping the same piece of snow.

"Help me with the big fellow." It was the voice of the doctor. "Dead—done for long since."

Schlegel's voice said, "No goggles—snow blind and concussed. Have you got a needle with you, Doc?"

Somewhere nearby there was another signal flare and I could see that all right. I struggled to get free.

"Wasted effort," said the voice of Schlegel. "Carrying him all that time—what a state he's in."

"Probably wasn't dead when they started."

"Maybe not, Doc."

"Let go of Foxwell." It was Schlegel shouting again, and this time his face was only inches from me. "You stupid bastard, let go of him, I say!"

Chapter 21

PRINTOUT (pink sheet total) is the end of game. Subordinate, aggregate and continuous play not included in PRINTOUT are not part of the game.

RULES. "TACWARGAME." STUDIES CENTRE. LONDON

Several times I had almost awakened into a hazy snow-white world of ether and antiseptic. Through the window bright sun shone on a world of dark-green pine forests, the trees sagging under layers of snow.

Someone lowered the blinds so that the room filled with soft shadowless light. There was a table with fruit, flowers and newspapers on it. The newspapers were in some unreadable script. At the end of the bed sat a man I recognized. He wore a dark suit and his face was elderly and slightly blurred.

"He's waking up again."

"Pat!"

I groaned. And now another figure came into view, looming over the end of the bed like a sun rising over the Arctic wastes. "Wake up, sweetheart, we've got other appointments."

"I'll pour him some tea," said Dawlish. "There's nothing so reviving as a nice cup of tea. Probably hasn't had a proper one since coming in here."

"Where am I?" I said. I didn't want to say it but I wanted to know where I was.

Schlegel smiled. "Kirkenes, Norway. A Norwegian chopper brought you off the submarine a few days ago."

"Is that right?" I asked Dawlish.

Dawlish said, "We were worried."

"I can imagine you were," I said. "I carry about ten thousand pounds in government insurance."

"He's getting better," said Schlegel.

"If you'd rather we went . . ." Dawlish offered.

I shook my head very gently in case it rolled under the bedside cabinet and we had to prod it with sticks to get it out. "Where's Ferdy?"

"You know where Ferdy is," said Schlegel. "You did your best for him—but Ferdy's dead."

"What for," I said, "what the hell for?"

Dawlish smoothed out his English newspaper. The headline said: GERMAN TALKS END WHEN RED KATYA WALKS OUT.

Dawlish said, "Stok's people arrested Remoziva's sister yesterday morning. Only thing they could do really."

I looked from Schlegel to Dawlish and back again. "So that's what it was all about—the German reunification."

"They're cagey blighters," said Dawlish. "They weren't convinced that the Admiral was coming over to us until they saw that corpse you took out there. They're cynics I suppose, like you, Pat."

"Poor Ferdy."

"It was only thanks to Colonel Schlegel that you were saved," said Dawlish. "He thought of using the radar, and bullied the Captain into using it so close to their monitors."

"Bad security, Colonel," I said.

"We brought some fruit for you," said Schlegel. "You want a grape?"

"No, thanks," I said.

"I told you he wouldn't want it," said Schlegel.

"He'll eat it," said Dawlish. "In fact, I wouldn't mind a grape myself." He helped himself to two, in rapid succession.

"You encouraged them to snatch Ferdy," I accused Schlegel.

"These grapes are good," said Dawlish. "Must be hot-house at this time of year but they're awfully sweet."

"You bastard," I said.

Schlegel said, "Ferdy was deep into Toliver's set-up. He needn't have gone on the trip at all, but he insisted."

"So you two have been conniving all down the line?"

"Conniving?" said Dawlish. "Sure you won't try a grape. No? Well, I mustn't eat them all." But he helped himself to another. "Conniving isn't at all the word I'd choose. Colonel Schlegel was sent to help us sort out the Toliver complication—we appreciated his help."

". . . got it," I said. "Use Colonel Schlegel to beat Toliver over the head. Then if Toliver complains to the Home Secretary you say its the C.I.A. doing it. Neat, but not gaudy."

"Toliver came near to knocking you off," said Schlegel. "Don't shed any tears for that bastard."

"Well, I'm sure he'll be taken care of, now."

"He's discredited," said Dawlish. "That's all we wanted."

"And all the hard work is being done by Russian security," I said. I picked up the newspaper.

TWO JOIN SOVIET POLITBURO, THREE OUSTED

Moscow (Reuters)

The first Politburo shake-out since the ousting of Nikita Khrushchev was announced at the end of a two-day meeting of the Central Committee.

According to observers here the new line-up means the end of all hopes for the German treaty of federalization.

I pushed the paper aside. The stop press said the D Mark had already begun falling against the dollar and sterling. So that was it. A united Germany would have upset the status quo. Its agricultural East would make French agriculture suffer, with a resulting gain for the French communists. Meanwhile Germany got a share in the Common Market's agricultural share-out. Germany's contribution to NATO—something like a third of all NATO forces—would certainly have to be dismantled under the treaty's terms. U.S. forces in Germany would not be able to withdraw to France, which wasn't a member of NATO. And this was timed for a period when the U.S.A. would be changing to an all-volunteer force. It would inevitably mean U.S. withdrawal from Europe. Just as Russia had completed its big five year military build-up. Yes, worth a couple of operatives.

They both watched me as I finished reading. "And

the Russians arrested all the Remozivas just on the basis of us meeting that chopper?"

"*Sippenhaft.* Isn't that what the Germans call it?" said Dawlish. "Collective family responsibility for the actions of one person."

"Don't you care that you've helped to frame completely innocent people?"

"You've got it wrong, haven't you? It wasn't British policemen who went out arresting everyone named Remoziva the other morning, it was Russian communist policemen. And the people they arrested were working very energetically to strengthen, improve and expand this system that arrests people in the middle of the night on the grounds that they might be an enemy of the state. I don't intend to lose any sleep over it."

"Just to foul up the reunification, eh?" I said.

"They've got an analogue computer at the Foreign Office, you know," said Dawlish.

"What's that supposed to mean?"

"It's not supposed to mean anything. It's a fact. They put the German reunification on it and didn't like the scenario one little bit."

I helped myself to one of my fast disappearing grapes. Dawlish said, "You are bound to feel a bit depressed for a while: it's the drugs. You were in a bad way, you know."

"Does Marjorie know I'm here?"

"I've been trying to get hold of her, Pat. She's left the hospital." It was a softer voice he used. "She seems to have cancelled the bread and the milk deliveries."

"Did she go to Los Angeles?"

"We're not sure," said Dawlish, trying to break it to me, gently. "We've only just got her family's address in Wales. Quite a tongue-twister, it is. She might be there."

"No," I said. "Forget it."

I turned away from my two visitors. For a moment I saw the wallpaper that I never did replace and heard Marjorie greet me as I returned from a trip. The bookshelves would now be cleared of those damned anaemia books but I'd go on finding hairpins down the back of the sofa.

Self-pity reached in and grabbed my breakfast. It hurt, and if you want to say it was nothing but a self-inflicted wound, I can only reply that it hurt none the less because of that. Ferdy had gone and Marjorie too: the comfortable little world I'd built up since leaving the department had disappeared as if it had never been.

"Are they treating you well in here?" said Dawlish.

"Pickled fish for breakfast," I said.

"The reason I ask," said Dawlish, "is that we have a bit of a problem . . . It's a security job . . ."

I suppose I might have guessed that a man like that doesn't fly to Norway to bring anyone grapes.